DOING TIME

Anne,

Enjoy your time
with the book.

DOING TIME

A Novel

CHRISTOPHER KUNZ

Doing Time is a work of fiction. While Eau Claire, Wisconsin really exists and several buildings referred to in the book are real, all characters, and events portrayed in the book are fictitious.

ISBN-13: 9798618236195

Design by Carol Hollar-Zwick
Cover photo by Ken Zwick
Author photo by Michelle Kunz

*This book is dedicated to my parents,
Julie and Al, who still guide me from beyond,
and to my wife, Ellen, whose guidance is
much more tangible.*

ONE

Mike Newhouse spent his short ride from the courthouse to the Wisconsin Experimental Prison pondering one word—*experimental*. As his van neared the prison, Mike watched a hundred protesters block the van's route. Police in riot gear pushed and dragged several demonstrators off the street. At a different time, Mike might have been yelling for justice with the crowd. Now he could only listen to the sharp shouts and thick thuds.

Inside the prison gates, as the sound of the protesters faded, Mike returned to his circular thoughts—prison, confinement, experimental. Not until the guards delivered him to his cell did Mike end his contemplation. His new surroundings required all his attention.

"Word is you were stupid enough to borrow some rich guy's ID," said Lonnie, Mike's new cellmate, as a way of an introduction. Mike knew better than to try to explain the subtleties of his business model.

"How about you?" Mike asked. As identification, a prisoner's conviction mattered more than his name.

"Armed robbery, but I'm innocent." Lonnie gave a big crooked-toothed grin. "Shit, there weren't even any bullets in the gun."

"What's the deal with this place?" Mike's voice echoed off the hard surfaces. "And why is it so quiet? Is it library hour?"

Lonnie sat on his cot and gave the same crooked-toothed grin. "Unnerving, ain't it?"

The cells were smaller than Mike had remembered and glaringly bright, with an unpleasant sterilized stench. "I heard stories about this place. Prisoners missing. Lights flickering. My lawyer thinks it's haunted."

"It's haunted all right," Lonnie said. "But it's not the ghosts you need to worry about."

"What then?"

"That's the mystery."

Mike scanned the cell. "Anyone really missing?"

"See that cot?" Lonnie nodded at the other side of the cell. "That used to be Stevo's. Ain't nobody seen Stevo in ten months and he ain't the only one."

"What's your theory?"

Lonnie half laughed. "I ain't got no theory. Shit, I just don't want to find out first-hand."

"The guards aren't talking?"

"We barely see any."

At lunchtime Mike observed the common areas. Most prisoners sat alone without talking or even looking at one another. After lunch they moved outside for an hour in the yard. Mike breathed in the fresh air as if he were about to dive down to the bottom of the ocean. He smelled manure and freshly tilled dirt. In the distance chartreuse leaves unfurled from their buds in sharp contrast to the black soil. Spring had arrived in Eau Claire, Wisconsin and Mike wanted to sit in a boat on a nearby river, drink a Leinies, and watch a young woman tan in the inviting sun.

Instead, Mike stood next to Lonnie and waited for a challenge from a prisoner, some indication of the pecking order. He scanned the yard and found slumped shoulders and lowered heads and wondered what could make prisoners so docile. They reminded Mike of the homeless people he saw on Barstow Street—ghosts—seldom noticed.

Mike decided at that moment he wouldn't wait to become one of the ghosts, afraid of what might happen next. He did what he always had—pushed. Even though Barstow Street was only five miles away, Mike had no idea how far his pushing would take him beyond his cell, Eau Claire, and reality.

But he didn't have to wait long.

With each protest he voiced and every question he hurled at retreating guards, his journey accelerated.

On his fifth morning, two guards approached Mike's cell door and called his name. *This can't be good.* Mike turned to Lonnie, who nodded, confirming Mike's fears.

"They came for Stevo too," Lonnie said, staring past Mike.

"How many others?"

"You're the fifty-eighth. Some before Stevo, some after. No one's seen any of them." Silence lingered until Mike's ears rang.

A guard tapped the cement wall with his baton. Mike stood, smiled, and met the guards at the cell door.

"I understand the mix up," Mike said as they began to walk. "I was hoping for a better cell, something lakeside, with a Jacuzzi." The guards remained silent, the only sound, hard-soled shoes on linoleum. They continued down the long hallways, through several locked entrances, until they arrived at a handsome solid oak door with the word *Warden* stenciled on it. A guard pushed open the door.

The warden's office looked light and cheery, painted a pale salmon with plush tan carpet that hushed the guards' shoes as they escorted Mike through the door. The warden, Dr. Maxwell Jennings, sat behind an antique desk polished to a high gloss, empty except for a writing tablet and a stained-glass reading lamp. The guards stood on either side of Mike as he sat in the only empty chair.

Sunlight blazed through the wall of windows, giving Mike the impression he had left the prison. On the floor in the corner, looking equally out of place, sat a three by four-foot sandstone rock fragment covered with what appeared to be native art engravings in the form of simply drawn animals with four stick legs and a slash mark for a body.

Dr. Jennings looked more like a college professor than a warden, wearing crisp slacks and an angora sweater over his shirt and tie. He signaled the guards to leave. They paused for a moment, then left the room and closed the door. Dr. Jennings, a slight man, smiled and picked up his tablet.

"Mister . . . Newhouse, how good of you to join us."

Mike appraised the warden's smile and saw nothing to make him feel at ease. "The pleasure's all mine."

"Forty-four, originally from Minneapolis, and a graduate from right here at the University of Wisconsin-Eau Claire, with a degree in philosophy of all things." Dr. Jennings shook his head. "I see you plan to stay with us for a while."

"I'll be glad to leave whenever you like," Mike said, keeping up the warden's repartee.

"I must say Mr. Newhouse, the idea of babysitting you for the next forty to fifty years bores me." The warden stood with his back to Mike as he walked to the windows and looked at the prison yard and rolling hills beyond. "Luckily for both of us, we take a much more creative approach to incarceration here."

"I bet."

"Well," the warden said as he walked back to his chair and sat down, "incarceration isn't quite right. Technically speaking, we do the opposite. What I'm saying, Mr. Newhouse, is I'm letting you go."

"You're just going to let me walk away?"

"I'm setting you free. What do you think about that?"

Mike looked into eyes that held a small measure of curiosity, but enough arrogance to make Mike feel like a lab rat used in experiments before cutting out its brain. Mike turned on the smile that had won him misplaced trust from any number of business partners.

"Great, I'm all packed. Guess I'll be leaving now. Call the guards to open the front gate." Mike stood, but Dr. Jennings held up his hand and gestured for Mike to retake his seat.

"As I said, we take a more creative approach here. If I let you walk through the front doors, I'd have to answer to a lot of people who'd believe justice wasn't served." The warden shrugged. "I think you'll find our approach more . . . innovative."

"You aren't going to make me milk cows are you?" Mike said.

"Nothing like that Mr. Newhouse." Dr. Jennings made a few notes on his tablet. "I meant it when I said I'm letting you go, but we don't let prisoners simply walk out the front door. It's more complicated than that."

Mike kept his eyes on the warden and waited for him to get to the point.

"You look confused," Dr. Jennings said. "You probably think this is a trick."

"Sure, I'm free to go. I just need to climb over the wall without getting shot."

"You're right, Mr. Newhouse. There's a bit of deception on my part, but it doesn't involve *where* we release prisoners. It has to do with *when*."

Mike thought he had finally figured out the warden's trick. "Like in forty to fifty years."

"In fact, you leave tomorrow morning." Dr. Jennings paused, goading Mike to ask a question. When the silence grew, the warden continued. "It's not the time you *depart* that matters, although I imagine it has a minor significance. What makes all the difference is the time we *send* you to."

Dr. Jennings studied Mike. Mike had no idea what he was talking about.

"What I'm saying is that your sentence isn't measured in the number of years you spend in this prison, but the year we choose to send you in time." The warden waited for Mike to respond, but Mike knew when to remain quiet.

"Far enough back where you can't cause much trouble, before the use of guns, when most resources were needed simply to survive. The greater the crime, the further back in time you go. The cost is minimal and, as you've observed, no overcrowding. Prisoners get a second chance, the tax-payers save money, and our shareholders make a profit. It's a win-win-win."

Mike waited for more information. When none came, he responded, "Bullshit."

"Am I to infer from your comment that you don't believe in the cost-saving potential, or that you're not fully convinced of the possibility of time travel?"

Mike realized the warden was serious but, more importantly, the warden controlled the conversation. If Mike wanted information, he had to play Dr. Jennings' game. "Let's say I don't believe in time travel."

"Fair enough. It is a bit of a stretch, and technically it's time manipulation. It can be difficult for some to grasp. I'll keep it simple." The warden stood and Mike watched him, looking for some indication this was a joke as the warden paced. "I take it you've heard of the Large Hadron Collider and the discovery of the Higgs boson or what many have referred to as the God particle?"

Mike nodded, but the warden stopped pacing and motioned with his hand, beckoning more of a response.

"It gives sub-atomic particles mass," Mike added.

"Very good. Scientists have discovered other particles, one in particular that gives sub-atomic particles their place in time, dubbed the Time particle. Its discovery has been classified, so I can't tell you much more." The warden sat on the edge of his desk. "Except we've learned to manipulate this particle and move people through time."

"I'm supposed to believe that?" Mike watched the warden, more interested in his expression than his words.

"In the end, it doesn't matter what you believe. You'll find out soon enough."

Dr. Jennings' complete confidence concerned Mike. He had fabricated enough facts to know the difference between true confidence and bravado. Either the warden had told the truth or he believed he had. Mike also knew reality was a tenuous thing for good con men who often believed what they needed to. Mike needed to do the same and changed his reality to one which included time travel.

"How long would I stay in the past?"

"The simple answer is that prisoners don't come back. That's the whole point of the program—a fresh start."

"How do you know it works? Where's the proof?"

"You sound like our investors, Mr. Newhouse. Proof. Proof. Proof. We are dealing with a certain amount of theory. Gravity is a theory. But if you want proof . . ." The warden gestured towards the rock in the corner. "See that stone?"

Mike had noticed it coming in and took another look at the reddish rock slab with the curved top, looking like a deformed version of the Ten Commandments.

"They found it while digging the foundation for this prison three years ago. According to an archeologist and using carbon dating, the markings on the stone are roughly eight hundred years old and do not conform to any known tribes that existed in the area."

Mike took a third look at the stone and noticed a word at the top—*days*—scratched with an uneven hand. He reexamined the drawings and recognized them, not as deer or horses, but as slash marks in groups of five used to keep score or . . . the number of days a person survived in isolation. The first bead of sweat formed on Mike's forehead. *What would make a prisoner delirious enough to claw his daily existence in stone?* He counted the slash marks—forty-three.

"We happened to send a prisoner back eight hundred years. Bone fragments also found at the site confirm they belonged to prisoner fifty-three." The warden looked at Mike. Mike was re-counting the slash marks when he became aware of the warden's gaze.

"Have you ever noticed humanity's fascination with fire or explosions?" the warden asked, then waved away any response Mike might give. "It's not destruction that fascinates us, but dramatic change, especially when that change happens to something or someone else. Tornados, car chases, we can't get enough of them."

Mike refocused on Dr. Jennings' face. "Why here?" Mike asked out of desperation, scrambling for reason. "Why now?"

Dr. Jennings sighed. "This is a new semi-isolated, for-profit prison with shareholders to appease and a whole new frontier to explore. If you're asking why we use prisoners, I think we both know the answer. We're saving tax dollars while advancing science with people nobody's going to miss. As to why now, is there a better time?"

"Why am I here?" Mike said. "To give my approval?"

"Nothing like that. You are a bit unique yourself—at least, your situation is. Your journey will be different from the first fifty-seven prisoners."

"More unique than time travel?"

"The procedure works." The warden motioned to the stone again. "It's the mind that gets in the way. Most of the prisoners who died during the process, did so because their minds couldn't make the leap. That is why you are here, not to get your approval, but to prepare you for the biggest leap to date as we enter Phase Two of our experiment."

"What does that mean?" Mike asked.

"Information from your psych tests and background indicates a greater degree of flexibility in your perceived reality. We are not sending you back in time, but forward." The warden studied his tablet, then Mike. Mike looked back, pretending indifference. "Mr. Newhouse, you will be our guide into the future. The past is established and predictable. The future is unknown territory. Nobody worries about the past. The future on the other hand . . . scares people."

Mike felt his future become more worrisome by the minute. "You want to send me into the future. OK, I'll play along. Perhaps I'll get my own hovercraft and a robot to do my dishes. What's the catch?"

"Let me explain the *catch* to you, Mr. Newhouse. When going to the past, your knowledge is an asset. But in the future, your ignorance is a curse. It isn't about gadgets and conveniences. The future is about adapting. It's about change. You won't be watching the fire this time. You will *be* the fire."

"Are you insane?" Mike asked, genuinely interested in the answer.

"Now that's the question I've been waiting for. No, I'm not insane." Dr. Jennings beamed. "Think about it. Technology you can't begin to imagine, a whole new set of rules and expectations you know nothing about. You could literally lose your head by entering the wrong access code for your hovercraft."

"How do you know what—" Mike heard his voice rise, then caught himself. Composure was power and Mike's success in the past often depended on him being in power. "I'm sorry," Mike said in a calmer voice. "How do you know what the future will be like?"

"I don't. That's where you come in. You'll find out for us." The warden removed an invisible speck of lint from his desk. "I merely postulated from known parameters. The details are irrelevant, while the outcome is quite predictable. You will struggle. You will try to manipulate others, but it is time that will transform you. You might have gotten away with breaking rules here, but the future won't be as easily deceived."

"How many more people do you plan to send to the future?" Mike clung to the comfort of shared misery.

"For now, only you, but if you survive the process, you could be a pioneer for thousands. Intriguing, isn't it?"

"How will you know if I survive?"

"Does it matter?" The warden shrugged.

Mike pushed away the question and struggled to gain a grasp on the conversation and his future. "How far into the future are you sending me?"

"Another excellent question, Mr. Newhouse. You are getting the hang of this. Calibrating time travel is not an exact science. Since you are the first person to be sent to the future, we don't even have a reference point. But our target is one hundred years. That should do the trick. You'll be as helpless as a newborn."

Dr. Jennings stood and opened the door. "Your journey starts tomorrow."

Mike studied the warden again and looked for some crack in his composure to judge the level of intimidation. He determined it was the worst kind, a threat given quietly, relying on substance rather than delivery. As Mike stood, he kept his next question simple. "Do I have a choice?"

The warden laughed lightly through his nose. "We all like to think so."

TWO

Mike did not return to his cell, but one identical to it, alone, separated from the rest of the prisoners. He had no view outside, not even of the highway, only a small patch of cement wall. "This is what I call exclusive," Mike said to the retreating backs of the guards.

Mike never slept well in prison, but spent most of his time meditating, a skill he learned on the streets of Eau Claire. After graduating college Mike drifted. His parents had divorced when he was thirteen, making his mediocre home life lonelier—his mom depressed and his dad gone.

He encountered a former psychology professor known as Guru, an eccentric man who was rumored to live under a bridge and led groups of street people, prostitutes, and office workers through Tai Chi in the park. Mike became engrossed in long philosophical discussions with Guru about the nature of the world.

"What about personal responsibility?" Mike said. "These rich bastards do whatever they want, but if I get caught, I have to pay the consequences?"

"Mikey," Guru said, "are you responsible for the day turning to night? Remember cause and effect, cause and effect. You control nothing." When Mike asked Guru how he dealt with all the shit happening around him, Guru simply replied, "What shit?" He taught Mike how to meditate and it changed Mike's life, allowing him to see areas he couldn't before, from a perspective most people could never imagine.

Mike sat on his prison cot, arms at his sides, eyes closed and relaxed. He observed his cell from an aerial view, the small room, storage, locked doors, and empty space between him and the other prisoners. He looked into cells in other blocks and watched fellow prisoners sleep. Flying over the guards' office, Mike studied monitors and observed the two guards sitting erect. He traveled outside, scrutinizing scenery he'd never glimpsed—a prairie and a lake reflecting the star-filled sky.

If he found himself thinking about prison or confinement, he waited for a gentle breeze to blow those thoughts away and remained outside with the wind in his hair and freedom all around. As night continued, he rested peacefully under the moon and only stirred when thoughts squeezed in of missing prisoners or decades behind bars. He thought he could also see an alternative, as if he could simply walk out of this life through the prairie to a new one as he had done numerous times before—new apartments, clothes, personality, bank accounts.

· · · · ·

Mike opened his eyes the next morning to the sound of the guards' grinding heels as they turned the corner to his cell. He wondered what his future would hold and hoped to survive the day. Following the guards to a processing center, he showered alone, then put on thick unbleached natural cotton underwear, socks, pants, shirt, and slipper-like footwear.

He didn't complain about the loose-fitting clothes, hoping they'd accompany him to the future. Mike didn't want to make the trip naked, one of the many issues he fixated on, along with whether he should hold his breath or close his eyes or if time travel would be painful. And what did the warden mean by "if you survive the process?"

The clothes were not standard prison issue. They had no labels, tags, elastic, zippers, synthetics, and absolutely no style. He looked like a hippie dressed in hemp, ready for an outdoor concert.

"Peace, brother," Mike said to the guards who never changed their expressions. He acclimated to the feel of the fabric as he moved to a table for breakfast—scrambled eggs, pancakes, and orange juice.

Mike had a strong stomach, disconnected from his nervous system, which allowed him to eat and enjoy his meal. Savoring the pancakes, he licked his fork and let the sugar dissolve in his mouth, imagining a lazy Saturday morning in a diner with nothing to do.

"So what do you guys have planned for today?" Mike asked the silent guards to keep his diner illusion alive. "I've got to run a few errands and go to the future. I hear parking's a nightmare."

He wasn't in irons, not even handcuffs. Mike figured the more he complied, the easier the process would be, and the longer he could live in his own fantasy. He finished his meal and waited, letting his anxiety move through him like the wind gently bending the tall grass during meditation. He had made similar leaps in his life—transforming from middle-class entrepreneur to bank executive or radical in the blink of an eye. He simply needed to adjust his reality. He wasn't walking to his death, he merely lacked plans.

The guards remained silent and moved only when a man and woman entered the room.

"Drop your pants," said the woman in a white lab coat, the first woman Mike had seen up close in well over a month. Despite her stern expression and latex gloves, Mike felt a tingle at her touch. "I'm giving you a few wide spectrum inoculations for diseases we know about and something for anxiety."

"What if I don't want them?"

She smiled and gave him injections in the butt and in both arms. She checked his blood pressure and pulse, looked into his eyes and ears. "Take another deep breath . . . look to the right, now the left." A man stood in the corner, typing on his computer. He said nothing, but when he nodded, the woman stood back and the guards escorted Mike out the door.

Farther down the hall in a room beyond double doors, Mike saw a heavy metal chair, slightly reclined, flanked by panels of lights and a pile of wire. Bolted to the floor, it had oversized restraints for both arms and legs and a sleek circular apparatus that hung above the entire chair. He didn't want to think about how it worked or what it did.

He waited with three guards who stood perfectly still, but who gave away their nervousness by glancing at the door repeatedly.

"Expecting someone?" Mike asked.

The guards didn't know it, but they helped Mike relax. He calmed down when others around him became nervous. The trait had probably developed in Mike as a child when his parents fought and Mike believed if he remained calm and relaxed, he could change the mood in the room. If his parents were quiet and content, he worried when the peace would end. It was perfect training for a Social Justice Entrepreneur.

15

Mike had called himself a Social Justice Entrepreneur, preferable to identity thief or money launderer. He was perfectly suited for this self-appointed title, neither handsome enough to dislike nor self-assured enough to annoy. His average height, brown hair, brown eyes, and medium-to-slight build worked to his benefit.

Mike had wheeled and dealt in possibilities and enjoyed breaking rules for a good cause. He kept score as most people did, with money, and used deception as his own form of civil disobedience. Now he had to readjust again.

The double doors finally opened, and the warden walked in with a man Mike had not seen before. A team of eight other people followed and quickly disappeared into the control room. The warden stood alongside the man with gray, thinning hair, dressed in baggy pants and a buttoned cardigan. They spoke quietly before the man walked towards the control room.

"Excuse me, John," the warden said. The man stopped and turned. "I'd like you to meet Mr. Newhouse. He's our guest for today's scheduled journey." John looked at the warden before he turned to Mike and nodded an acknowledgement. He was about to turn away when the warden spoke again. "Mr. Newhouse, Director John Mason is the genius behind time manipulation and your host today. Think of him as Father Time." Mason studied the warden a few seconds longer, then turned away from them both and proceeded to the control room.

"Shall we begin?" the warden asked Mike. Mike nodded, not sure if his head actually moved. He hoped to remain calm and maintain some control over his body. He didn't want the guards to force him into the chair. He needed it to be his move.

The warden's composure concerned Mike, until he noticed the warden glance one too many times at the control room, reminding Mike of the nervous guards. Mike relaxed, but as the anti-anxiety medication altered his perception, he didn't feel right.

"Ready, Mr. Newhouse?" the warden asked. Mike answered by walking towards the chair. As he walked he became aware of his stride, making it harder to move his legs.

He reached the formidable chair, climbed in, and sat on the reclined metal surface, surprised to find guards on either side of him. Mike didn't look at either of them as he put his arms in the heavy arm restraints. The guards locked them closed with a clank of metal. Mike did the same with his feet. Mike leaned back in the uncomfortable chair as a two-foot thick circular metal tube, resembling a halo, lowered around him and began to spin.

Mike had the sensation of spinning at first until the apparatus picked up speed. It began to hum as the speed increased and Mike felt as if he was giving a speech in high school, naked. He tried to ignore the flashing metal surface spinning around him and its irritating hum and focused instead on the statement the guard read.

"The State of Wisconsin, in conjunction with the Wisconsin Experimental Prison, does hereby sentence Michael J. Newhouse to no less than one hundred years on this day, April 21, 2020."

Mike closed his eyes and meditated, emptying his mind as he focused on his breath, but the drugs interfered. He opened his eyes when the warden addressed him by name. "Mr. Newhouse," the warden said, waiting for Mike's eyes to open. "Mr. Newhouse, is there anything you want to say before you're released into society? Any final words?" The warden gave a condescending smile.

Mike thought of an injured eagle, released on its first flight to freedom, but he only saw himself as a prisoner about to be executed, a form of release. Death or time travel, he tried to distinguish the two—both were unknowns where he'd leave his current life behind and enter a new world, a new existence. *Perhaps death is time travel.* His blurry mind conjured images of heaven and hell. Either way Mike wanted to make a statement.

"Time is time," he said. "People are people. I have been whatever I needed to be, while you . . ." Mike had been glancing around the room as he spoke, but now looked directly at the warden over the metal tube spinning around his chair. "You are stuck playing the role people expect of you, limited by what you know, what makes you comfortable. Ignorance isn't a curse. Sometimes it's the only thing that gets me through the day."

Mike had more to say, but with his mind racing and shutting down at the same time, he forgot. Instead he closed his eyes and hummed a song to himself, recognizing it as *Happy Birthday* the second time through. He enjoyed the feel of the vibration in his ears and continued, aware of the warden watching him. He heard the warden walk towards the control room and give the signal to proceed. A few seconds later an electrical zap echoed in Mike's ears.

THREE

"Do we have audio yet?" Dr. Jennings asked again as he paced back and forth in the cramped control room filled with screens, computers, audio apparatus, and enough blinking lights to guide in a 747.

"Be patient. It's been less than an hour," Mason said. "I told you this could take a while. Go back to your office and I'll let you know when we hear something." He knew the warden wouldn't leave the control room, much less stop pacing, until he had confirmation the audio transmitter injected into the prisoner's arm functioned. The problem, as Mason saw it, wasn't *when* the link would work, but *if*. Time manipulation was difficult and, given the lack of peer research and minimal testing, unpredictable.

"Did it work?" Dr. Jennings asked twenty minutes later as he looked through the window at the empty Time chair. "Did we send him to the future?" Dr. Jennings liked to ask questions with no clear answers, more interested in the reaction than the response.

"We technically didn't send him anywhere," Mason said, avoiding the real question. "As I've said before, this isn't time travel. It's time manipulation. We're *setting* his body at a particle level to a different time, not sending him."

The overall Time project had succeeded, but not without major setbacks. The first few attempts at time manipulation involving prisoners ended in disaster, with a messy cleanup of body tissue, the process too slow for the larger human mass, compared to that of a ferret. Of the seventy-five trillion cells in the human body, if as little as one-hundredth of one percent failed to convert at the same instant as the other cells, the body ripped apart.

On the third attempt, the process worked, and they converted a prisoner's atoms to a different time, 239 years in the past. The goal had been a hundred years, but they still celebrated. Unfortunately, the only proof of success involved a few graphs, a piece of stone, and missing prisoners. Investors had forbidden sending technology to the past for fear of contaminating timelines, but the future didn't hold those same restrictions.

"With all those numbers you're caressing over there," Dr. Jennings said as he continued to pace, "you must have some indication of where you *set* him?"

"The numbers are on target, but you know better than anyone, they only tell half the story. Even *Father Time*," Mason said as he turned from his numbers to look at the warden, "can't determine with certainty the exact time reference."

"I couldn't resist," Dr. Jennings said. "I wanted to see his reaction to meeting you, but the look on your face was even more entertaining."

"He did seem calm for a man about to have every cell in his body altered."

"He couldn't possibly appreciate the complexity of the procedure."

Can you? Mason thought.

Dr. Jennings, a successful psychiatrist in the discipline of anxiety had joined the project early in the planning stages, when experiments with ferrets resulted in mental abnormalities—animals that wouldn't eat or gnawed on themselves or died unexpectedly. The mind was a tricky organ to move in time because of its ability to anticipant and remember. Dr. Jennings assumed the position of warden as well and used his broadened powers in an experimental prison system to influence the project and ignored the growing protests outside.

"We're past the difficult part," Dr. Jennings said. "He still had a heartbeat when he left, and his blood pressure was manageable."

Dr. Jennings' top priority was to weed out high-risk candidates and prepare prisoners for the reality of time travel. Based on the experiment's short timeline and the prison's small sample size, he often failed both objectives.

"If the audio transmitter doesn't work," Dr. Jennings said, pacing again, "it won't matter if he survives. We'll have no proof."

Mason concentrated on the numbers before him and composed himself, knowing it was the warden's style to say the most direct and emotionally charged statement possible. "I would like to think that it matters if the subject survives, with or without proof."

"Why? This project has already killed five people," Dr. Jennings said. The two sound technicians looked at each other, then up at the ceiling. "For funding to continue, we need proof, not computer printouts and stone etchings."

Unfortunately, time manipulation to the future was more difficult. Changing a particle to a past time reference was relatively easy compared to manipulating a particle to a future reference point that didn't yet exist. They had attempted to manipulate one other person into the future, prisoner fifty-seven, but he died from stress of the recalibration process before completion.

Mason and Dr. Jennings had watched from the control room as prisoner fifty-seven's eyes widened in terror when the metal tube began to spin. His faced drained of color and sweat erupted from his skin. Dr. Jennings knew adrenalin and calcium must have flooded the prisoner's heart and caused the abnormal rhythm that abruptly stopped it from beating.

When the time manipulation cylinder spun beyond thirty rpm it began to hum and recalibrate cells in the body either a few microseconds back in time or forward, depending on the final destination. Only after every cell, all seventy-five trillion, had reached cellular resonance—cells vibrating in perfect sync—was instantaneous particle manipulation possible.

Recalibrating every cell back a few milliseconds felt slightly disturbing, like any change, but manageable. Recalibrating cells a few milliseconds forward was extremely jarring. Like standing on a cliff with feet hanging over the edge, moving back a millimeter or two could be nerve wracking, but ultimately comforting. Moving forward could be deadly. Some people were better equipped to manage the stress. Both Mason and Dr. Jennings hoped prisoner fifty-eight was more adept than prisoner fifty-seven.

"When will we know if the audio transmitter worked?" Dr. Jennings peered over Mason's shoulder. Asking questions was an occupational habit.

"I told you," Mason said, trying to keep calm. "It will be a minimum of two hours before we hear a signal, maybe three, if it works at all."

Mason had created a miniature time manipulation chip, small enough to inject into a human body for the purpose of capturing two hours of digital sound waves. The device would return the two-hour files and continue the process every two hours, providing a constant stream of recorded data after the initial two-hour lag. But the only way to determine its success was time.

"Is it possible we'll get a signal sooner?"

"Anything's possible." Mason punched his computer keys. "But highly improbable."

"You really need to relax." Dr. Jennings began pacing again.

The warden's pacing and continual questions reminded Mason of driving to Lake Tahoe when his kids were young and they asked every thirty minutes, "are we there yet?" It was benign at first, but after a while, he wanted to drive off a cliff.

FOUR

Mike landed hard on the ground as if someone pulled his chair out from underneath him. This unexpected collision caused the words *happy birthday* to erupt from his mouth. He opened his eyes, rolled to his knees and threw up eggs and pancakes. His first official action in the future was to eliminate everything from his past. He tried to appreciate the fresh start. As he looked at the hundred-year-old pancakes on rotting leaves, he became aware he was no longer within the prison walls.

He rose to his feet, looked for threats, and immediately grabbed his head with both hands as he attempted to stabilize his brain from sloshing between his ears. He tentatively turned from side to side, and with no immediate danger in sight, only trees, he stood still, taking deep breaths, waiting for clarity.

A steady breeze rushed through the trees with a temperature of over fifty degrees Fahrenheit. He stood in a forested area that reminded him of the woods he'd explored as a kid. It even held the same faint mossy smell of decay. Mike wondered where the prison had gone, but he saw no structures and put it out of his mind.

He listened and heard only the breeze, not the hum of a distant highway or a single airplane. He had envisioned a future filled with flying vehicles, but this sky fit neither past nor future.

He considered sitting down, but wanted to get away from his current location, unsure exactly of how he got there. The woods thinned to the right, so he headed in that direction. He looked back once at the remnants of his breakfast, the only indication of his past and the starting point of his future.

Mike walked through the forest as it gradually turned to open field. The wind blew stronger and helped clear his head. A tall ridge partly shaded the field, gently bending away from him where the sun rose in the sky. Mike continued to walk until the grasses thinned and he noticed a building. He froze, then backtracked into thicker cover to observe what appeared to be a long-abandoned strip mall.

Remnants of road, barely noticeable in the grass, consisted more of weeds than asphalt. It looked like decades since anyone had used either the building or road, as nature reclaimed its space, prying up tarmac and poking holes in structures. After five uneventful minutes, he kept moving and found more strip malls and houses, all equally deteriorated.

Tired and thirsty, he had crossed a small stream fifteen minutes back, but decided not to drink the water until he knew more about the environment. He thought of nuclear war and radiation fallout and began scratching his skin.

Mike walked down the middle of deserted streets, a stick his sole weapon as he looked to the ridge on the other side of what remained of the city. He had avoided the ridge at first, concerned about keeping hidden, but now he wanted to see everything.

"I heard the grass is always greener on the other side." Mike talked to distract himself from the empty buildings and desolate surroundings as he stepped toward the ridge.

The terrain changed back to all grass as he made his way up the long incline, and he felt better leaving the decay behind. Mike grew tired, but the thrill of cresting the rise propelled him forward. Halfway up the ridge, he looked to the top and noticed a big green sign—*Welcome to Eau Claire Population 112,932*.

Mike stopped. The name surprised him, and the population seemed way too high. He couldn't help but think he was in some foreign country, as if time travel was its own location. He smiled. Eau Claire, Wisconsin had represented many challenges for Mike, confinement and incarceration the most recent. But now it offered familiarity, a connection, as if he'd run into a demanding neighbor in a foreign country and was glad to see a familiar face. The sign was his only documentation, adding context to the empty buildings. He walked the remaining two hundred feet to the top and wondered what had happened to all the people.

Still thirty feet from the sign, he reached his hand towards the rusty marker, wanting to touch something of color that had survived the years. Movement, a flash of light, caught his eye and he dropped to the ground. Crawling on his hands and knees to the sign, he peered between the two metal posts. Over the ridge at the bottom of the hill a half mile away, arose a mass of buildings with sharp crisp lines.

"Shit," Mike said at the unexpected intrusion. The sight so surprising, so jarring and yet so welcome, he had to take a breath and recalibrate his view of the world. Mike crawled through the grass, torn between curiosity and concealment, to get a better look at this Eau Claire.

He stared at his city. He didn't take in any details at first, watching movement, the sun reflecting off white walls, and shadows falling on red brick. It reminded him of peeking inside a clock with all its intricate parts, trying to determine what caused the hands to move. What he saw changed by the minute as his understanding grew. What were walls and people became a city. The more he observed, the more Eau Claire looked like a mirage, a cityscape surrounded completely by untouched prairie, as if a giant came along, gathered up the sprawling city, and compressed it into a compact ball, a few miles in diameter. But it was softer, greener, more organic than cities he knew, as if it could get up and walk away.

If he focused on any small section, the city looked familiar, brick buildings, stone structures, and trees, no flying ships, not even a hovercraft. He might've recognized a few of the buildings, but everything appeared to be in a different configuration.

Nothing looked futuristic until he took it all in, including the pristine wilderness surroundings. He thought he saw some of the structures move until he recognized them as a train, and saw it traveling along the city's edge.

Numerous turbines and wind catchers bordered the city in a variety of sizes and styles. "How could I have missed those?" Mike said, as he watched the turning wheels and spinning cylinders. He turned back and looked at the starting point of his relatively short journey and saw the extensive forest and fields with I-94 barely visible, but unnaturally straight, running through the countryside. The concrete, crumbled and overgrown, had large gaps and a faded yellow line still visible in places. Mike saw no usable roads or other signs of human existence in any direction, only a single train track leading into the city on the other side of the ridge.

Mike kept himself concealed as he moved closer to the city. Within a hundred feet of the train track, he perched himself on a steep rise. He didn't see any cars or room for them.

"I know I parked the car around here somewhere," Mike said, smiling at his own joke. What he first thought were parking lots, appeared to be vegetable gardens. The buildings clung together, mostly two or three stories tall and none more than six or seven. Mike couldn't tell homes from offices as one structure blended into the next with older buildings attached to newer ones and trees obscuring his view.

A ribbon of steel made up the train track, creating a dividing line between city and wilderness so stark Mike assumed some type of barrier kept it that way. He threw a rock that cleared the train track and nearly hit a building as it traveled much farther than he'd expected due to his elevated position. Mike looked around to make sure no one had seen him.

"That was me," Mike said under his breath, sticking his hand up slightly, sure he went unnoticed. "My fault, won't happen again."

Entering places where he didn't belong was Mike's specialty. It took some knowledge and an understanding of authority, but Mike's success came from a willingness to step over the line. He had once walked the red carpet at the Academy Awards, convincing security he was Reese Witherspoon's boyfriend to demonstrate something important that he could no longer remember.

The Academy Awards Ceremony had a line, some sections covered with high security, but most of it protected by an imaginary line, an area where people didn't go unless they had a reason. The trick was to find the imaginary line, then be the person to step over it with purpose.

Mike descended the steep slope, climbed over the track, and walked casually through twenty feet of prairie grass that lay before the gardens.

Bracing himself for some type of security, he stepped through the knee-high grass, and crossed the imaginary line. Nothing happened. He took five more steps before he heard an alarm. Mike's first instinct was to run, but he knew better. He turned to face out from the city and casually backed up into the garden area, looking in either direction for a perpetrator.

After a few seconds the alarm stopped, Mike shrugged his shoulders, and the people nearest to him returned to weeding gardens and gathering herbs. Mike pretended to pull weeds from a random garden as he took a closer look at the fifteen people around him, the closest thirty feet away. Most people wore muted natural colors, light browns and greens with darker patches on the fronts of long-sleeved shirt and pants, all in similar loose-fitting styles, making it difficult to tell men from women. Mike's clothes, thick light-brown cotton, stood out more for their sloppiness, but they weren't as conspicuous as they would have been in his own time.

He tiptoed between garden plots, careful not to step on any plants, and stopped to examine the vegetables. He recognized some—eggplant, green peppers, and tomatoes. Mike was no gardener, but as he looked at hundreds of small plots bursting with vegetables, he wanted to be one, if only to get his hands on some food.

He walked between buildings as he touched the nearest one and ran his hand along the smooth surface. He didn't mind if he looked like a tourist, but he didn't want to appear like the time-traveling invader that he was. He reduced his gawking.

He attempted to start a conversation with several people walking by. "Hello, I'm looking . . ." The people kept moving as if they hadn't seen him. "Excuse me," Mike said as he stepped in front of a woman. She nearly walked into him, startled by his presence. Mike thought his clothes distracted her or maybe it was his slight accent. "I'm new in town and looking for the best restaurant."

"The best *what?*" she said.

"The best restaurant. You know, the best place to eat." She looked at Mike with greater alarm as he mimicked eating by spooning food into his mouth. She stepped around him and walked away. Mike looked around, excited and confused by his first conversation.

He searched for high-tech gear, flashing lights, flying objects, and hoped to learn more about the city through the tools they used, like an anthropologist who studied arrowheads and clay pots.

Mike heard kids chasing each other and light conversation, but missing were the mechanical noises of engines idling, buildings rumbling, and lawnmowers running. The main walkway mesmerized him, raised about an inch higher than the area around it with individual sections that move up and down when people stepped on them.

The longer Mike stood, the more he noticed what wasn't there. He didn't see any trash or trashcans, no newspaper racks, no signs except those painted directly on windows, no streets or street signs, no fire hydrants, no poles or wires, no advertising. Mike attempted to decipher his surroundings from the void created by absent items and wondered what else he had missed.

FIVE

Mike stood a few minutes longer between buildings as he enjoyed his last uninvolved moments before plunging in. He followed an older couple and walked purposefully with his hand behind his back. He looked ahead, studied people, their hats, distracted expressions. He reached the main walkway and felt the unstable surface under his feet, but he continued without pause. He took five unsteady strides on the undulating path when each new step he took sounded like glass breaking. The older couple ahead of him increased their pace. A younger man smiled as he walked faster alongside Mike.

"Sounds like someone needs a Bio Boost," he said as he passed, looking in Mike's direction, but not at him. Mike stopped. The man continued another step or two, then he stopped too. He turned and walked back to Mike. "You don't want to use Energy Squared," he said. "They're stuck in the seventies." Mike looked confused. "A Bio Boost," the man said, tapping an iridescent ribbon around his right wrist similar to a watch in size, but more contoured. "You're not getting your energy points. That's what the noise means."

Mike continued to stare and waited for the right time to comment.

"It's an easy fix. Here, let me see how you've constructed yours." He pulled up Mike's shirt sleeve and studied Mike's empty wrist. "What, you a lefty?" The man then searched Mike's left wrist and again found nothing. "Garbage. Don't worry. We'll locate it." The man walked back the way they came, then stopped when Mike hadn't moved. Mike studied the man as he walked back to him. He was tall and lanky with an open face, carefree attitude, and the enthusiasm of a child.

"What's your name?" Mike asked.

The man peered at the device on his wrist. "Stanley Lou Desmer," he said as he continued to study both his wrist and then Mike.

"Hi Stanley. My name is Michael John Newhouse. You can call me Mike." Mike held out his hand, Stanley hesitated for a moment then shook it. "Look Stanley, I don't have a device." Mike pointed at his wrist.

"What?" Stanley said.

"I never had one."

"Never had a Bio Pulse? How?" Stanley stepped backwards. But then he seemed to notice Mike's outfit, his hatless head. Mike remained quiet. Stanley glanced around. Mike liked that the conspiratorial gesture had not changed. "Are you from the Outside?" Stanley whispered. Mike didn't know what the question meant, but he liked its simplicity and nodded his head.

Stanley appeared to be doing long division in his head. "Follow me," Stanley said before he walked back the way they came. Mike paused for the slightest moment and determined Stanley to be the safest person he had ever met. After five noisy steps they walked on a gravel path that led to buildings. Two different people ran into Mike along the way.

"Why do people keep bumping into me?" Mike said as he caught up with Stanley, dodging another person.

"They can't see you."

"What do you mean?"

"Without a Bio Pulse you basically don't exist, electronically anyway."

"How can they not see me?" Mike waved his arm around.

"If they looked, they could. It's called sensory blindness when we rely solely on data input."

"Why can you see me?"

"The energy relay alarm on the walkway helped."

Mike heard a door unlock as they neared the third building. They entered and walked up four flights of stairs in a broad and sweeping stone staircase. Mike ran his hand along the smooth railing and thought he might have been in this building before, but it was filled with offices then. They walked down a hall lit by interior windows running high along the wall. Stanley remained quiet and seemed to study his surroundings as much as Mike. A door unlocked and they entered.

Stanley darted into another room while Mike tried to figure out where he was.

"Here, put this on," Stanley said when he returned. "I mean, please." Mike looked at the instrument, a thin iridescent ribbon of semi-transparent material, and was curious enough to try it on. His wrist tingled in a pleasant way, warm and electrifying. Stanley took Mike's wrist, moved his fingers in front of the device, and waited.

"Except for high levels of polymers and a few missing antibodies, you don't appear to be a health risk." Stanley relaxed his shoulders, removed his hat, and sat. Mike took another chair and looked around. The apartment was small and sparsely furnished with a nice view and plenty of natural light.

"Are you really from the Outside?" Stanley asked. "And before you answer, you should know your BP is set to give an audio alarm if you lie, and that's a pretty good model you're wearing. I built it myself." As an after-thought he said, "Sorry."

Mike thought about the question. "I walked into town from over the ridge." His Bio Pulse remained quiet as Mike let Stanley lead him to the truth, or at least answers that made sense.

"No BP," Stanley shook his head, talking more to himself than Mike. "I've heard stories of people who lived on the Outside. I've never seen any, but I've always wanted to meet one."

"Do you have anything to drink?" Mike asked.

"I'm sorry." Stanley moved his fingers over his Bio Pulse. "I'm so excited. I have water or tea." Mike drained his first glass of water and drank his second while Stanley watched. "What's it like, the Outside?"

Mike thought of an honest answer. "Windy, lonely, and bleak," he said.

"Are you a landfill miner?"

"A what?" Mike asked.

"I only ask because of the high levels of polymers in your body. I figure you've been mining for treasure in the landfills."

"No, I'm not a landfill miner," Mike learned more with each question.

"What are you then?"

"To tell you the truth, I really don't know anymore. I've been out wandering around looking for a city."

"But why were you out there in the first place? Are you an isolationist, or a technophobe, or a privacy nut? I don't mean to pry. I know you're not mentally ill because the Bio Pulse detects that, but that doesn't mean you're necessarily sane either."

Mike had to think about the question. "I guess you can blame it all on my parents," he said. His Bio Pulse remained quiet.

Stanley looked confused, used to getting his information electronically, not deciphering the nuances in conversation. "What do you think of the Bio Pulse?"

"It's great," Mike lied to see what would happen as his Bio Pulse beeped. Mike didn't know much about the Bio Pulse, but he knew he didn't like anything that detected lies.

"This might sound kind of crazy," Mike said, "but what year is it?" Seeing the concern on Stanley's face, he added, "There's no way of keeping track on the Outside." He had been wondering the year since his ass first hit the ground and couldn't wait to find out any longer.

"Eighty-four," Stanley said as if Mike were joking.

Mike didn't know what to make of the number. "Do you mean 2084?"

Stanley had the panicked look he'd worn when they'd first entered his unit. "How long have you been on the Outside?" he asked. Mike gave the universal shrug for I don't know. "It's the eighty-fourth year since the end of the Poly Plagues." Mike showed no signs of comprehension, so Stanley continued, as if he were talking to a three-year-old. "It's the year 2151, as some people still refer to it, or 84."

"Oh." Mike tried to look nonchalant. "My parents never told me about the plagues. I feel like I don't know anything." Mike calculated in his head—131 years. *Holy crap.*

"Do you have some place to stay?" Before Mike could say anything, Stanley answered his own question. "Of course you don't. You're from the Outside." Stanley looked at Mike from his hatless head to his funny shoes. "You should stay here." He smiled. "We have an extra room."

"I'm not sure," Mike said, playing out the conversation.

"It's no big deal. We have someone staying with us all the time. It's more sustainable than the city hostel which is probably full and people from the Outside haven't always been welcomed there."

"Why not?" Mike asked.

"Well," Stanley paused, then continued without looking at Mike. "You know, Outsiders have stolen energy, spread contaminants from the landfills, often carry diseases, and have occasionally thrown things at the city."

"But I didn't mean to . . ." Mike said, not knowing how to finish, as he thought about the rock he had thrown to check for a force field.

"I know. We've let Outsiders starve and die of things we could've cured, but that was decades ago, when cities struggled with consolidation and some outlying communities like Chippewa Falls and Menomonie tried to hang on by raiding Eau Claire for food and energy. Outsiders couldn't just walk in then."

"I didn't steal anything," Mike said.

"I'm saying some people can't let go of the past."

"Are there a lot of Outsiders?"

"I don't think so." Stanley gave a big grin. "You're the only one I've ever met."

"Why aren't you more afraid of me? And why would you let me stay here?"

"You don't look scary. I thought someone from the Outside would be dirty and speak some other language, but you look more harmless than dangerous. My BP also has a couple of protective settings and I've wanted to meet someone from the Outside all my life."

"How do I know if I'll be safe here?" Mike asked, but he didn't really need an answer. Compared to prison, his current living arrangements were the best offer he'd had in a while.

"When I was younger, my friends and I talked about taking a year off and living on the Outside. Everyone talked about it, but I don't know anyone who did it. I stayed on the Outside once, for half a day. Sara, my girlfriend, wanted to have a picnic Outside. For the first hour I could almost pretend I turned down my BP, but then it seemed to get harder to breathe. After a few more hours even Sara wanted to get back to the city."

"What else does the Bio Pulse do?" Mike didn't want to talk about the Outside anymore. He had too much new information to learn.

"Everything. It has three main functions—feeds information to the wearer, interacts with the city, and maintains optimal health." Using a series of eye movements and finger manipulations in the air, Stanley showed Mike how to access general information on his Bio Pulse, including a holographic screen with features similar to a computer. "That's the manual interface to make specific inquiries," Stanley said. "No one uses it. Most pertinent information is always available, but the BP you're wearing is calibrated to my requests."

Stanley applied a small piece of material behind Mike's ear. "That's to hear the audio from the Bio Pulse." He took Mike back out in the hallway and reentered the unit, allowing Mike to experience the information exchange system.

Kevin and I are at Twisted. Come and join us. Otherwise we'll be back at 8:00. The time is 5:36. Temperature twenty. Don't forget to water the herbs. Paul's schedule this week is . . . The voice Mike heard through the Bio Pulse with Stanley's.

"Are those your other roommates?"

"Yeah, the BP can project their holographic images, but most people don't bother. It uses too much energy. Do you want me to turn on that feature?"

"No," Mike said more forcefully than he'd intended.

Stanley skimmed over how to interact with the city. "It'll be easier to show you later." He used his own BP to demonstrate the health features. "Yours will give accurate information. But it can't analyze the data without an established history and baseline scan."

"What kind of data?"

"It constantly monitors your body looking for any warning signs—abnormal cell division, high blood pressure, increased level of hormones—and either makes an adjustment or directs the user to the proper remediation."

"Do all Bio Pulses use your voice?"

"The voice recall system is usually programmed with the user's own voice." Stanley sent a few messages, giving Mike a minute to test his BP. Mike didn't have a chance to do any in-depth searches. He barely knew how to operate it. Learning the system would take longer and Stanley had already moved on to a tour.

"This is one of thirty-six living units in this building." Stanley moved to the door on his right. "Here's a bedroom. Each one looks about the same." It was tiny, roughly eight by ten feet. "Here's the study."

Mike saw, through a window in the study, no books, but two stationary bikes. They walked through the living room to the bathroom, a small intimate space. Back in the living room, Stanley pointed to the tiny kitchen that looked more like a science lab in the corner.

"Only about ten percent of the units have kitchens. It's more sustainable to centralize cooking activities."

Intricate murals covered the walls, depicting colorful vegetation and smiling people. The floors looked like wood, but were softer, squishier. The couch appeared sleek and minimal, with two similar chairs, each well-worn but clean. A petite garden, green with herbs, grew in the kitchen. Running the length of the living room wall, hovered a two-foot-wide garden filled with what looked like wheat grass.

"Let me show you how to access background information on my other two unit-mates." Stanley used Mike's BP.

Paul Bodden, thirty-one, a bio-mechanic, originally from the Philadelphia Region, and a Green member of the Magnetic Line . . . Kevin Wong, thirty-three, an organic chemist from Eau Claire, and a painter . . .

"I'm right here." Stanley selected a small glowing icon of himself. *Stanley Lou Desmer, thirty-six.* Mike thought he looked more like twenty-five. *From Eau Claire, a botanist, and guest chef at Beta Carrotene . . .*

"Do you have anything to eat?" Mike asked after learning about Stanley's guest chef status.

"I was on my way to the food market when I ran into you." Stanley looked around at an otherwise empty room as if to make sure no one but Mike could hear him. "Why don't we go to a health store? No harm in that?"

Mike couldn't tell who Stanley was talking to. "What's a health store?"

"You know." Stanley looked concerned again. "A place to get something to eat."

"I haven't eaten since ..." *Was it seven hours or one hundred thirty-one years?* "I'm starving."

Stanley examined Mike's Bio Pulse. "Your body is beginning to break down muscle tissue. That settles it. We have to get you something to eat." Stanley walked towards the door, then paused. "I know the sun is pretty low and the energy gain won't be great." Stanley looked up and down at Mike's clothes. "But we can't take you out in that. Walking around without solar receptive clothing isn't city savvy. Follow me." Stanley walked into a bedroom, grabbed clothes from a built-in dresser, and walked through another door. "Here, this will be your room." Stanley laid the clothes on the bed. "Try these on and I'll get you some shoes."

The clothing had heft. The outer shirt wrapped around itself similar to an incredibly tailored bathrobe. The pants were made of thick tweed, but smoother, same as the outer shirt. Mike liked the hat, glad to see they had come back into fashion, even if functionality outweighed style. It reminded Mike of an old felt hat he had worn in college when he wanted to be interesting.

Stanley's clothes fit him better, and Mike could tell each piece was custom fitted. When Mike reached to put his hands in his pockets, he discovered he had none, at least not on the pants, only the outer shirt had two, low on the sides. Mike didn't know what to do with his hands as he hooked his thumbs in his shirt pockets and felt ridiculous. He put them behind his back instead. The shoes were the best part of the outfit. They opened, similar to a clamshell, to hug his toes in a brushed material, like thick moss. They were lightweight and massaged his feet as he walked.

"No need to mention you're from the Outside," Stanley said. "We don't want to alarm anyone."

SIX

Two and a half hours into the experiment, the silence in the control room erupted with distorted sounds from the future. Everyone in the control room froze, including Dr. Jennings in midstride. They listened to static as two sound technicians isolated the distortion, adjusting the frequency and phase.

"I need you to confirm the signal is from prisoner fifty-eight," Dr. Jennings said.

"It's confirmed doctor," a sound technician responded. "It's his signal. The distortion confirms it. This wave cycle is intense."

Dr. Jennings didn't know anything about wave cycles, but he knew success when he heard it. He wanted to celebrate but didn't know how. He reprimanded himself for not buying champagne for the occasion.

"Can you clear up the audio?" Dr. Jennings asked.

"One more adjustment," another technician said. They listened. But all they heard was Mike's heartbeat. "Sorry. I forgot to filter out interior sources." The technician moved.

"Wait." Mason held up his hand and listened to the strong, steady heartbeat of the prisoner, a human subject, believed to be over a hundred years in the future. Mason

41

thought he had never heard anything more wonderful. The technician tried to ask him a question, but Mason pushed away her words. He stared into space and breathed in the future.

Dr. Jennings watched his colleague, a bemused smile on his face. "Would you like us to dim the lights and turn on some romantic music? Or are you ready to move on?"

"Make the final adjustment," Mason said as he came out of his trance and smiled to the technician.

The outcome was silence. For the next twenty minutes, they heard Mike make involuntary noises of exertion. He said a few words out loud, then began talking to himself with greater frequency. "Where is everybody?" Ten minutes later, "Do I drink the water?" Followed by, "Stop scratching your skin. You're fine." The two technicians looked at one another thinking the future didn't sound so great. Mason and Dr. Jennings smiled to themselves, excited the subject displayed higher cognitive functions.

"Are we recording?" Dr. Jennings asked. The technician confirmed the digital documentation.

For nearly two hours the only sound was Mike's utterances, "Look at that," and "What the hell is that?" His voice reverberated from twelve speakers in the small control room while lights danced across multiple screens.

When they finally heard a different voice, a woman saying "the best what?" to Mike's question about restaurants, several lab technicians clapped their approval.

"It's as if we discovered a new planet," Dr. Jennings said when they heard Stanley speak.

"More like exploring the future blindfolded, without visual cues or background data," Mason said, as he adjusted several sensors, "attempting to build a dinosaur from a description of its fossils." He couldn't stop smiling.

When they heard the year, the room exploded in cheers. The Bio Pulse became a break-through discovery for Mason and Dr. Jennings.

"I want to hear what he is hearing on that device," Dr. Jennings said to a sound technician. After adjusting the internal sound dampeners, they heard Stanley's BP voice.

The speakers danced with background data as a continuous stream of information flowed from the Bio Pulse, creating an endless commentary. Paul's background information continued for five minutes and overlapped with Kevin's profile while general news about Eau Claire filtered in. The data never stopped.

"How can a person listen to all of this?" Dr. Jennings asked.

"I don't know yet, but the Bio Pulse must continually feed overlapping information to its user," Mason said. "Instead of asking for data through searches and apps, I assume the Bio Pulse learns what information a user wants, then over-supplies." He looked at the computer that analyzed the audio information. "In the last twenty minutes, the system has stored over sixty gigabytes of data."

Dr. Jennings looked at the same computer. "What are we going to do with all the data?"

Mason smiled to himself. "Build our own version of the future."

SEVEN

Mike stumbled along the walkway, glad to have a guide. He looked in all directions while Stanley walked faster and paused frequently for Mike to catch up. Mike wanted to know more, but his brain was overwhelmed with what he had already learned, his memory of past Eau Claire, and the continual stream of data from his Bio Pulse.

Jason, a friend of Kevin's is coming into range on your left . . . one energy point earned . . . current temperature is nineteen . . . Second Skin is looking for a cellular engineer with experience in stage-two development cells . . . Carolina Allspice is in bloom ahead.

"How do you turn this down?" Mike pointed to his ear.

"Tap it," Stanley said. Mike tapped the fabric and the rolling commentary lowered to a whisper. "But listen for the energy points. Whenever you walk on an energy walkway, your downward pressure exerts a force that's converted into energy." Stanley demonstrated by rocking back and forth between two raised platforms in the walkway, depressing them with his weight. "Your BP registers that energy in your name along with solar energy from your clothes." Stanley smiled. "Well, actually it registers it in my name." Mike partially listened to Stanley, distracted by the exotic plants

44

growing in impossible areas and people moving around them.

Is it my imagination? Women kept looking at him. *Do I look different? Do they know?* Mike found his answer when a woman walked up and gave him a long kiss on the mouth. Stanley stepped between them.

"A misunderstanding here. Wrong setting," he said to the woman, who looked annoyed before she walked away. To Mike he said, "Sorry about that," as he moved his fingers in front of Mike's Bio Pulse. "I forgot I had that particular date feature set on this one. Won't happen again."

"Don't apologize," Mike said, enjoying the future.

Each step brought a new perspective. One minute, Mike saw nothing but vegetation, multiple small garden plots, trees, and flowers. Several steps further, he thought he'd walked into a small Italian piazza with shops surrounding a small square. The next vista might have been Eau Claire's historic downtown, except gardens and walkways replaced roads and parking lots. In the distance, Mike could see rows of houses, but where a road should have been, taller buildings stood.

In eight more steps he saw a child move floating numbers in the air. "What's that kid doing?" Mike asked.

"I don't know. Looks like algebra."

"What's that shop? Or that one with the fancy balcony? Are those apartments?"

"That's a BP accessory shop." Stanley pointed to the first. "The one with the balcony is a studio, and most of those upper spaces are living units except for a few immediately above the main entrance. See, that one's a repair shop."

"How can you tell?" Mike saw no signage, only large murals and intricate patterns done for artistic reasons, not commercial.

"My BP is more sensitive than yours and I don't have the sound turned down," Stanley put his hand on Mike's shoulder. "Why don't we get something to eat, then I'll give you a tour."

"Sure, I'm starving, remember?"

After walking another five minutes they arrived at Beta Carrotene. Mike could swear it used to be a hair salon, but now it reminded him of a cross between a New York deli and an Italian café, with lingering aromas and warm character, but no clutter. It held no more than sixty people with fifteen small tables, a counter, old creaky wood floors, and brick interior walls.

"Grab a glass and silverware," Stanley said, as he selected from a collection of glasses of varying sizes and shapes. "What do you want to drink? The solar tea is good." They cleared two spots at the counter and sat down on stools that spun.

Stanley and Mike listened to menu choices through their BPs along with names and backgrounds of the chefs, a harvest report, and ingredients.

"That's good," Stanley said after the pecan salad description, followed by, "that's one of my favorites" and "you have to try that" after nearly every item. Each item was four credits.

Stanley nudged Mike ten minutes later and they retrieved their food at the counter. They had both ordered the chef's special, vegetables in a spicy tomato sauce.

"What do you think?" Stanley said when they sat down and ate. "This has got to be a treat after eating moths and wild onions or whatever you eat on the Outside."

"It's different." Mike forced himself not to wrinkle his nose. Even with his hunger, the food tasted off, too much like spinach. The sauce was thin and needed salt, a lot of salt. The serving size was tiny.

"What *do* you eat on the Outside?"

"Moths?" Mike said. "I guess I'm used to eating more meat, like rabbit or squirrel."

"I think moths would be better." Stanley drank water, Mike assumed to wash the taste of squirrel from his mind. Stanley picked up a pepper with his hand and held it out for Mike to see. "It's like chewing on sunshine," Stanley said before popping it into his mouth.

Mike stabbed his last pepper and chewed it with determination. He wanted a big burger and fries served to him at a table by the window.

After their meal a woman came out from the kitchen still carrying a knife and gave Stanley an intimate hug. Mike wondered if this was another of Stanley's BP date settings, but as they held each other, Mike guessed they were more than digital acquaintances.

"Stanley, who's this? Another botanist?" the woman said with an eager look, slipping the knife into a holder in her shirt.

Stanley looked at Mike then back to the woman. "Not exactly."

"And why is he wearing one of your BPs? I thought only kids still swapped them."

"He's from the Outside," Stanley whispered, looking expectantly for a big reaction that never came. After an awkward pause, he continued, "This is Mike Newhouse. Mike, Sara Watson." She gave Mike a hug as well. Sara had the kind of smile that made others smile in return without knowing why. Even while holding a knife, her calm and inquisitive demeanor encouraged Mike to tell her his life story, and given time, he might have. She stood at five foot two with shoulder-length dark brown hair worn in a ponytail.

"It's nice to meet you Mike," Sara said before turning to Stanley. "Not everyone broadcasts their whole life history like you." She turned back to Mike. "I like a man of mystery."

"That's me," Mike said.

"Stanley thinks anyone who doesn't include their favorite herb in her display information must be from the Outside." Sara looked at Mike's BP. "I see you're a better sport than I am. He tried to get me to wear a BP of his, claiming mine was too old and poorly constructed. I almost poisoned him." Sara smiled. "Are you new to the Region or to Eau Claire?"

"The Region. And Stanley has been kind enough to show me around."

"Don't forget to show him my favorite garden," Sara said. She kissed Stanley goodbye before she rushed back to the kitchen.

"I thought we weren't going to mention I was from the Outside," Mike said in a whisper.

"Sorry. I wanted to show you off." Stanley loaded their plates and glasses into a metal rack. They left the health store and Stanley started Mike's tour of Eau Claire.

"This is an interesting garden up here." Stanley pointed to a plot that looked much like all the rest to Mike. "They're growing heirloom melons. Not the most sustainable, but look at the size of that melon." Mike saw the big familiar oblong watermelon he knew as a kid.

"This cocoa tree," Stanley pointed to a tree Mike had never seen before, "produces the best chocolate in the city. Can you smell it?"

"It smells like a rancid pumpkin," Mike said.

"You need to experience what it's like around here when they roast the beans. Everyone walks by with a smile on their face for a week." Stanley had Mike turn up his BP to receive similar information electronically, but Mike turned it down immediately, getting genus, species, age, gardener, and a string of additional data about every plant near him.

They zigzagged through gardens and stopped at one of many outdoor cupboards. "I hope you don't mind." Stanley grabbed an instrument from the cabinet. "I need to weed a small section and check the soil."

Mike pulled plants Stanley pointed out as weeds, enjoying the power to pluck one plant and let another grow. "Is this your garden?" Mike asked.

"It's Beta Carrotene's. I'm just helping." Stanley pointed. "Over there is a special variety of carrot I created. They've got a great spice."

"What's the date?" Mike asked. He figured after asking the year, the date was almost reasonable.

"March ninth. Why?"

"I'm no gardener, but it seems early in the season to have such large vegetables already."

"Maybe on the Outside, but here, in the city, the temperature is controlled at all times, and with additional engineering we can manipulate environmental properties to grow whatever we like year-round." Stanley threw their weeds on a compost pile in the middle of the gardens, returned the tools, and continued the tour.

Most of the buildings appeared the same to Mike. He couldn't tell a lab from a repair shop or old from new. The buildings weren't identical—each had unique qualities in the stonework, size, color, windows, or the materials used— but not a single building had a sign or logo to differentiate it.

The sun sank and lights gently illuminated the city. Mike stopped, surprised by the glow. He examined the source, and found flat light panels attached to benches, buildings, and trees.

"The lights pick up energy directly from solar panels." Stanley pointed to solar panels overhead that had retracted for the evening. They walked again. "That's a food market and that's a library."

"What?" Mike thought libraries would be the first casualty of the future. "Can we go inside?"

"Sure," Stanley said as if he didn't fully understand the question.

The library appeared familiar to Mike from the outside except for the abundance of glowing lights and the vegetable gardens that surrounded it. Inside the two-story building, books decorated an expanded area, displayed like artwork on low sturdy bookcases. Chairs, most of them filled with people, were the only other items in the library. Mike could hear the faint sound of readers turning pages. Stanley played with his Bio Pulse. Mike noticed the running BP data had stopped.

"The library is one of the few BP-free areas in the city." Stanley watched people reading. "It's kind of creepy." They walked by rows of books and Mike stopped at random spots.

"I read this book." Mike had pulled out *A Prayer For Owen Meany* by John Irving and flipped through the pages.

"Are you going to read it now?" Stanley asked.

"I'm surprised to see it, is all." Mike gazed at the book again, wanting to sit down and lose himself in it. He liked the fact that libraries still existed and thought if libraries survived the future then maybe he could too. Mike closed the book. "Let's leave before you go into BP withdrawal."

As they exited the library, they saw a crowd had formed near a group of gardens off the square. They found a gap in the crowd to see what had captured people's attention. A small pile of garbage, no more litter than Mike had seen on any particular day in his past life, lay on the ground. People scrambled to get a better view of the mess, but no one stood closer than twenty-five feet, creating a wide circle around the pile.

"What's the big deal?" Mike said. "It's just a little trash."

Stanley turned toward Mike. "Don't say that too loudly."

Mike knew when to be quiet and watched as more people gathered. Two people brought in equipment and the crowd moved further back.

Mike and Stanley moved with the crowd. As Mike repositioned himself, he noticed a piece of handmade paper sticking out of his shirt pocket. Surprised he hadn't noticed it before, he pulled it out and saw his name printed clearly on one side: *Mr. Newhouse.* The other side read: *Welcome to the future and beware of men pouring beer.* Mike jammed the piece of paper back in his pocket before scanning the crowd. He concentrated on his breath and wondered if anyone noticed him reading the note, but the crowd continued to focus on the pile of garbage.

Mike stood stunned, appearing as fearful as the people around him, but for a different reason. He pulled out the note and read it a second time, folded it, then hid it back in his pocket. He felt compromised. He found the *men pouring beer* part odd, but he was more concerned with how anyone could possibly know who he was and when he came from. He hardly knew where he was himself. As he played with the piece of paper in his pocket, he tried to decide if the note and the garbage were a coincidence. His BP buzzed with information about the garbage. Then he heard the word *Outsider* and knew this was no accident.

"Let's get out of here." Stanley pulled Mike from his trance. They took a maze of paths to a quieter part of town where the passageways narrowed and the gardens grew larger. "One more thing to do," Stanley gestured ahead.

Mike heard a door click as he followed Stanley into a small lab.

"I need to make one adjustment to the lighting on a few plant trials and record my findings. Here take this." Stanley handed Mike a gadget that looked like something a doctor used to check inside a patient's ears. "Go like this," Stanley said, showing Mike how to clip off a piece of plant, "and the Celluscan will record the numbers."

The lab was roughly twenty feet by twenty feet with another room behind it. Several different lights hung from the twelve-foot ceiling.

"These plants," Stanley said while they worked, "are hybrids of the same plant your clothes are made from. Fascinating stuff, grows fast, it's incredibly strong and easy to work with. I'm collaborating with thirty botanists around the world to determine the best method for growth in every climate." Mike didn't care about the details, but enjoyed taking samples, giving his mind a chance to catch up. "Finish the last row, then I think it's time for a refreshment." As Stanley headed for the door, he looked over his shoulder. "Do they drink beer on the Outside?"

"I think I've heard of it," Mike said, smiling until he remembered the note in his pocket.

They walked a short distance before they stopped at Barley Belly, a bar packed with over a hundred people. Again, the building exterior felt familiar while the interior appeared completely foreign. The bar had eight beers on tap, but when Mike searched for men pouring beer, he found no bartender in sight. People stood on either side of long, tall, skinny tables, holding ceramic mugs. Stanley grabbed two mugs from a shelf while Mike surveyed the crowd. He searched for anything out of the ordinary, without understanding what ordinary was.

"Tell me about the beers," Mike asked. "Are any of them local?"

"You have your BP turned down, don't you?" Stanley looked like Mike's mother when she caught him skipping school. "All the beers are local like nearly everything in Eau Claire. That's the point of being sustainable." Stanley handed Mike a mug. "If you really feel adventurous"—Stanley pointed to the second tap—"this one is made from compost piles." Stanley filled his mug. "This next one"—he placed his hand on the third spigot—"uses oat husks. And that one"—pointing to another—"is supposed to have the best hops." Mike picked one that Stanley hadn't mentioned, thinking the less he knew the better, much like the last ten hours.

After his first sip, Mike grimaced at the lukewarm beer that tasted like watered-down pond scum.

"How do you like it?" Stanley asked. "I think it tastes better in the fall, but nothing beats compost-pile beer." Stanley took a big gulp.

"It's different." Mike took another sip, testing the foreign flavors, and realized it wasn't much different than the first time he tried beer in his friend Nathan's basement when he was thirteen. They drank warm Grain Belt and Mike thought it was the worst thing he'd ever tasted, until he eventually became a connoisseur. He took another sip.

He looked around at the young crowd and for a moment had the sensation of going back in time, not forward. Mike remembered his college days, spending so much time in bars that he became a bartender. For Mike, bars illuminated people, allowing him to see inside them, learn how they work. Now everyone appeared opaque. Body language had changed. Women didn't look away when he stared at them.

"How . . . ?" Mike started but didn't know how to finish.

"If you want to meet someone, link your city scan to Barley Belly and the system will identify your best match in the place—most compatible, fewest conflicts, or best sexual partner." Mike was intrigued. He didn't think he had a city scan, but knew from Stanley's expression that he should.

With Stanley's help, Mike heard the backgrounds of several individuals in the bar, including Julia Bergman: *Twenty-eight, cellular biologist, leather repairer, drummer in Gorgeous Roots, cheesemaker* . . . But the piece of information Mike found most interesting was *Currently in training to be a parent* . . . He walked up and introduced himself the only way he knew how, by shaking hands. She seemed to find it awkward. Mike ignored her discomfort.

"What's it like training to be a parent?" he asked.

"It's wonderful," Julia said without hesitation. "The hardest classes I've ever had. I'm halfway through. I still have another year to go, but I can't wait. Although I haven't decided if I'm going to get pregnant or work at Child Care. It depends on the numbers."

"What numbers?" Mike asked.

Julia's smile faded. "The population growth projections. Eau Claire is slightly high," she shook her head. Mike couldn't tell if her disappointment came from the numbers or his question. He assumed it was the numbers.

"Does it mean that much to you to have a baby?" Mike asked. He was wrong.

"What do you think I am? Some self-centered ownership freak? That I'd have a baby outside the numbers?" She turned her back on Mike, knocking over her beer, and walked away.

Mike wiped away beer that had splashed his face and thought of the last time a drink flew in his direction. His wife, Carol, had thrown it. They had been married less than a year.

Carol knew little of Mike, having met and married quickly after a chance encounter at the grocery store when Mike had returned to Minneapolis after college. Mike had made her dinner, dazzling her with chicken fricassee, philosophical musings of the Greeks, and his ability to listen so completely that people told him everything. Mike didn't pretend. Carol was smart and adventurous, but also serious in a way that made his life more real.

They were happy until the FBI asked her several incriminating questions about Mike. They had no proof yet, but it was enough for Carol to piece together the rest of her husband's dealings. She had made plans earlier in the week to have dinner with him at a nice restaurant. She wanted to tell Mike she was pregnant and hoped to celebrate. Instead she confronted him.

"Cut the crap, Mike. I spoke to the FBI."

"They're trying to make trouble. Natural gas is a political hot potato."

"And the two other times you were in prison?"

"I was a kid, basically arrested for protesting."

"You pretended to be a bank employee and embezzled two hundred thousand dollars from the bank president."

"Which I gave to the families the bank was trying to foreclose on."

"And now?"

"I've been selling mineral rights in this natural gas boom. Most of these guys are so slimy they don't care about people's land or the environment. They want to make a fast deal. I give them what they want which turns out to be mineral rights I don't actually own. I'm doing a favor to all the families these guys ripped off."

"Is it legal?"

"That's not the point. At least the families don't lose their land." Mike looked down at his wedding ring and spun it on his finger. He felt nervous and excited to finally tell the truth to the first woman he ever loved. Until her drink ran down his face.

The FBI arrested Mike a few months later on reduced charges, but it ended his marriage and kept him in prison until after his daughter's birth. He learned he was a father when the court forced him to sign papers to give up his rights to his daughter's life. He held his daughter once. She smiled and Mike felt a pain he could not describe nor find its physical origin.

Mike watched his daughter grow from a distance, but he never had another chance to hold her or explain to his ex-wife or find anyone else who made him feel as honest and real. He eventually moved back to Eau Claire, another new start.

EIGHT

Stanley walked over to Mike, smiled, and wiped off the table. "We'd better go before you give my Bio Pulse a bad name." Stanley's smile faded when two people rushed through the doors. Conversations paused as nearly every bar patron turned, anticipating a confrontation. Stanley led the way out the other door with a mug of water in one hand and Mike at his heels.

"Who were those people at the door?" Mike asked once they entered the walkway and it was clear no one had followed.

"Security volunteers. Those two volunteer all the time. He runs a farm market and she's a soil engineer. They're a bit too eager for me."

They continued to walk in no particular direction. Mike still wanted to see more and overindulge in new experiences. They wandered into an open fourth-hand store. Mike and Stanley were the only ones in the sparse shop. Two couches and five chairs made up the bulk of items available. A single table contained two incomplete sets of china.

Mike tapped his foot against a terra cotta pot filled with coins. "What's this stuff?"

"Items salvaged after the Poly Plagues. If a chair needs repair, you can drop it off and pick out a replacement." They left without taking anything. Stanley suggested they ride the train back to their unit.

"Why are you carrying a mug of water?" Mike asked. Stanley had been carrying it since they left the bar.

"It's for the train," Stanley said, leading Mike to believe the train ran on water.

Boarding the train in the dark, Mike had the sensation of entering a subway, but inside the train lights glowed, illuminating flowers and plants perched along the seats in miniature gardens, making the train smell nothing like a subway. Most people stood, but Mike and Stanley found two seats. Stanley tended to a few gardens he could reach. He poured water from the mug he carried and returned thinned plants to the empty mug.

They looped in the opposite direction of their unit before cutting through the middle of the city. Stanley told Mike how the train divided the city into four districts. "Right about . . . now," Stanley said, waiting for the train to reach the center of the city, "we're in all four districts." Mike watched several couples and groups of young people kiss and looked at Stanley. "People kiss at the center," Stanley shrugged. "They always have. It's tradition."

Stanley described the four districts—Art, Park, Research, and Garden. Each district had developed a specialty over the years, but also included labs, studios, parks and gardens along with all the other shops.

"Our unit is in the Park District. That's where we have the Fair," Stanley said. "It also has the most bars of any district."

"Why not call it the Bar District?"

"Because it's called the Park District."

"Which district is this?" Mike pointed out a window on the left side of the train.

"That's the Art District. It has a small bohemian section and the best clay deposits for pottery."

"What district were we just in?"

"My lab is in the Research District. Eau Claire's college is in that district. It also includes the biggest neighborhood of houses in Eau Claire."

"Why don't you live in a house?" Mike asked.

"It's mostly for younger people. I lived in one years ago, but having ten unit-mates isn't for everybody."

"What's the other district?"

"The Garden District," Stanley said. "It has the biggest gardens and more animals—mostly chickens and goats."

Mike looked out the window, watching the lights go by. The train ran silently, making it possible for Mike to listen to several conversations at once. A young man explained to the two women he received kisses from at the center of the city that his unit-mates were gone and at least one, if not both, should keep him company. Mike was listening for a reply when he heard a group of six discussing the garbage incident.

"I've never seen that much garbage in one place," said a tall man, shaking his head.

"I can't wait to get back to my unit and stand under a Steri-Light for a full minute," said a woman wearing a hat.

"I bet it was an Outsider," said a man with a shaved head.

"Come on, when's the last time we had an issue with an Outsider? A decade?" said a woman with a flattop haircut. "It was the Fortune Tellers. Who else dumps garbage?"

"I tell you, Outsiders are still dangerous," said Shaved-Head.

"You wouldn't know danger if it welded a relay onto your ass," said a burly man.

"Nothing's wrong with Outsiders," said Flattop. "And everyone knows the PLM hang out in Eau Claire."

"Where was the prediction then?" said Shaved-Head.

Mike reached into his pocket, knowing exactly where the prediction was.

"Anybody want to stop off at Hops Scotch Bar? I'm volunteering," said the shortest one in the group.

The train stopped several times as people transferred on and off. Mike waited for the group of six to leave before talking to Stanley.

"Do you know what they were talking about?" he asked. "What's the PLM?"

"It stands for Prolong Life Movement. The fancier the name, the bigger the statement they want to make."

"What's their statement?"

"They want to extend life for everyone, double life expectancy to over two hundred years."

"That doesn't sound bad."

"It's not sustainable. As nice as it'd be to live longer, it would mean either an imposed zero birth rate or an increased population leading to overcrowding, pollution, disease, and eventually a pandemic worse than eighty-four years ago, possibly ending human existence on the planet."

Mike thought about what Stanley said, not sure he fully understood the argument, but he did understand the passion behind the words. "Why the garbage and why did that one guy call them Fortune Tellers? Can they really tell the future?"

"They dump garbage from old landfills to bring attention to their cause."

"How does garbage get them attention?"

"You saw the crowd. We're all strangely attracted to what frightens us the most. People were sending messages and we're sitting here still talking about it."

"But doesn't the garbage prove your point that you'd poison yourselves in the end?"

"They think we're killing ourselves now, polluting ourselves with fear."

"That doesn't make sense," Mike said. He looked around to see if anyone else was listening, but other passengers were either in conversations or stared straight ahead, presumably listening to the constant stream of BP data.

"Since when do terrorists make sense?"

"Let me guess," Mike said. "The PLM can see into the future, so they know they're right."

"They make predictions written on crudely pressed paper that sometimes comes true. At least one did." Stanley played with the discarded plants in his cup. "They gave the names of every person who would die in Eau Claire before the next Fair."

"Are they killing people?" Mike pressed the note between his fingers in his pocket.

"No. These deaths weren't a shock. The people were all old and died naturally, but to list the exact names of all the dead is unnerving. Most BPs can pinpoint an elderly person's death maybe three days before, but not two weeks."

Mike remained quiet. He didn't want to hear or see any more and closed his eyes. He thought about the note in his pocket, the future, the garbage, his past, and how great his feet felt in his borrowed shoes. Stanley nudged him when they came to their stop.

On the short walk back to their unit, Stanley put a hand on Mike's shoulder to get his attention. They stopped and Stanley turned to Mike, sliding his feet back and forth in the gravel. "We need to talk. I don't mind having a unit guest. Someone from another Region is always staying with us."

"But," Mike said.

"But I can't stop thinking about the polymer levels in your body and the pile of . . ."

"Garbage. You think I had something to do with that?"

"No. You were with me the whole time. Look, I haven't been in a library for years, but you made it an adventure. I like that. I like you. But I don't even know your favorite color."

"It's blue."

"Blue?" Stanley asked.

"Sapphire blue. Do you feel better now?"

"I guess I'm mad at myself. I should've had you check in with the city for a real scan when we first met, but I was having too much fun."

"I'm not dangerous." Mike thought of the note in his pocket.

"Probably not, but this has more to do with your health. My Bio Pulse can't protect you."

"I don't need protection," Mike said.

"You can stay with me as long as you like. I really want to find out more about the Outside. But the Bio Pulse won't work properly for much longer without some baseline readings." Stanley hesitated before asking the next question. "Do you exist in the database?"

"Look Stanley, if it's about credits, don't worry. I'll pay you back."

"It's not the credits. The Bio Pulse you're wearing can't even access them. All you're doing is earning more energy points for me. If you're in the database, it's a simple process, but I don't know what to do if you're not."

"Am I doing something illegal?" Mike asked.

"Well, no. I don't know. I don't think so." Stanley looked less sure the more he talked. "Anyone can live on the Outside. I heard of a guy who spent a year roaming. He was a legend. Even gave lectures."

"Does everyone need to wear a Bio Pulse?" Mike asked

"Well, no. I don't think anyone *has* to wear a Bio Pulse, but how would you function? It's not illegal to hold your breath either, but everyone breathes."

"What does that mean?"

"I'll ask around, but tomorrow morning we need to stop at City Office and get you officially integrated into Eau Claire." Stanley bounced on his feet. "I had fun tonight."

"I appreciate your help," Mike said. "I don't mean to be a problem. I'll be on my way tomorrow." Mike had turned off the lie detector feature on his BP or at least he hoped because he wasn't planning on going anywhere yet.

"You're welcome to stay as long as you like. That's not the issue. The question is how do we connect you to the system?"

That's a good question. Mike had been searching for the answer his whole life.

NINE

Technicians swapped shifts throughout the day and evening, but Mason and Dr. Jennings didn't leave the control room the first day. Now that Mike slept, Mason recalculated numbers and tried to make sense of the overwhelming amount of data they had already collected, almost glad when Mike took off his Bio Pulse to sleep.

Dr. Jennings sat in silence with his head pounding from a sea of words spoken more than four generations in the future. He remained in his own bubble of existence, contemplating his unique version of future Eau Claire.

"I'm surprised he was able to slip into the city undetected," Dr. Jennings said. "I thought the future would extract its own punishment." He had worked hard convincing each prisoner of the rehabilitative power of time. He believed it himself, to the point of religion.

"It didn't sound that easy to me and he's not officially in the city yet. What were you expecting?" Mason found himself, if not liking Mike, at least rooting for him. Mike was Mason's future, his baby. He brought Mike into this new world and like any father he was willing to overlook his faults to live vicariously through his offspring's achievements.

"I expected that time would be better at confining prisoners than any prison cell—constrictive to the point of changing behavior."

"How so?"

"If I locked you in solitary confinement for ten seconds would it make an impact?" Dr. Jennings didn't wait for a response. "Of course not. But after a week you'd be hallucinating and banging your head against the wall. What's the difference? Time." Dr. Jennings sat up, alert.

"Send a prisoner a week ahead in time and he might not even notice, but a hundred years, his brain can't make the leap. He falls as if he leapt from a hundred-story building." Dr. Jennings smacked his hands together. "Time controls us like nothing else, holds us in place. Interrupt that control and we're lost until time catches up and strangles us to death."

Mason marked a spot in his work and looked up. "I always saw the future as a positive thing, a vision of hope."

"You would. But everything I know about fear and anxiety reinforces the concept of time as an effective jailer. The biggest, most pervasive fear is what?" Again, Dr. Jennings didn't wait for an answer. "Fear of the unknown, stemming from humanity's anxiety over death. Uncertainty and change, the main byproducts of time, are also the dynamic duo of most dysfunctions that I've made my living analyzing and treating. Do you know what my success rate is for significantly reducing debilitating anxiety?"

"Psychiatry is a difficult discipline."

"Less than twenty percent, which is high in my field. The unknown is a crafty foe." Dr. Jennings took Mike's successful first day as an insult, an attack on his reputation, his religion.

"What do you think of this PLM group?" Mason asked to change the subject.

"They seem harmless and if they scare the prisoner, they can't be all bad." They had agreed to refer to Mike as either *the prisoner* or *prisoner fifty-eight*. Dr. Jennings found it easier to avoid any emotional connections, just as he never named the rats in his experiments.

"I mean, what do you think about extending life?" Mason asked. "How old is too old?"

"I don't see why anyone would be against it. We spend trillions of dollars every year to live longer and look younger. Look at what we do to the terminally ill to squeak out one more month of a minimal existence."

"It's hard for me to put it into perspective," Mason said. "I'm fifty-eight and I'd like to live longer, but if overpopulation is responsible for the plagues, I can understand their apprehension."

"Think of what you could accomplish in a couple hundred years."

"The question is, would I care? Would particle manipulation matter to me anymore or would younger scientists, unsaddled with old concepts, leapfrog over me? I've reached success. I'm not sure I'd want to spend another hundred years defending it."

"What do you make of the death predictions?" Dr. Jennings put his feet up on the console. He had nowhere else to go but the tastefully designed home he seldom used.

"You're the expert on fear," Mason said. "The PLM's death predictions remind me of people who constantly predict the end of the world. They hope to create fear by the topic rather than results."

"I expected the future to be more high-tech," Dr. Jennings said, moving to a new subject. "Everything clean and orderly."

"I imagined greater advancements in science myself, but there appears to be a fairly sophisticated layer of data here." Mason looked at the information collected on his computer screen. "Think of the changes that must have taken place. Plagues and destruction and our Eau Claire, in the middle of nowhere, thriving." He started a sketch of Eau Claire. Mason was visual, peering inside molecules and picturing worlds that no one knew existed.

"What are you working on over there?" Dr. Jennings stood and stretched.

"We've calculated the prisoner to be at least four hours behind our time," Mason said. "Assuming he sleeps until first light we shouldn't hear anything until about 11:00 in the morning."

"I bet he sleeps late, just to make us wait. Most of the prisoners would sleep all day if we let them."

"Technically speaking," Mason said, as he finished his math equation on the corner of his drawing, "he's 130 years, 11 months, 11 days, and 20 hours ahead of us. It could be argued, he's the one waiting."

TEN

Mike woke early the next day, saw his small room, and thought he was back in prison. He closed his eyes to get more sleep, opened them, then smiled as he remembered the day before. He replayed bits of yesterday in his head and it occurred to him he didn't know anything about the world outside of Eau Claire. He needed perspective, beyond his room, beyond Eau Claire.

He secured the Bio Pulse to his wrist, too afraid to sleep with it on, and remembered what Stanley showed him yesterday. He struggled to access historical information about the Poly Plagues. The logic appeared to emphasize current, local, Eau Claire-based data. The only useful information he found involved the trains. From the Eau Claire railway, he accessed the Minneapolis railway which linked to other Regions, connecting cities across the continent.

Cities were one of three sizes, with Eau Claire the smallest and most common size at 92,000. No listing existed for smaller cities or towns. Mike didn't know whether they were too small to receive train traffic or if, like the landscape Mike had seen on the Outside, they simply didn't exist.

In major metropolitan areas, cities congregated near each other. Chicago had nine distinct cities, some as large

68

as 142,000 people, named Chicago One, Chicago Two and on. Mike became lost in the data, thinking about traveling from city to city. Travel time from Eau Claire to Chicago was two hours and Minneapolis took less than one.

"Would you like to take the 9:00 train to Minneapolis, Mr. Desmer?" asked Mike's BP in Stanley's voice.

"Yes," Mike said to see what would happen.

"I'm sorry Mr. Desmer, but we can't authenticate your request. Please confirm your DNA signature on file."

Mike learned a Green Member of the Magnetic Line referred to a person with living quarters on the train. The rail system reserved Green Member status for people required to perform their unique skills on-site. Regional trains were a city in themselves with their own energy source, gardens, and water purification system. Mike listened until his bladder forced him out of bed. He heard no one in the unit stir as the sky lightened on his first full day of his new life.

Mike never lingered in the bathroom, like some, reading novels or contemplating the day. He was usually efficient, in and out. Today, he lingered. For the first time he understood the appeal. The bathroom offered a cozy spot, with curiosities to explore and much to think about.

He opened the toilet lid, surprised by the glow inside the bowl and tentatively sat down, enjoying the way the light tingled his skin. Slowly and luxuriously he crapped out his past and enjoyed the sensation of his old life leaving the body, eliminating everything he no longer needed. It was the last physical evidence of an earlier time, clues of how he lived, buried in the waste of over a century, a hint of life's former frustrations in the smell of his past.

He reached for toilet paper, but found none, only a panel to adjust the light that surveyed his exposed area. While

Mike normally liked to play with buttons and make unpredictable adjustments, he refrained. He sat thinking, feeling the remaining evidence of his former life dissolve by the light with an occasional splash of water. Eventually Mike's sense of bathroom efficiency returned, and he lowered the lid. The light extinguished and Mike heard the comforting sound of water swirling counterclockwise.

He stood where the sink should have been and stuck his hands in light rays cascading down. Looking in the mirror, he stared back at a face he had forgotten and spent time memorizing it again—the faint lines he seldom paid attention to, a few sun spots, his light brown hair soon in need of a haircut.

He left the bathroom and saw Stanley standing in the study, waving Mike in with a smile. Floating pictures of people filled the room and talked when Stanley touched their image.

"What's all this?" Mike asked.

"I sent messages last night, asking if people are required to wear Bio Pulses. I also asked, for example, what someone from the Outside does to become a citizen. I got messages like this."

"Stanley, are you crazy? You wouldn't last a minute without your Bio Pulse," said an unknown voice.

"I probably received a hundred of those. But listen to this." Stanley moved the floating icon. "This is from an old unit-mate of mine who works at City Office."

"Hey Stanley, you thinking of going native on us? You might as well try cutting off your arm. But hey, if you're really interested, let me know what you're thinking. We have 123 people off the grid. There's a garbage pile of regulations and procedures to follow. But whatever illuminates your light. Hey, before I forget . . . about Outsiders."

"This is the best part," Stanley whispered.

"We don't get many around here anymore. I hear most of them have taken over the abandoned coastal areas. We use a standard form to build up their background information, run your basic scans, and review citizen expectations. You'd be surprised how some of these people live. Last I heard, we give Outsiders a Bio Pulse with a hundred credits. I hope that helps. Maybe I'll see you at Beta Carrotene soon. Hey."

Mike stared at the now frozen image. After hearing that Outsiders could simply sign up and join the community, Mike was disappointed. He appreciated the ease with which he could incorporate himself into the city, but a part of him romanticized his role as an agitating Outsider, an underdog, battling an unjust government. As a Social Justice Entrepreneur, it was a dream scenario, the perfect rationale to behave badly and believe it to be for the good of the community.

He'd have to find some other injustice to battle in order to appease his conscience. In the past Mike had borrowed money from those who had too much. It wasn't an elegant plan, but it did have its benefits, money being one of them, but also a self-righteousness he appreciated. He hadn't seen any wealthy people yet, but he had no idea what people hoarded or valued now, making it hard to tell who was rich.

"We're all set for City Office this morning," Stanley said. "This is going to be great. Maybe we should invite more people. Make it a party?"

"They'd get in the way and diminish the experience," Mike said, wanting minimal witnesses to his morning of planned lies.

· · · · ·

They entered City Office, on the first floor of a brick building distinguished from a lab or repair store by the words *Eau Claire* painted on the front window. Mike remembered buying subs and ice cream out of this same building. Now the inside resembled a bar with several tall round tables, stucco walls, and tile floor. A man approached, full of energy, with wide shoulders, and a knowing smile that could make people blush.

"Hey Stanley, you haven't changed a bit. I see mint ice cream is still your favorite," Dave, Stanley's old unit-mate, said as he slapped Stanley on the back. "This must be Mike. From the Outside, hey?" Dave looked at Mike, analyzing him like a piece of art. "Come with me. Come with me."

They walked past the tables to the door farthest on the left and went in. "Mike, I'm going to have you see Dr. Fanning. He'll run a few scans and make sure you're up to code. It'll only take a few minutes. When you're done, step over to my office." Dave pointed to the other side of the main room.

"OK," Mike said, apprehensive about a physical. Right then the doctor walked in looking young and shy.

"I'll have numbers to you shortly," the doctor said to Dave as he escorted Mike to the scanning area where Mike stripped down to his underwear and undershirt. His underwear came from the prison and Mike saw the doctor pause as if he wanted to ask a question about his cotton briefs, but a second later resumed his tasks.

The scanner reminded Mike of a car wash with columns of lights running around his body, bathing him in a low-intensity glow. He didn't like how the doctor stood in another room while the lights moved around Mike, making him wonder what type of rays bombarded his body. After the scan Mike waited for the doctor to poke and prod him, but

72

the exam was done. The doctor handed Mike two green cubes and told him to chew them. They tasted similar to last night's beer. Mike dressed and found Dave's office, but listened outside the open door first.

"Do you really think he's from the Outside? He doesn't look rough enough and you think everyone's from the Outside."

"Wait until you see his numbers," Stanley said. "He wasn't wearing a Bio Pulse or sun sensors, and he didn't know what year it was or anything about the Poly Plagues."

"Is he wild, aggressive, paranoid?"

"No, he's quiet, nice. I like him. We walked by the library and he had to see the inside. You'd think he'd found a rainforest by the astonished look on his face."

"You went in the library? When?"

"We walked out of the library and a crowd had already formed," Stanley said. "I was with him for at least three hours before that. He had nothing to do with the garbage." Before Dave questioned Stanley more, Mike walked in.

"How'd it go?" Stanley asked.

"Fine. The doctor told me I could see my results here."

"Give me a minute," Dave said as holographic numbers and images filled the room. "We'll pull most of this information directly into your application. I don't see any real issues." Dave slid images through the air. "Hey, look at your polymer content. I've never seen one that high. It appears the doc gave you a fungus to compensate and two courses of antibodies."

"What are these numbers?" Mike gave a small fungus burp and pointed to data floating off on the side.

"Blood, lipids, molecular makeup, the works. I see plaque, an FB, abnormal liver enzymes, high carbon infusion, a stressed autoimmune system, overall inflammation, and a strange phase variance." Dave paused before continuing.

"All your numbers are skewed, but the doc has stabilized you. Medically speaking, we have everything we need." Mike was amazed at the amount of medical information presented from a three-minute scan, including detailed brain activity he couldn't begin to understand. Instead of trying to make sense of each number, he took a broader approach.

"What's the average life expectancy in Eau Claire?" Mike asked. Stanley looked at Dave.

"As of last month, Eau Claire's life expectancy broke 119 years. That's in the top ten percent for this region."

Mike asked his next question quickly, afraid to hear a whole presentation on the above-average performance of Eau Claire. "Based on my medical numbers, will my life expectancy be a lot lower?"

"Hey, you're not helping us win any awards," Dave said before looking from Mike to Stanley and softening his response. "It's not the best start, but you have plenty of time to rehabilitate. You probably added ten years in this one day alone based on the fungus the doc gave you and the Bio Pulse programming."

The room remained quiet for five seconds, the longest silence Mike thought Dave could tolerate. "Hey, let's get some background information for the system, starting with your age. What's your date of birth?"

Mike knew he could make up any age, with no one to verify it, but he also knew he looked older for his age compared to people in Eau Claire even though many had considered him young looking a few days ago. He also knew he couldn't give his real birth date of June 13, 1975. He had no time to lie. It took too much brain power to work out the math. "June 13, 2106."

"How about relatives?" Mike needed more time to think, but didn't have it. He gave Dave his parents' names, changed their ages, and misspelled their first names slightly.

"They were born on the Outside. I don't know where."

"No problem," Dave said. "It looks like they were born right after the Poly Plagues ended. Data's a bit sketchy around then. How about any other relatives?"

Mike wanted to move on until he thought of his daughter and decided to incorporate her into the data. "My great-grandmother is the only one I can remember and probably the most likely to be in any database." He gave his daughter's name, Samantha Sullivan, her actual date of birth, and social security number, which he'd hacked in order to establish a secret college fund. He didn't think they still used social security numbers, but it had to be part of the old database.

"The data's much more stable back then," Dave said, moving multiple images. "And luckily for you, I'm able to locate one living relative, Sonia Hartman. She lives in the Denver Region."

"Can you pull up her picture?" Mike asked. And there she was—an eight-year-old with eyes like his ex-wife's and a smile, reminding him of his daughter's. Mike thought he might see his daughter again. Instead of finding her pictures on the school website or watching her on the playground, he could see her through 131 years and several generations.

Stanley raised his finger near her face, "She's cute."

"No need to dwell," Dave said. "Everything is downloaded into your new BP. You can access it any time. Hey, let's get your work background and overall skills." Dave slid more icons around. "What was your last job?"

Mike extrapolated his entrepreneurial experience to a more mainstream occupation, then converted it into a believable skill from the Outside, a place he knew nothing about. Part of it was easy for Mike, who often described his bartending job as if he were the Marketing Manager of a large corporation, but converting his skills to a plausible Outside job was pure guesswork.

"We didn't have job titles, but I enhanced our group's ability to survive," Mike said, "by evaluating new opportunities and ensuring effective communication."

Dave and Stanley looked at each other. "Sounds like an Area Strategist," Dave said.

"What's an Area Strategist?"

"It doesn't really matter. The brain scans are so complete now. They give us most of our useful information."

"Then skip the background information," Mike said.

"Hey, are you from the Outside or something?" Dave smiled at Mike and Stanley. They did not smile back. "Sorry, old joke. Background information is required."

Looking at the holographic application floating in the air, Mike picked the responses he liked best instead of making up his own. Dave beamed, excited to fill out the application so quickly. For education Mike selected Bachelor of Arts in Philosophy, the exact degree he had and forgot to enhance his educational credentials as planned.

"The next thirty-five questions are in reference to your knowledge and preferences," Dave said. "Touch the icon that best represents your answer within five seconds." Mike moved closer to the floating images, feeling competitive. "Do you associate more with the Earth, people, plants, or vegetables?" Mike touched the people icon. "Do you see numbers as theoretical, absolute, convoluted, or beautiful?" Mike selected theoretical. He continued for thirty-three more questions, and then another set of thirty-five questions focusing on general skills and abilities.

"According to the data," Dave said, while Mike still thought about changing his last answer, "your skills best suit Eau Claire's needs as a Chef, Entertainer, or Data Analyst. Pick one." Dave's cold efficiency surprised Mike.

"What do you mean pick one?" He looked at Dave. "Aren't there any more options?"

"Why? You can't pick from the three I gave you?"

Mike thought that maybe Dave had a point; more options hadn't helped him in the past. "But what if I don't like the job?"

"We've matched your preferences, skills, experience, physical attributes, and brain scans with the city's needs. The expectation is that everyone does what they are capable of. You are capable of all three. Pick one."

"Entertainer," Mike said without understanding anything about the position except that it sounded the least boring.

"Perfect." Dave touched several images in the air. "Lola Simpson will be expecting you tomorrow morning."

"I just got here. I hardly know where I am."

"If Stanley," Dave said, turning to look directly at Stanley, "had brought you here yesterday, like he should have, you'd already be a citizen. This would be boring detail."

"Sign me up," Mike said and gave his weakest smile. He figured he had to ride out the orientation portion of his stay, similar to his first day in prison when he realized he couldn't talk his way out of giving up his tater tots.

"Hey, I just sent you your garden plot location, the name of the child you'll be mentoring, and over thirty education recommendations. You have some catching up to do."

"Wait a second," Mike looked from Dave to Stanley. "What about mentoring a child?"

"She's not a child. She's fifteen." Dave touched icons and moved forward with the application. "Everyone mentors at least one child."

"Why this ch—I mean, fifteen-year-old?"

"I don't pick them, the system does, based upon your profile. Usually mentoring starts at five or six, but we're always augmenting based on need."

"What if I don't want to mentor a child?"

"Hey, your application is complete," Dave said. "We'll match it with your DNA signature, and you'll be all set." He tested Mike's BP without acknowledging Mike's question. "Some of the higher functions won't be accessible until we establish some history, which means you'll need to come back for a follow-up visit in about a month."

"Am I free to go anywhere I want?" Mike thought about leaving Eau Claire and their expectations behind.

"You need to remain in Eau Claire for a year, after which time you're free to travel anywhere." Dave moved icons and paid no attention to Mike. "In the meantime, familiarize yourself with the city's Citizen Expectations and, hey, welcome to Eau Claire."

"That's it?" Mike asked, thinking he didn't even get to enhance his past, but was satisfied with leaving most of it behind. "Do I get more information or time to catch my breath?"

"No. That's it for now. You should have everything you need."

"But . . ." Mike started, not sure what to say next.

78

"It looks like you have a place to stay, but we'll work with you if you want something different." Dave moved more icons. "There's also the issue of education, volunteering, and hobbies. Stanley can help you with your transition?" Stanley nodded his head. "Hey, I think you're in good hands."

Mike played with his new BP, glanced at the Expectations, startled to hear his own voice as part of the audio feedback. To Mike it was like talking to himself with two conversations going on at the same time and he didn't understand either one.

ELEVEN

"You look the way I feel when Sara tries to explain literature to me," Stanley said on the walkway outside City Office.

"I'm still trying to catch up. But look at me." Mike waved his arm with the Bio Pulse over his head. "I'm an Eau Claire citizen."

"I need to deliver some produce for the Fair and look in on my research." Stanley gazed at their surroundings. "Do you mind waiting here for me?"

Mike didn't know exactly where he was.

"Why don't we slow things down for you?" Stanley put his arm around Mike and walked him to a bench, protecting him like a fragile seedling. "Sit for a while." Mike let Stanley move him and thought even relaxation in the future was abrupt.

"This is a favorite spot to relax and take in Eau Claire." Stanley showed Mike some potentially interesting destinations in the area on Mike's BP. "I'll be back here in a couple hours. Enjoy the city, our city." Mike sat on a bench and watched Stanley walk away, glad for the opportunity to stay in one place.

He took a moment to evaluate his situation. He sat in a great people-watching spot with a spicy citrus smell coming from a nearby tree. The sun shone in a triangular courtyard filled with gardens, walkways, and plenty of people relaxing just like Mike. Kids jumped from raised section to raised section on the energy walkway as if playing hopscotch. Mike couldn't help but smile.

He rubbed his legs, smoothing out the soreness from all the walking yesterday. He had run these streets and enjoyed the meditative aspect, but sitting in a cell had weakened his endurance. He noticed how lean and tall people were in this Eau Claire. Women in particular seemed taller and more muscular than in his past, similar to men. A few people sat on Mike's bench, but quickly moved to another area. A couple swerved around Mike and several people walked faster when they neared him. He felt exposed.

A woman walked up to Mike. "Your preferences are showing," she said. Mike looked around wondering if she was talking to him, then looked down to see if his pants were unzipped. He didn't even have a zipper. She smiled as she sat down and took his arm. "Your personal preferences." She worked her fingers over his BP. "I'm not sure you want everyone to know that you like to be on the bottom." She gave him a wonderful smile.

"I know that wasn't a question they asked at City Office," Mike said. "Can you show me how to turn it off?"

Her smile deepened, and while still holding Mike's arm, she slid her body towards his until their legs and hips were touching. She adjusted Mike's BP. "That's me," she said and didn't let go of Mike's arm or move her body.

After a month of incarceration, Mike was on fire. He heard his own voice describe her through a haze of chemical distractions filling his blood stream, *Gina Elliott, forty-six, Environmental Engineer, guest librarian, loves the color orange* . . . Mike moved away from Gina, to clear his mind, and to see her more clearly. Mike knew how to read faces and he liked what he saw.

She looked younger than her age, like everyone he met in Eau Claire. He saw kindness, composure, and confidence. Her hair was short, light brown. She had a tiny, slightly up-turned nose, bright wide brown eyes, and dramatic eye-brows that danced on her forehead keeping time with her playful smile. Her clothes had the tiniest fleck of orange and like most, clung to her body at just the right places while remaining loose-fitting everywhere else.

He introduced himself even though she appeared to know more about him than he wished.

"Are you really from the Outside?" She looked him straight in the eye with a warm smile.

"I was from the Outside. Now I'm a . . . I'm an Eau Claire citizen." Mike pointed to the Region listed as *Outside*. "Is there a way of turning that off too?"

"Nope, prior Region is a required field. It comes from the main system. Besides I think it's kind of sexy."

"Is everyone in Eau Claire this forward?"

"Only the smart ones." Gina stood. "Welcome to Eau Claire. Have you seen the water retrieval system? It's fasci-nating. I'd love to give you a real tour of the city. I grew up here. I'll show you things you've never seen before." Again, she gave her knowing smile. Mike found himself standing, excited to explore the water retrieval system. She wrapped her arm around his and led the way.

"I need to be back here in a couple hours and I don't re-ally know where I am." Mike noticed she was an inch taller than him.

"Don't worry, I'll take good care of you," They walked arm-in-arm as Gina pointed out structures designed not to be seen—moisture collectors, runoff basins, heat conductors. "We utilize all of our resources to control the environment within the entire city. We radiate collected heat at night, adjust the length of sunlight, and manipulate atmospheric moisture levels."

"Is that something?" Mike asked, pointing to a five-foot-wide opening in a small rock outcropping.

"A semi-natural geothermal opening. It helps cool the city in the summer." Gina tightened her grip on his arm. "You're pretty good at this."

"I know interesting things when I see them." Mike watched Gina and waited for her to meet his gaze.

"Tell me about the Outside," Gina said.

"You'd hate it. They throw away everything."

"I don't know—sounds like a challenge."

"I try not to think of it much. It's hard to compare the Outside to this." Mike waved his free hand towards the trees overhead. "I'm better at new beginnings."

"How about endings?" she asked.

"It's the middle I struggle with."

Occasionally they simply stood, looking at their latest discovery—solar collectors or a community ladder. In their silence Eau Claire asserted its peaceful stillness. Mike could hear a garden spade slice through the dirt thirty feet away.

Gina led Mike down alleys hidden from sight and walkways barely three feet wide. Mike looked for connections to his old Eau Claire, but everything moved too fast. They continued their erratic tour until Gina reached her destination.

"This is what I've been working on for the past three years. It's one of four water stations in the city. This one separates, purifies, and recycles all the water and refuse from the Park District, making the city a neutral water user, only adding water when it rains."

Water. Mike finally realized what else was missing—water. Eau Claire had always been dominated by rivers, another aspect Mike had taken for granted. Translated to English, "clear water," the city's French name spoke of the importance water played in shaping the city. He took a fresh look around and remnants of rivers were everywhere in the etched stone, bridges, and ravines, used mostly for gardening. The water plant sat in a dried-up river bed. Mike shook his head.

"What?" Gina asked.

"It's an amazing building."

Skylights provided generous lighting and, similar to the surrounding area, a faint scent lingered, reminding Mike of fresh-mowed grass. Rushing water echoed off large flat surfaces. Gina put her lips on Mike's ear to speak without raising her voice.

Gina's warm breath and dynamic dialogue held Mike's attention. She showed him the whole operation including the filtration and purification systems.

"Water dissolves more substances than any other liquid. Up to a hundred gallons a minute rush through this station, coming out pure and at a perfectly neutral pH."

It was exactly as Gina had described, fascinating. Still in the building with the waste from a quarter of the city spinning and separating behind them, Mike turned towards Gina. She put her arm around his neck.

"This has been wonderful, Gina." It was the first time Mike said her name and it felt as new and exciting as the future. He kissed her, thinking that kissing hadn't changed much in 131 years, until Gina tightened her grip around the back of his neck. Gallons of water purified during the short kiss. Mike noticed none of it.

They continued to gaze at one another. "Everything is so intense here," Mike said.

"It depends on who you're with," Gina said with that smile that Mike already understood to be both playful and provocative. Eventually they left the building and continued their casual walk. Mike asked to feel her bicep and she proudly flexed for him and explained the water plant levers and cranks didn't always move by themselves.

Stanley sat at Mike's bench when they returned, looking neither impatient nor concerned. Mike and Gina stopped a short distance from Stanley. They both waved. "Do you think you can find your way from here?" she said.

"How do I find you again?"

"I'll make it easier." She took his arm and moved one image on his BP from right to left. "Just say my name and tell me where you'll be and I'll find you." She gave him a kiss on the cheek. "It was fun meeting you, Mike. I hope to see you again." Mike watched her walk away and needed a moment to catch his emotional breath before joining Stanley.

"It looks like you're making friends," Stanley said when Mike approached. "I take it you've recuperated from this morning's meeting?" Mike smiled in response. "Good," Stanley retrieved a basket of food next to him. "I saw one of your occupational preferences was chef. Let's see what kind of cook you are."

TWELVE

"What kind of city is this?" Dr. Jennings yelled in the control room. "No verification. They didn't even use their lie detector feature. They simply gave him the keys to the city." He put his face up to the audio receiver. "He's a criminal, people. Wake up."

"They made him take a job." Mason found himself defending Mike.

"You call *entertainer* a job? Sounds like a license to goof off. Hell, he lied about everything."

"What do you think their system would choose as your profession?" Mason asked.

"A medical doctor I suppose."

"It didn't sound very demanding or highly respected. The doctor didn't even provide results."

"Then maybe a city administrator or whatever it is this Dave does because he thoroughly disappoints. I also wouldn't mind being a teacher and work with people who are normal for a change. That or an architect."

"Why does everyone want to be an architect?"

"Who wouldn't want to build new, clean, crisp buildings?" Dr. Jennings framed a skyscraper with his hands, looking up at his imaginary structure. "What would you be? Something in particle manipulation?"

"Either that or an artist."

"You could work with the prisoner."

"He has an imagination. Maybe he'll make a good entertainer." Mason studied his computer screen again. "At least we're accumulating massive amounts of information. It won't help me calibrate time any more accurately, but the data we picked up from that one scan alone might take a year to understand."

"What about the prisoner mentoring a child? How did that happen? We send him forward in time, thinking he'll spend every waking moment struggling to catch up to the future. Instead he's guiding youth into their future?"

"Well, she's fifteen," Mason offered as some kind of consolation. "Maybe it's like those Scared Straight programs you were involved in years ago where kids learn from a criminal's bad choices and consequences."

"But there aren't any consequences for this chameleon. He jumps through time while the rest of us are limited to a short existence, trudging through every single day. He's meeting women, going on tours. He's treated like a celebrity."

"He only met one woman and you heard what that other woman called him. He certainly isn't viewed favorably by everyone. Prejudice has survived."

"Are we listening to the same transmission?"

Mason endured Dr. Jennings' outbursts. They were tedious but harmless. He waited to respond and let emotion seep out of the room. "We definitely hear things differently. I think it's called diversity."

"It's a common statistic that each year behind bars decreases an inmate's life expectancy by two years." Dr. Jennings slammed the counter. "But this prisoner extended his life by ten and has a good chance of living longer than either of us."

"We knew medical advancements would be dramatic in the next hundred years. Look at what's happened in the last couple of years with stem cell research."

"I figured we would create just as many advancements in disease and ailments." Dr. Jennings fiddled with two antacids in his pocket. "We continually find new ways of killing ourselves."

"You've always been the optimist."

"Spend some time with criminals once. After hearing a seventeen-year-old tell me how much he enjoys killing, it's hard not to see the worst in everything."

"Why do you stay in the criminal justice system? You could be listening to executives whine about their overwhelming lives."

"Yes, and you could be doing fulfilling research in paper manufacturing and golfing every afternoon."

"I've always hated golf. Never played it. I can't even stand watching it on TV."

"Aren't we a pair?" Dr. Jennings took a sip of his coffee. "Sitting in a prison, listening to a convict lie his way through the future."

"It sure beats golf."

THIRTEEN

Mike's surroundings were novel, but the concept of cooking hadn't changed in millennia, and he looked forward to doing something immune to time's influence. Stanley volunteered to be sous chef and awaited Mike's orders.

"I see these are mushrooms," Mike pointed to six different types of fungus ranging in color from white to brown to black. The biggest mushroom looked like a small boulder.

"Smell the smoky aroma of this one." Stanley pushed a reddish-brown mushroom towards Mike and described the texture and flavors of each one.

"What's that?" Mike pointed to a pile of weeds on the counter.

"Dandelion roots. They have a fantastic flavor."

As Mike began to cook, he felt intimidated until he picked up an onion. Its shape and heft were familiar, connecting him to something primal that reached back 131 years and a few thousand more. He asked Stanley to make the salad while he continued with the mushroom sauce for fresh pasta.

"Stanley," Mike said, as he chopped roots with his back turned, "do you like living in Eau Claire?"

Stanley ripped lettuce and eventually answered. "I've lived in five different cities, but I grew up in Eau Claire and I missed the community that brought me up. I probably became a botanist because of the people here. Two of the mushrooms you cut up were developed in Eau Claire."

The kitchen became quiet again except for the sound of knives chopping and sauce thickening with a bubble ending in a low pop. It created a soothing sound that, along with busy hands, encouraged conversation.

"Each city seemed the same to me in my twenties," Stanley continued, "but as I got older and volunteered in kitchens and planted gardens, I couldn't help but think of roots. Now that I've met Sara, I understand the importance of community I heard so much about as a kid." Stanley peeled long strips from a carrot. "Why? What do you think of Eau Claire?"

"I don't know. In some ways, it's completely different from what I know." Mike set his knife down and stirred the sauce. Cooking relaxed him. "Other times it seems no different. I met Gina today, and it felt like I ran into an old friend." Mike tasted the sauce and added a pinch of salt. "How do relationships work around here? Does everyone meet electronically?"

"I'm no expert on relationships and I don't know how you'd have one on the Outside without a BP."

"How did you meet Sara?"

"On my first day volunteering at Beta Carrotene, I hadn't been there more than an hour, and in walked Sara." Stanley examined the pepper in his hand. "She didn't say a word and started working, but I could tell she was watching me. It was her kitchen." Stanley held his knife in mid-cut.

"I couldn't cut this particularly tough root and struggled. Sara walked up behind me, held my knife hand still, and said, 'Watch out, you might hurt somebody.' I can still feel her body against mine as she took up a cleaver and in ten seconds minced the root into perfectly uniform pieces. She smiled, handed me my knife, and went back to washing celery. She didn't say another word until the end of the night when she asked me to try her vegetable soup. She cupped my hand and held the spoon, and . . . well, that's how I met her."

Stanley's unit-mates returned with two bottles of wine in plain brown bottles, marked with white writing on the side. They set the table with mismatched plates and glasses. Paul was shorter, bulkier than Mike with a ready smile, reminding Mike of a CEO from a California tech company—pompous, but in a hip way. Kevin was about the same height as Mike and had a similar trim build. He came across as a grad student who stayed in school because it made him a higher class of hippie. Mike and Stanley brought food to the table while Kevin poured wine and Paul found the silverware.

"So Mike," Paul said when they sat down, "what's it like on the Outside? Is it as dangerous and tough as they say?"

"Well," Mike thought after taking his first bite, "for me, it was lonely, dirty and the women were a lot less friendly. What about you Paul, what do you think of Eau Claire?"

"It's too small and out of the way. I was a Green Member. I've been to more cities than anyone. Paris Three, now there's a city if you are looking for friendly women, but those solar ships are slower than an apple tree bearing fruit."

"Who are you kidding, Paul?" Kevin said. "You told me the other day how great the beer is here and how you've never been to a place with lower energy expectations. Don't listen to him, Mike. I've been to a few places myself—we all have. Every city has great aspects and things that suck. Eau

Claire is no different. Just beware the horseradish here. It's wicked stuff."

"This is great sauce, Mike." Stanley took another bite. "You were right about the thyme. It's perfect."

"What?" Paul and Kevin said in mock horror.

"Do we have another cook in our midst?" Kevin protected his plate with his hands. "Stanley, why didn't you warn us? Hide the herbs."

"It's good sauce," Paul said. "Maybe you'll be able to temper Stanley. He's been trying to get us to cook for the last couple of years. You can't make a nuttybutter sandwich around here without Stanley suggesting a few raisins or a slice of apple."

"Heathens," said Stanley.

"I've been curious." Kevin held a forkful of food in front of him. "I heard on the Outside, people collect things, strip the abandoned buildings, gather as much stuff as they can."

"Well." Mike thought about how to answer, hoping his past and the Outside were similar. "It's true. A lot of people hoard stuff. They think the more they have, the happier they'll be." His three new unit-mates looked skeptical. Mike continued. "On the Outside everyone is on their own, so you need a lot of resources to deal with each possibility. We were taught to use it up before somebody else does."

"That's crazy," Paul said.

"In Eau Claire and just about everywhere," Kevin said, holding the same forkful of food, "the person who consumes less and creates more energy is the one people look up to."

"I know a guy who can't even take a date back to his unit because his building uses too much energy," Paul said as he poured more wine. "Last time he tried, his date took one look at the building rating, and left. Just so you know."

"You can't believe everything Paul says," Kevin said. "Just so you know."

"Like hell you can't."

"I was wondering something." Mike wanted to change the subject. "Do people get married in this city? Because everyone seems to be single. You guys are all single, right?" Stanley, Paul, and Kevin looked at each other like Mike's question was the stupidest one they had ever heard.

"Of course people get married," Paul said. "Happens all the time."

"At what age do people get married?"

"What would you guys say?" Stanley asked his two unit-mates. "Around sixty or seventy?"

"Sounds about right." Paul and Kevin said as they nodded.

"What about kids?"

"What about them?" Stanley said.

"Women have babies by themselves? No fathers around?" Mike thought he should be the last person to ask such a question. Again, his unit-mates looked at each other.

"I don't know if they explained this to you where you come from," Kevin said, "but a baby requires both a mother and father. The applications wouldn't be accepted otherwise."

"What applications?" Mike said, reminded of the convoluted conversation with Dr. Jennings two days ago. *Was that only two days ago?*

"I can't believe we are sitting here talking about where babies come from. Stanley, you explain the birds and bees to our guest while Kevin and I clean this up." Paul pointed to the kitchen table. "Then I suggest we catch the Fair." They looked at Mike.

"I don't know what the Fair is, but it sounds good to me."

. . . . .

The Fair consisted of a series of venues, each separated by stone or brick walls of various sizes and styles. Mike thought he might be in old Carson Park, but without rivers and lakes as guides, he was lost. Along a wide walkway, actors, musicians, and artists lined both sides. Live performances made up half of the shows while the other half were a mixed media of images or sounds, often with strong audience participation.

"Everyone, send me your scans," said the performer, as he projected a fifteen-foot face that looked like everyone and no one. "Now engineers only." The face changed. "Child Center volunteers." The image changed again. Mike saw one more face transform before his group continued on to watch another performance.

A woman walked past juggling drinking mugs. One show recapped the history of the solar collector; another featured an acoustic band not unlike many bands Mike had heard in past Eau Claire. At least two different groups performed Shakespeare, one as a holographic parody, the other a shortened play performed by five-year-olds. Mike didn't understand either one. He had always struggled to appreciate Shakespeare.

Mike marveled at a high energy mathematical band that played long algebraic equations, the lead singer rapping out formulas, sometimes breaking into a word problem while musicians played in time, their beautiful melody solving the equation.

Mike and his unit-mates moved from site to site, never staying to see an entire show. Paul led the way. Kevin lingered behind and caught up as the other three moved on. Mike loved it, wanting to stay for every performance while still seeing everything.

Some time after dark, people wandered over to the Furnace. "What's the Furnace?" Mike asked. Kevin and Paul looked at Stanley.

"You guys go ahead. I'll explain it to him." Stanley pulled Mike aside. "Every couple of weeks, enough heat accumulates in this rock formation." Stanley motioned to a rock outcrop at least a hundred feet long. "It provides the citizens an ample heat source to work metal and glass, fire clay, and," Stanley said as he turned from the rock to look at Mike, "burn the dead."

"It's a funeral?" Mike asked.

"Yes and no. It's also a celebration." They walked again.

"But I can't possibly know any of these people."

"It doesn't matter. The bodies are symbolic."

Mike had been to one funeral when he was young. He remembered how eerie his uncle looked laying in a coffin with pillowy white satin around his head. "I'm not sure I should be here."

"Nobody celebrates alone." Stanley opened his arms to show the mass of people. "The entire city joins in. Each life that ends makes room for another to begin. It's the cornerstone of our sustainability." They continued to follow the crowd. "For the thirty-four people honored in death tonight, thirty-four babies, born over the last two weeks will be their gifts to the city."

"What do we do?" Mike asked and thought of all the things his parents told him not to do at his uncle's funeral.

"Look." The area around the Furnace came into view and the same festive mood carried over from the Fair. "This is something we look forward to. Relax."

The same heat that dissolved century-old bodies produced functional artwork in a fiery visual display. Mike and

Stanley walked the entire hundred-foot length of the Furnace. Eau Claire residents of all ages said goodbye to people who had lived through the Poly Plagues, welcomed new arrivals, and celebrated life in general.

The glow from the Furnace cast shadows across the landscape, creating the centerpiece of the fairgrounds. Over fifty thousand people danced and talked, celebrated and created, while toasting those who had died. Kids moved through the crowd and darted together like flocks of birds, reading signals through some old form of communication. Adults hugged every child within reach. Adolescents lingered just out of grasp, preferring to ignore the friendly acknowledgements while still enjoying the attention.

They found Paul who had commandeered a table as Kevin returned with four beers in ceramic mugs. "Perfect timing," Paul said. They drank and talked while artists and amateurs blew glass, hammered metal, and threw clay into mugs similar to the ones they drank from. Kevin took a turn at the potter's wheel, produced a large pitcher, and brought the still-damp piece to the table where the unfired creation wouldn't survive the evening.

"It's time one of you showed some artistic flair." Kevin looked at his unit-mates. No one moved. "How about you Mike? As the newest citizen of Eau Claire, I think it's time you demonstrated some responsibility and got out there."

Mike stood up. "OK, what do I do?" Kevin explained the informal process and within a half hour Mike's new unit-mates cheered him on as he blew his second gather of glass, turning the pipe to keep it symmetrical and smiling between breaths.

After his third piece of glass broke, Mike returned to his unit-mates.

96

"A Renaissance man." Kevin slapped Mike on the back. They drank and talked. Friends wandered up to their table and pulled the conversation in different directions.

"I didn't understand a single joke that guy told about elephants," said Kevin's friend, "but the tour of molecular structures was cool, especially when you reached the neutrons."

"I missed it," Kevin said. "I tried to keep up with Paul."

Stanley discussed Mike's history as an Outsider with two of his friends. "Right when I saw him, I knew he was from the Outside. Didn't I, Mike?"

"You must be an Outside expert," Mike said wanting to help Stanley after all the help he had received.

"Stanley thinks everyone's from the Outside," said one of Stanley's friends.

"He was bound to be right at least once," said the other as they both walked off to another table.

A heated discussion picked up between Paul and the people at the next table about the winner of last month's energy challenge. "Numbers don't lie," said the woman a few feet away.

"That's complete garbage," Paul said. "He takes the train nearly every day. How's he going to accumulate those kinds of numbers?"

Everyone moved around until Mike found himself at a table full of people he didn't know. He thought it odd to be in Eau Claire barely twenty-four hours and already distinguishing between friend and stranger.

The conversation grew lively and broke into three or four separate yet weakly connected discussions. Not surprisingly, Mike found himself in a philosophical debate about the city's volunteer recommendations.

"One area of interest isn't enough for these fascists," said Madeleine as she flattened Kevin's deformed pitcher. "What about an individual's right to self-actualization?" Mike looked eagerly at the others, hoping to find some dissent or at least rebellion. He was disappointed.

"It's a recommendation, Madeleine," said a man with graying hair and weathered skin. "You don't have to volunteer in three different areas. Stick to one if you like." Madeleine tried to regroup and form a rebuttal, but for all of her passion, she lacked any evidence of a dictatorship or personal injury on the part of the city. *I hear you sister.* Mike struggled with similar issues, wanting to justify not playing by the rules.

Mike found conflict, but not the kind he'd hoped for when two young men walked up to him and poured their beers on his lap. He jumped to his feet more startled than angry, but the anger caught up. "What the—?"

"We thought you'd feel more at home sitting in your own filth," said the bigger one.

"We don't like stinking Outsiders giving our city a bad name," said the smaller one whose eyes looked through Mike and his smile made Mike feel cold inside. "Take your trash and leave."

Mike was about to act unstable to diffuse the situation when Paul and a few of his friends came to Mike's aid and stepped in front of the beer pourers.

"You're the one giving Eau Claire a bad name, my friend," Paul said to the bigger one. "Why don't you two go hammer some metal and put that energy to good use?" The two looked at Paul and the people gathering behind him and decided to pursue other interests. "Sorry about that Mike, but there are bound to be a few people dumb enough or afraid enough to see you as a threat. Don't let them get to you."

Mike dried his clothes close to the Furnace. He considered whether he represented a threatening Outside influence or the last holdover of personal greed and waste and smiled at both options until he realized—*those must have been the beer pourers from the prediction.*

He saw Stanley and Sara sitting at a table with a group of kids around them. Stanley waved Mike over.

"I'll see you three tomorrow," Sara said, pointing to three teenagers in the group as they ran from the table.

"I heard you had fun tonight," Sara said.

"If I don't think about my new job tomorrow and everything I don't know, I sometimes enjoy myself."

"Stanley will help you tomorrow." Sara elbowed Stanley. "Won't you Stanley?"

"Sleep in tomorrow. Those guys," Stanley said and pointed in the direction of Kevin and Paul while he pretended to wince from the pain of Sara's elbow, "won't be up until the solar collectors have absorbed half the day's energy. Sleep in, relax, catch your breath."

"What about Lola? I need to meet her in the morning."

"Morning's a relative term, especially after a Fair."

FOURTEEN

Mike sat in bed the next morning and attempted to remember first where he was, then how to use his BP. Listening to the city's thirty-five citizen expectations, only seven appeared substantial. Expectations such as *be courteous and helpful* were generic while others like *show the proper decorum when using Clean Screens* were confusing, as Mike had never heard of a Clean Screen.

When he accessed the list of open jobs in Eau Claire, the number and variety of positions overwhelmed Mike. The list of volunteer opportunities continued even longer. He turned down his BP.

Instead he projected his great-great-great granddaughter Sonia's hologram and stared at the five-foot-tall picture of her. He thought about the four generations of people between him and her. Years he skipped. Lifetimes he missed.

"What was your mother like? Your grandmother?" Mike asked out loud, lying on his bed with his hands behind his head. "Would you know your great-grandmother, or my daughter, your great-great-grandmother?" He looked at her image until nothing remained for him to discover.

He got out of bed and put on his only set of clothes, which reminded him of another task he needed to complete soon.

His one small sense of accomplishment came from the four energy points he'd earned yesterday.

As he walked into the living room, Mike's mood showed on his face, which was unusual. He didn't travel 131 years in the future often, so he brooded with gusto.

"What's wrong?" Stanley asked.

"I have a new job I don't understand, and my voice continues to tell me things I don't want to hear."

"You can reprogram the audio response on your BP if you like."

Mike ignored Stanley. It wasn't his voice that bothered him, it was the constant barrage of information. "I'm supposed to work, mentor a child, volunteer, produce energy, tend a garden, and I'm wearing the same clothes as yesterday and they're not even mine." Mike attempted to fasten his outer shirt then gave up and let the tie hang loose. "I think I'll go back to bed."

"I know I encouraged you to sleep in, but what if we address a few things first?" Stanley operated Mike's BP and moved holographic images around. "You can put in a couple of hours with Lola, meet Florence—she's the fifteen-year-old you're mentoring—then volunteer at the library. I also sent your scan to the tailor. Choose a style."

Mike saw six different life-size holographic models of himself, each wearing a slightly different outfit. He spun them around and examined the neckline and cuff types. Each selection led to a series of other choices until he saw an image of himself wearing an outfit much like the one he had on, minus the hat. Mike's hat-wearing days had passed him by. Stanley helped Mike finalize the order, adding the slightest fleck of blue to the otherwise brown outfit.

"You're all set. Everything else can wait. Feel better?"

"Thanks." Mike looked down at his clothes. "How do you keep these clean? I've been wearing this for two days straight."

"We'll take care of it. I'll walk you over to Lola's on my way to the lab. How about a vegi-protein shake on the way?"

Mike felt better after he acquired his own shake, which tasted better than it sounded.

"You might want to finish that." Stanley pointed to Mike's shake as they approached a covered section of the walkway. "The Clean Screen up ahead filters and intensifies the sun's rays to kill surface bacteria and break down residue several layers deep. It will destroy your shake. And don't look up." Mike gulped the rest of his shake. Stanley took off his hat. As they walked through the Clean Screen, Mike thought he felt a slight tingle on his skin, but it was over too fast to know for sure.

"I read about these in the City Expectations," Mike said.

"Every day it seems, someone uses it as their own personal shower and takes off their shirt or runs through naked." Stanley looked back at the Clean Screen. "Mostly it's kids, but you'd be surprised what you see go through there."

Stanley collected Mike's now clean shake glass from him. "Here's how to find Florence and get to the library." Stanley showed Mike on his BP. "Several good health stores are along the way. If you have any questions or get lost, send me a message." Stanley left Mike standing in front of Lola's at an unmarked door. Mike knocked, but no one answered, so he walked in. He was alone in a small front room, and about to leave, when a curtain flew back and in glided a stately woman.

"Mr. Newhouse, you will be doing an interpretive performance of life on the Outside at the next city Fair," Lola said in a booming voice before she gracefully turned and walked back through the curtain. Mike stood and stared, unsure what to do next. After a minute Lola stuck her head back through the curtain.

"Mike, you want to haul it back here?" Lola asked in a more casual voice.

Mike walked through the curtain into a much bigger room filled with twenty people practicing. Three people acted out an elaborate scene with no props. A woman looked as if she was singing, but she made no sound. Mike looked away, then back again.

"Sound-dampening enclosures," Lola said. *That explains the band in the corner.* The sweaty drummer comically moved over her drums with her arms dancing and her head rocking to a beat that Mike couldn't hear or feel.

Along the back wall, people manipulated holographic images, prodding them to move according to their plans. Mike's Bio Pulse whispered their names to him, but like most information, he ignored it. Before Mike explored more, Lola demanded his attention.

"It should be at least two weeks before the next performance, depending on how long it takes the sun to reheat the Furnace. You can use any medium you like, but get input from the other performers since they will be the ones reviewing your work. Any questions?"

"What happens if I don't want to perform?"

Lola turned as if on stage and delivered her lines flawlessly. "If you fail to perform or if your performance does not meet the expectations of the group, you will have violated your commitment to the city's expectation." Lola used all of her training to project. "Which, unlike the Outside. Comes. With. Consequences." Lola walked away. The acrobats balancing nearby stood as still as Mike. A couple danced in Mike's direction.

"Welcome to the group," said the male dancer.

"Don't mind her," said the female dancer, moving to a silent rhythm, both in each other's arms, as they circled Mike.

"She has a thing about the Outside," said the male dancer.

"She lost her older brother on the Outside," said the female dancer.

The conversation continued as Mike picked up information in alternating sentences from the couple that never stopped moving.

"It was thirty years ago."

"He left with a friend for a year on the Outside."

"He was never heard from again." The dancers twirled elaborately.

"Do you have any advice about getting started?" Mike asked, but the dancers glided away. Mike walked over to the acrobats, a man and two women. A woman balanced on each of his outstretched arms.

"What do I do next?" Mike asked. He looked at his BP to address them by name.

"We don't wear BPs when we perform," said the woman on the man's right arm. "That's what makes us special. No one else will take the risk." She asked Mike if he could sing or dance or act. He shook his head. As they moved into another position, Ivan, a holographic performer, put his arm around Mike and steered him to the back of the room.

"You must have some skill," Ivan said. "Nobody ends up here by accident."

Mike struggled to think of a talent. "I can tell stories."

"Well, isn't that what entertaining is all about?" Ivan was the oldest in the group with white hair and one of the few men Mike had seen with a beard. Ivan saw Mike noticing his beard. "You should get yourself one," Ivan pulled on his white beard. "Make you look more like an Outsider. It's all about the illusion." Mike liked him. Ivan had a way of describing concepts in terms Mike understood.

Ivan used holographic shapes that morphed into other shapes, telling stories with color, texture, and form. He explained the tools and the process as he called over the rest of the holographic operators.

"I want everyone here to help Mike," Ivan said to two men and one woman. "Anyone who can upset Ms. Simpson is welcome here."

"Ivan," Mike said, "what happens if I can't do this?"

In response, Ivan pointed with his head to the holographic images he brought up. A three-foot red cube bounced up and down, waiting its turn while five smaller blue spheres made several trips over a green triangle jump, propelling them over an elongated yellow rectangle. They eventually stopped to allow the red cube a turn. The red cube flipped itself over awkwardly towards the jump before it gave up all together. Once the cube stopped moving, the five spheres combined into one big eight-foot sphere and rolled over the cube, leaving a flattened red smear similar to a pool of blood. Ivan shrugged while the rest of the group smiled apologetically.

Lucas, the shy one, worked mostly with animals and nature scenes. Lily, young and the most outspoken, used large images of everyday objects in compelling ways. Thomas worked with monsters. He was the youngest and the best animator. He offered to assist Mike to create a library of images, but Mike first needed to decide what types of images to use. It didn't take Mike long to figure out he was best at manipulating people.

Thomas made creating holographic people easier than Mike thought possible and Mike produced fifteen within a few hours. Several holographic women bore a striking re-semblance to Gina, each with progressively larger breasts.

"Looks like you got a case of fantasy drift," Thomas said.

"What?"

"It's common with beginners," Thomas reduced the breast sizes on the women Mike had created. "The power of creation can be overwhelming and lead to unrealistic dimensions. That's why I stick with creatures. No one can tell if I over-exaggerate." Mike reexamined his creations. He liked the changes Thomas had made but felt as if he had been caught window peeping.

Thomas went back to his work and left Mike alone to continue his progress. Mike stared at his images without much progress until hunger gave him an excuse to quit. He snuck out and had lunch alone.

He stopped at Beanery, a health store Stanley recommended, and decided to tinker with a social system he didn't yet understand. He pretended to have difficulty with his BP, which caused three people to shake their heads in disgust, but as Mike had hoped, an older gentleman came to his rescue.

"It's probably the interface. They can be tricky at first," the stranger said, stretching out his arm. "Here, use mine." Mike did and thanked the man for his help. As he ate his ill-gotten black bean burrito, Mike debated how to apply what he had learned and wondered what in the city needed to be fixed.

"They let Outsiders in here?" he heard a woman say to no one in particular. Mike smiled and savored the last of his burrito.

He walked towards the Park District, in no hurry to arrive. He eventually came to a brick Victorian house with a large front porch and admired the building before he walked up the stairs. On the porch a woman approached.

"Florence will be glad to meet you," she said. "Well, no she won't, but you know what I mean."

"Who are you?" Mike asked.

She looked at him, then her BP. "I'm Kali Bello. I run the house. My information's in the system."

"Of course," Mike said, pretending he understood.

"I'll bring Florence out."

A teenager stepped onto the porch. She couldn't have weighed more than ninety pounds and had short, light brown hair and piercing eyes. She approached Mike, who sat on the railing.

"Don't tell me we're going to be the best of friends and don't call me Florence."

Mike looked at her. She didn't look away. He smiled, not to be friendly or inviting, but because he understood the tactic. Intimidation was beginner stuff. He had seen the same look on rich, insecure people who tried to bully their way through life. It was also how each new inmate under twenty acted on his first few days behind bars.

"Do you want to go for a walk?"

"No," she said, trying to make the word a weapon.

"OK. I enjoyed meeting you Florence. Maybe I'll see you later." Mike walked down the stairs and was not surprised to see Florence walking alongside him. "Florence, that's a tough name. What do you want to be called?"

"Ren."

They walked in silence for a while. "Ren, what's your deal?"

"Are you really from the Outside?"

"Yep."

"Do they use BPs on the Outside?"

"Nope."

"I don't want to wear my BP and everyone thinks I'm suicidal."

"Who's everyone?"

"I don't know. Ms. Bello, my parents, the city, teachers, any of ten different mentors I've had over the last year."

"Are you suicidal?"

"I just don't want everyone looking into my stuff."

"Get over it," Mike said. Ren kicked him in the shin and ran towards the house and up the stairs. *Maybe she's not quite like a new inmate.* Mike rubbed his shin.

Mike thought about not volunteering at the library, but after the free burrito and poor showing with Ren, he could hear his old homeless friend, Guru, whisper in his ear about the cosmic payback of life. Besides, Mike looked forward to the library's quiet walls. It was the same building he visited his first day. He could see barriers still surrounding the garbage site.

As soon as he entered, he felt he had gone back in time a hundred years with nothing but books to indicate the era. Another volunteer showed Mike around.

"There's really not much to do," she said. "If anyone gets too loud or unruly, threaten to take away their book. That usually works."

"How do you know where to re-shelve each book?" Mike asked.

"We try to shelve them by author's last name, but put them wherever you can find space. Some of our fancier books go in the gallery section. It doesn't matter where in that section. Make it look nice."

"How do I know which books are fancy?"

"Anything big, heavy, or with a pretty cover. This isn't tree surgery."

"What about non-fiction books? Do you still use the Dewey Decimal System?" Mike made a bet with himself, fifty-to-one odds, that the archaic system hadn't survived.

"The what?" she said and Mike shook his head in a dismissive fashion. "There aren't many non-fictions. We put them back there." She pointed to a bookshelf in the distance. "It doesn't matter where."

Mike walked through the library and looked for the most comfortable chair, then re-shelved a few books. One book, *The History of Eau Claire*, created in 2072, caught his attention. He sat down and read the handmade book, looking at original sketches. He learned Eau Claire had incorporated in 1872. He grew bored with the history of sawmills and farming and skipped to the beginning of the twenty-first century. He looked for information about the downtown, the university, and even the prison, but found none. He followed Eau Claire's history starting with the industry boom in 2028. *Growth was fueled by an increase in tourism and the addition of several larger businesses, predominately in the food industry.*

The book mentioned a few wars with little impact on Eau Claire, except for the Water Wars. *A series of conflicts in the western states that moved to the Great Lakes area and intensified, eventually stripping the flow of water to the city, changing the landscape.*

Major population growth coincided with increased oil costs. *The ban on fossil fuels in 2043 benefited Eau Claire due to its fertile soils and investments in solar power, securing Eau Claire as a link on the Magnetic Highway.*

The population in Eau Claire peaked at 142,490 in 2050, shortly after the Interior Migration. Over half of the country's population was on the move as coastlines flooded. Mike pulled his feet off the floor. *A series of pandemics known as the Poly Plagues—due to bacterium that mutated from plastic polymers once prevalent in the human body— started in 2052 and finally ended in 2067, changing Eau Claire dramatically.* The drawings were bleak, filled with suffering.

An early adopter of bio filters, Eau Claire experienced a thirty-five percent mortality rate, while the effects of the Poly Plagues were far more devastating in other parts of the country. Mike looked up from his book, thinking he might find the library empty, but discovered it full of healthy people. *In 2068 Eau Claire established itself as a Tier-Three city in the Minneapolis Region as part of the zero-growth population plan.*

Mike sat in his chair for another thirty minutes with the book still open, unable to move, waiting for the years of history to reach equilibrium in his body. After skipping 131 years, history was no longer the subtle impression made over a lifetime, but a tidal wave threatening to engulf his entire life in a single moment. He eventually set the book on the arm of the chair and numbly walked out of the library, with a new appreciation for the past.

FIFTEEN

Mason and Dr. Jennings now listened to the Tapes separately, the warden in his office, and Mason more frequently at his home in Eau Claire, away from the warden's influence and the growing protests at the prison. They called the audio recordings the Tapes, even though the information was stored digitally, and contained terabytes of data in the form of charts, graphs, and reports extrapolated from the audio file.

With an extended delay in the project, waiting for politics and protesters to come to some agreement or simply lose interest, Mason and Dr. Jennings focused more on the Tapes than time manipulation as they attempted to reconcile their two views.

"I can't help but think they've gone backwards," Dr. Jennings said, sitting in the Time lab. "People either walk or take mass transit. How's that better?"

"No pollution."

"No privacy."

"No marketing."

"No enterprise."

"No poverty."

"We can't be sure of that," Dr. Jennings said, "but no luxuries either."

Mason thought of several other positive aspects, but didn't mention them, knowing his colleague would counter each one. "What do you do with your free time?"

"I still have a prison to run." Dr. Jennings updated his prisoner list and wrote a future date in front of each prisoner's designation, fantasizing about the punishment each sentence would bring.

"I've been walking downtown," Mason said. His wife had left him years ago in the middle of his first obsession—exploring space within atoms. Most people couldn't understand him, his wife least of all. His kids had grown, mostly without him, and lived in other states. "I've been here three years and I'd never seen the downtown before." Mason incorporated a drawing of the Masonic Ballroom into his sketch. "I think many of these buildings are the same ones in future Eau Claire."

"It seems impossible that anything from this hick city would survive."

"Why? These buildings are in relatively good shape and built to last." Mason turned from his sketchbook back to his computer. "In Europe, it's not uncommon to find buildings five hundred years old and older."

"But with technology, they would've built more modern buildings."

"That doesn't seem to be their philosophy. Here, let me play you a section of the Tapes." Mason played a preselected section on his computer.

"All Fibers harvests its material monthly. Currently we have an open field blend offering a medium green hue and a durable rating of twelve. The current wait for tailoring is . . . Built in the Classic Revival style in 1928, this Neo-classical structure . . . Seedy Reeds will be performing in twenty-three minutes."

"Did you hear it? 1928 Neo-classical structure. With at least one reference point to a building here, I can start overlaying the two cities."

"For what purpose?" Dr. Jennings pulled out his prisoner list again, already bored.

"To envision what Eau Claire would look like with gardens instead of parking lots. Imagine the space with no streets," he tapped his sketch pad. "Science is about exploration, envisioning things we can't see. Besides, I think I've found it."

"What?"

"A reference point."

"How?"

"I simply extrapolated the size of future Eau Claire from the current downtown as if it were a nucleus, expanded it in all directions. By applying known parameters with the latest research on city density and agriculture, I determine future Eau Claire to be about twelve square miles."

"There are places in New York with ten times as many people in twelve square miles," Dr. Jennings said, not quite sure if it was true.

"Perhaps, but they have taller buildings and few if any gardens which is not sustainable. I settled on a two-mile radius with the downtown at the center."

"What's the reference point?"

"You just heard it, the 1928 Neo-classical structure. It has to be the Masonic Ballroom."

"What next?"

"I fill in the detail, depict future Eau Claire by better understanding our Eau Claire."

. . . . .

Mason's daily routine now included walks through downtown Eau Claire with sketchbook in hand. He listened to the
Tapes as he recreated Mike's steps. *This apple tree is the
Golden Eau Claire cultivar, planted April 11, 2149. It produces . . . Lucas, a close friend of Kevin's is within fifteen
feet . . . currently serving alfalfa, kale, apple, walnut, berry
shakes ... Sesame Court is approaching on your right.*

He heard locals talk about him. "One of those Government guys, probably writing all of our names down," said a
man with his name embroidered on his shirt.

Within the two-mile radius he believed the future Eau
Claire comprised, lived only half of the sixty-five thousand
residents of current Eau Claire. Strip malls and fast food
restaurants pulled at the nucleus, stretched the city, and
weakened its structure. "How had I never noticed this before?" Mason said to himself.

He did find one spot that reminded him of Mike's Eau
Claire, a quaint diner, called The Farm, in an old building
two blocks east of downtown. He believed it was in the same
structure as the fourth-hand store. The food tasted earthy,
real, where farmers and businesspeople mingled in a
friendly environment. The waitress who first called him
mister, now referred to him as John.

"How about the special, John? It's got those little red potatoes you like."

"Thanks, Debbie."

"What do you think of all those new buildings they're
putting in by the highway near the mall?" Debbie asked, setting the coffee pot on his table. "People are going to forget
we have a downtown."

"I don't think they should build anything north of Highway 12," Mason said, believing it to be near the northern

edge of future Eau Claire. "Why do they build new buildings when beautiful ones sit empty?"

"What are you drawing?" Debbie tried to peek at the pages. Mason showed her a few of the same drawings he showed anyone who asked—current sketches of downtown. He never let anyone see his version of future Eau Claire or what he thought these buildings looked like in the future.

· · · · ·

Dr. Jennings researched Mike's background and, like Mason, created his own sketch, not of the city, but of the man. For Dr. Jennings, prisoner fifty-eight had first been an oddity for his lack of susceptibility to time's influence. His interest in the prisoner grew into an obsession as Mike defied the warden's guiding principles of justice and consequences. With no new Time trials scheduled, Dr. Jennings turned his energy to study Mike, in the hope that he might learn what made him—and time—tick.

Dr. Jennings started at the beginning. He visited two bars Mike had worked at years ago while attending college in Eau Claire—the jumping-off point for his entrepreneurial career. No one at the bar knew of Mike. Too much time had passed, but they all knew of a man who might have some answers. Guru wasn't hard to find, but Dr. Jennings clearly saw he wasn't a pushover.

"Excuse me, are you Guru?" Dr. Jennings asked when he approached an eighty-year-old man with perfect posture in clean but tattered clothes.

"I have been called that." Guru bowed slightly.

"My name is Dr. Max Jennings. I'm a psychiatrist, I specialize in the treatment of fear and anxiety and I'm attempting to analyze the effects of deterrents on identity theft." Guru remained quiet. "I can interpret the data, but I need help understanding the motivation."

"How can I help?"

"I've been told you have a vast amount of knowledge about motivation."

"Step into my office." Guru walked through a gap in the bushes and led them to a quiet park with a chess table. He sat on the black side of the table. "Do you play chess?"

"It's been a while," Dr. Jennings said. They played several moves rapidly.

Guru took the doctor's pawn with his knight and held the pawn in his hand. "Why are you really here, Doctor?"

The question didn't surprise Dr. Jennings. Up close he could see Guru's clothes were high quality if well-worn and the man possessed an authority beyond simple appearances. "I'm sorry. I haven't been completely truthful. I am a psychiatrist, but I'm more interested in one identity thief in particular—Michael Newhouse."

"Ah, Mikey. How is he?"

"Mr. Newhouse is under my care, and—"

"I find it hard to believe," Guru interrupted. "Mikey was particularly strong-minded. I don't believe he would seek your services."

"Let me try again. Mr. Newhouse is under my state-mandated care."

"I see," Guru said, as he looked from the pawn in his hands to the doctor. "What do you want to know about Mikey?"

"Mr. Newhouse isn't a typical identity thief. He appears to have some delusion that by pretending to be other people, he is saving the world from . . . I don't know what."

Guru studied the pawn again. "I can tell you this. Mikey liked to use peoples' weaknesses against them. He focused on corruption in the world and attacked it. I tried to convince him to focus on love and grow it. We argued for hours. He could be quite passionate."

"Do you think Mr. Newhouse's behavior is rational?"

Guru redirected his gaze from the pawn to the doctor. "Mikey might've been happier if he didn't care what happened to other people. He saw it as a strange mission to help those who didn't fare as well in a rigged system and lost himself in the process. He used other's greed as a shield to protect him from his own misdeeds. He internalized the struggles around him and saw them as personal attacks. He fought injustice in equally personal terms and enjoyed the freedom righteousness provided without ever realizing how constricted, how isolated his life had become. It was very personal to Mikey, and it made for a tough life."

"What's the best way to help him?"

Guru handed the doctor his pawn. "Compassion."

SIXTEEN

In one week, Mike had changed. His transformation was not a sign of growth or acceptance, but simply a response to his surroundings. He watched people, not for weaknesses, but to understand their motivations. He found himself touching trees, running his finger through soil as he vaguely became aware of a deeper connection.

He still struggled. His Outside interpretive performance wasn't going well. He could perform, but not entertain. He knew when to smile, play his part, deliver his lines with rich emotion. He could convince people to give him things, but he had no idea what to give in return.

Mike wandered through Eau Claire in an attempt to generate ideas and found himself outside the Park District Water Plant.

"Imagine meeting you here," Gina said as she opened the door while Mike stared at it, wondering what to do next.

"How did you know?"

"Proximity alert." Gina tapped her BP. "And I know a great place for lunch." They took the train to the Garden District, ordered sandwiches, and ate on a bench surrounded by flowering herbs with a view of distant hills outside the city.

"Yeah, my mother was single." Gina said to Mike's question about her upbringing in Eau Claire.

"And your father?"

"He was single too. I stayed closer to my parents than most kids. They were both assigned as mentors to me, which is pretty rare."

"That's how kids grow up?" Mike asked.

"Sure. We're children of the community. Parents play a key role particularly in the early years, but mentors do the heavy lifting. One mentor showed me the mechanics behind the conveniences of the city, the secret to how things work. She changed my life."

"Is that where you learned your appreciation for water runoff and organic energy relays?"

"Partly. It's also why I find you interesting. So much is going on in there." She tapped Mike on the head. "I want to know more about the messy inner workings of Michael Newhouse, Outsider and new entertainer extraordinaire."

Mike had told her about his frustration with entertainment on the train. She seemed to be the only person who held any sympathy for him, although Mike had questioned her sincerity when she pinched his butt and said, "Now let's see what you've got."

In the middle of their casual lunch Mike fell asleep lying on the bench with his head on Gina's lap. He woke to find her smiling at him. "What?" he said.

"You talk in your sleep," Gina said. "You were trying to sell trips somewhere. Something about ten credits a year, one-way flights only. You can be incredibly convincing, even in your sleep. I wonder what that means. And who is Sam?"

"Sam?" Mike said. "Sam was my dog growing up." He wasn't ready to tell Gina about his daughter, but he wasn't prepared for her reaction to a dog either.

"You had a dog? I didn't think any dogs or cats survived the Poly Plagues."

"Well," Mike tried to look sheepish. "He was an imaginary dog who followed me around." Gina gazed down at Mike and he recognized the look. She knew he was lying. Instead of turning away as most people did, Gina watched his face and stored away his physical responses. *She recycles everything.*

They decided to walk back the entire way, not ready to say goodbye. When she kissed Mike outside the water plant, Mike regretted his lie until he noticed a pinched looked on Gina's face and wondered for the first time what she was hiding from him.

. . . . .

A few days later Mike ate a frequented spot, Stone Soup, waiting for inspiration on his performance. He liked to eat alone at the counter and watch people come and go. With the front wall removed, he had an expansive view of the walkway and gardens outside. Mike sat with his back to the counter and watched an old couple make their way from bench to garden as they weeded a larger plot in the square. They finished putting the discarded material on the compost pile when Mike turned back to his empty soup bowl.

Under his bowl sat a note made of the same handmade paper Mike had seen once before. He pretended not to notice it and turned back to watch the old couple, scanning the area for anyone out of place.

He casually picked up the note and put it in his pocket with the one he still carried. He didn't know how to get rid of the first note. Trashcans didn't exist. Even an open flame was something Mike hadn't seen, and it occurred to him that Eau Claire had disregarded the world's two biggest discoveries, fire and the wheel, at least in the ways he thought of them, in terms of barbequing and cars.

He left Stone Soup and five minutes later sat in a quiet spot where he examined the new note. On one side it read: *Mr. Newhouse.* On the other: *Garbage—soon they will be throwing it at you.* He looked around again but saw nothing unusual. He only thought about garbage for a moment because in smaller letters below the prediction was a comment he found much more disturbing: *You look great for your age. Not a day over 175.*

Mike looked around again, more as a primal self-defense mechanism in response to an attack. His first day in Eau Claire had been overwhelming; he had nearly forgotten about the note and didn't fully appreciate the implications.

Now that he had started to relax into his new life, the second note blew a hole in his sense of security. Mike had to do the math to confirm his real age. He would be 176 in a few months.

He put the second note in his pocket with the first, hoping to forget it as easily as the original. He debated who to tell, if anyone, as he walked to Beta Carrotene. He could have checked his BP for Stanley's location, but he needed a destination. While at Beta Carrotene, Mike ran into Sara.

"Stanley tells me you met somebody," Sara said as she cut vegetables. Mike shrugged as men sometimes do when they have nothing better to say. "Stanley and I are going to a health store this week. It's supposed to have the best pizza in the city. I want to steal some ideas. They use a solar brick oven, so it'll have to be a sunny day. Why don't you and your friend join us?"

"I don't know. I'm overwhelmed, and I just met her," Mike said, momentarily forgetting about the note.

"This isn't some holographic woman you created? She is real, right?"

"It's . . . we haven't even gotten in a fight yet and I don't usually introduce a girlfriend to others until after our first fight."

"What?" Sara asked.

"Women are unpredictable. I like to wait for them to be battle-tested before putting them on the front lines."

Sara swung her knife, and before Mike could move, stuck it into the cutting board an inch from his hand. "You're right, we are unpredictable. I'll expect to see you both at Solar Pizza this week." Sara walked away. She didn't wait for a reply. Mike felt the blade and decided to keep quiet about the notes.

SEVENTEEN

Rain fell the following day which postponed the pizza date, and drenched Eau Claire with big heavy raindrops. Mike walked the streets amazed at the multiple ways water pooled in depressions, ran along narrow brick paths, and filled higher elevations, awakening a water amusement park that laid dormant for weeks.

Walkways filled with people happy to get wet as they turned their faces to the sky with arms extended and enjoyed the unique sensation of water on their skin.

Wherever Mike turned, whatever he saw, reminded him of Gina, partly due to the playful way the water fell, but also the elaborate systems in place to wring out the rain's full potential. Mike thought this odd, to think so completely about a woman he hadn't known long. New places had a tendency to do that to him, amplify experiences beyond reality. *Perhaps that's why I seek so many new beginnings.*

The sun shown the next two days and their date at Solar Pizza proceeded. Mike wanted to invite Gina ahead of time, but Stanley assured him an advance arrangement wasn't appropriate. "I'm not sure how it works on the Outside, but in the city the only event you plan is your death."

Gina was able to meet them at Solar Pizza and had already introduced herself to Sara when Mike and Stanley arrived. Sara and Stanley spoke excitedly to the chef as Mike and Gina chose a bottle of wine on their way to an open table. They had a perfect view of the massive brick oven that encompassed the entire south wall.

"Gina," Mike liked saying her name, "I stood in the rain a couple of days ago and thought of you." Mike had a way of saying corny things and making them sound poetic.

"I'm glad I made an impression."

"I hope you don't mind," Sara said as she and Stanley arrived at the table, "but we ordered with the chef. We're going to try a sampling of his favorites." Sara's enthusiasm made Mike smile.

"Thank you for including me," Gina said.

"I've been looking forward to this." Sara stretched imaginary dough with her hands. "They make a unique crust and line their oven with garlic and other aromatics to infuse the pizzas."

"Gina, can you help me understand this love of libraries?" Stanley put his arm on Mike's shoulder. "Mike is no help."

Conversations still amazed Mike, starting in the middle, as if he missed the first three hours of discussion.

"I like that it's quiet," Gina said, "and the same people come every day, sit in the same chair, and read the same book day after day."

"How do you feel about plants?" Stanley asked Gina.

"I like to eat them."

"I think we're going to get along great," Sara said as she took her first sip of wine.

"Sara, is there anyone you don't like?" Mike asked.

"Anyone who doesn't appreciate my cooking." Sara smiled and looked directly at Stanley.

The meal progressed seductively. They took turns re-trieving pizza slices from the edge of the oven and present-ing them at the table like pieces of artwork.

"We have an exquisite pizza for your dining pleasure this evening," Mike said in a butchered Italian accent. "These four pieces," Mike set them down with a big arm flourish, "are unpretentious gifts with a light coating of artichoke hummus, thinly sliced tomatoes, fresh basil, a dusting of walnuts, drizzled with a reduced wine glaze."

They talked and ate and waved their hands to make a point as they held slices of pizza and drank wine. Each pizza was a journey as they tried to identify every ingredient and trace it back to its origin.

"The goat cheese and pesto taste great together." Sara chewed, looking up at the oak beam ceiling. "But there's an-other flavor I can't quite identify."

"I think it's pistachios used in the pesto," Gina said.

Sara froze, chewed, then smiled. "You're right. I can't be-lieve I missed that."

The conversation continued along the same path, with questions about the sun-dried peppers or the mushroom sausage, inquiries about the reduced balsamic, comments on the hint of cilantro. Mike enjoyed the food, his taste buds already acclimating to subtleties of some flavors and the punch of others. He didn't mind that most of the pizzas had no cheese. The wine was as weak as the beer, but still cap-tured the earthy dry complexities of the grape, if a bit meek.

After two hours, they still lingered, drinking hot dessert tea and talking about their interests. Gina discussed poetry, insisting an author must write it down and not simply tran-scribe it digitally. After some encouragement, she read a short poem written on a piece of hand-pressed paper like a work of art, pulled from deep inside her clothing.

Water trickles down the wall,
Gathering,
Carrying with it our impurities.
This universal solvent,
One day,
Will wash us all away.

The table fell silent while Gina tucked away her poem.

"It *is* better written down," Mike said, as he watched Gina hide the poem back inside her shirt, noticing the paper's similarity to the notes he had in his pocket.

"Mike, what have you been up to?" Stanley studied his BP. "You have no updates."

Mike rubbed together the two pieces of paper in his pocket and came back to the conversation. "I threw my first mug a couple days ago." He hoped he heard the question right. "It wasn't great, but I love the feel of the clay and how it changes shape almost like magic. How about you, Sara? What have you been doing besides cooking?" Mike often forgot to access information electronically and asked questions he should have already known the answer to.

"I tutor kids in math at the school," Sara said hesitantly. She looked at her BP, then at Stanley who shrugged before she continued. "One kid is so wickedly smart, I have to brush up just to keep her honest. But I love it."

"Sara's a wiz at math," Stanley said. "Could've done anything in the field."

"It was a lonely profession. I'd much rather cook." Sara made the first move to leave. "I want to work on some of these recipes while they're still fresh in my mind." She pulled Stanley with her.

"Now what?" Gina asked as she and Mike strolled in the opposite direction from Sara and Stanley.

"I don't know. It's your city. I love it when you show me new things."

She took Mike's arm as they walked. So much had been said over dinner, they both needed time to roll it around in their heads and digest the words along with their meal. They stopped for a moment in the middle of the walkway.

"Look at the moon." Gina turned her face up to the sliver of light in the sky. "It's what I call a first date moon. Only a tiny bit is lit up, the rest in shadows." They stood and admired the moon, lost in their own thoughts until Gina tugged his arm and they continued their walk.

"You know, this is the first time I've noticed the moon since I've been here." Mike looked from the moon to Gina's face. "I usually notice details most people don't, but you make me feel like I'm walking in the dark."

"Do I need to remind you that you *are* walking in the dark?"

They stopped at a building, distinguished only by its lack of windows. Gina opened the door. "This is a city water relay station."

"Where are we going?" Mike asked, as they climbed four flights of stairs.

"Up."

Like nearly all the buildings in Eau Claire, gardens filled the roof. But since this building didn't contain living units, one garden occupied the entire roof with a walkway around the perimeter and two paths through the middle. "Follow me." Gina moved forward.

On the walkway, too narrow to stand side-by-side, she walked in front of Mike and held her hand back for him to take. They walked to the far side where the path widened and they had a clear view of the moon again. Behind them grew a tall thick crop Mike didn't recognize. The building rose above its neighbors and allowed them an incredible view as they held hands, looking at the sky.

"Gina," he still loved saying her name, "how do relationships work in Eau Claire?"

Gina stepped in front of Mike, kissed his mouth, neck and ear. "Like that." She didn't step away or take her eyes off of his. "I wanted to do that since I first saw you tonight."

"Let me see if I have this straight." Mike returned the kiss, running his hands down her back and onto her butt.

"I think you're getting the picture," she said as she turned away, took his hand, and lead him back the way they came. Mike was unclear where they were going—her place, their separate ways—so he clung to her hand. Halfway back along the path, she led him through a small opening. They walked ten more feet to a clearing with a garden shed, supplies, and a sturdy picnic table.

Gina walked ahead of Mike, unfastened her shirt so it hung open slightly, and sat on top of the picnic table facing him. Mike watched and quietly approached until he stood next to her. Gina took his arm and interacted with his Bio Pulse.

"Interesting," she said. Mike was busy playing with the hair on the back of her neck with his other hand, and it took several seconds for him to react.

"What's interesting?"

"You have no pathogens, but you're fertile as a father. Most men take something for that."

Mike's hand stopped moving on Gina's neck. "Really? I'm still new in town, but I'll have to check into that." He kissed Gina on the neck, but she pushed him back and held up her arm.

"A gentleman would check a lady's Bio Pulse before going any further." She took Mike's hand and used it to activate her own BP. "See? I'm pathogen-free and, lucky for you, I'm not due to ovulate for another fifteen days." Mike took a closer look.

"What's this?" He pointed to a group of numbers on the side.

"That number is my blood pressure which has dropped slightly. Apparently blood is rushing to another part of my body." She let her comment hang in the air. "And the first number is my heartbeat, which you currently have raised to ninety-nine beats. But I think you can get it much higher."

"You keep showing me new things in the most unusual places," Mike said while he opened her shirt further. He kissed her neck again and worked his way to her bare shoulder, his arm grazing her breast. Under a first date moon, Gina continued to show Mike new things in unusual places.

. . . . .

Mike and Gina lay on the picnic table asleep under a landscaping blanket with their heads against sacks of seed. It was past one in the morning when Gina stirred and kissed him. "Get up. There's one more thing I want to show you." She pushed him again with little effect. Standing up, she pulled the blanket off Mike, and when he finally sat up, she flexed both biceps with the moonlight reflecting off her naked body.

"Now that's something to see." Mike was fully awake now.

"OK, two things." She held the pose. Mike began to move after she was fully dressed. On their way out of the building, Gina stopped to review settings on the filtration equipment and made a few adjustments.

Gina wrapped her body around Mike's, slowing their progress as they walked on the paths, quieter in the middle of the night.

"Gina, are you seeing other guys right now?"

She didn't pull away or stop walking like he thought she might.

"No."

"Do you think it's a weird question?" Mike stopped and took a half step away to look in her eyes.

She looked back with equal intensity. "Not for someone who seldom listens to his BP. How about you, Mister Frontier Man?" Gina smiled. "What have you been up to? I thought Outsiders clubbed each other to death, fighting over women too tired to care."

"That's not far off," Mike said. "Actually, I was married once." He saw Gina's smile falter. "It was ten years ago. People get married much earlier on the Outside." Scrambling to see the smile he had come to appreciate, he made things worse—much worse. "We had a daughter together and I have no way of knowing where she is." He didn't know why he said it. Once the words were out of his mouth, he knew how badly he'd screwed up.

The man who could keep a straight face and lie his way through fraudulent bank transactions became undone by the absence of a smile from a woman he barely knew. He waited for questions, accusations, yelling, anything, but she only stared at him until the first tear ran down her face.

Mike stood equally still, not knowing what to do. He was thankful when she turned and walked away because he couldn't stand to see the pain he'd caused.

EIGHTEEN

He wiped away his tears, surprised to feel them running down his cheeks. He hadn't cried when his wife left or when he broke three ribs slipping on ice. He wondered, why now? He felt like a teenage girl crying over lyrics about love and loss. Mason found himself yelling at the speaker, "Tell her you're from the past! Tell her!"

He needed to get out of the house. He hadn't left in three days. He lived on future Eau Claire time with his clocks turned back four hours and twelve minutes to hear Mike's broadcast in real time. He still recorded everything for detailed analysis, but he liked to experience events as Mike did, as they actually unfolded, listening to voices and BP commentary on his ancient speakers he almost forgot he had.

With only audio, he used every syllable to construct a surprisingly clear picture of future Eau Claire while Mike managed to hear almost none of it.

Mason put on his coat and grabbed his notes. He wanted to find the site of Solar Pizza. It was five in the morning, future Eau Claire time. Mike would sleep for a few hours, and though he did talk in his sleep, it was only occasionally insightful. Mason needed fresh air and to escape his computer. The plague scenarios he'd been running were depressing. Both of his children lived in the most affected areas with the plagues thirty-two years away.

He stepped outside and shut the gateway on future Eau Claire to explore *his* Eau Claire. Newly built mansions on the edge of town greeted him as he shook his head in disgust, knowing they wouldn't last. Closer to downtown, he found himself picking out houses and buildings he hoped would endure, beautiful bungalows with deep overhangs, a 139-year-old brick restaurant that had already survived the last city renovation.

As he walked along, he thought he found the site of Solar Pizza—an older stone Craftsman house with a visible rock formation in the backyard. He wanted the house to survive and considered buying it, even though it wasn't for sale.

Standing outside the home made him feel better, closer to Mike, to Gina. He had a need to repair their relationship and wondered if this was what people who spent too much time watching TV shows experienced. He reconstructed Mike's evening and, for a few indulgent minutes, placed himself at a nearby table with his own lovely date, thinking of nothing more than the food, company, and a mild walk home. The plagues would be history, not an impending doom for his offspring.

．．．．．

Dr. Jennings had ripped his speakers from the wall following Mike and Gina's adventure on the roof. He didn't know about their painful break-up until he talked to Mason the next day. It might have helped him deal with his anger and betrayal over the prisoner's enjoyment.

"Did Ms. Elliot slap him?" Dr. Jennings asked.

"No, she was more brutal than that." Mason stood with his arms full. He had stopped at the Time lab to pick up necessary equipment to build his own Clean Screen and hoped to leave unnoticed.

"Are you kidding me?" Dr. Jennings said. "He's living in a hippie commune with loose expectations, a terrible work ethic, and atrocious personal hygiene. He couldn't have it any easier."

Mason put down the transformer and UV light diode, knowing he would no longer make a fast getaway. "I've been a bit jealous myself. I've always wanted to own one version of the same outfit and wear it every day." Mason thought future Eau Claire was a paradise and grew wistful of Mike's relationships and lifestyle.

"I'm not jealous. I'm disappointed. I could envision the challenges for prisoners we sent to the past. It was a fitting punishment and a good solution, if a bit old-fashioned in its clumsy form of retribution." Dr. Jennings paced. "I thought sending prisoners to the future would be a more sophisticated approach, where they'd be confronted with the realities of taking shortcuts, of not being prepared, where they'd finally experience the limitations of brute force or charm."

"You should have heard his conversation with Gina," Mason said. "My blood pressure soared just listening."

"You know I originally wanted to send him forward only fifty years."

"I remember."

"But he seemed so adaptable. He pretended to be so calm. Now I can hear his pulse race like everyone else's. I was conned, manipulated to send him further forward." Dr. Jennings stopped pacing. "What do you think the plagues were like?"

"Catastrophic," Mason said. "More than half of the world's population—eliminated."

"What about the people who survived?" Dr. Jennings asked.

"They must have stopped helping those infected after the first few months. A vaccine would have been their only solution, something to prevent the disease before it destroyed the body. Cities must've separated the infected from the healthy, moved them to the outskirts of town in an attempt to create a windbreak as if fighting a forest fire. It explains the defined city lines."

"Yes," Dr. Jennings said, "but what was it like for the sick and the people that survived?"

"I can guess," Mason said. "But that's your area of expertise. It must have been horrible."

"I've envisioned the prisoner wandering around in the middle of this infectious mess." Dr. Jennings thought John Mason was brilliant but had no imagination for human suffering. "He would walk up to the first person he saw in hopes of charity, only to receive a deadly virus instead. That's justice."

"He wouldn't have survived long, and we would've missed a wealth of information."

"Instead he's having sex on a public rooftop with a woman he hardly knows." Dr. Jennings became furious all over again. He, like most in his field, chose psychiatry in part to heal himself. The profession was littered with doctors and psychotherapists crazier than their patients, working on issues from their childhoods in an attempt to correct some larger discrepancy in the way the world worked. Dr. Jennings focused on fear and ways to overcome it, to help him sleep at night. The fact that it turned into a lucrative career was a convenient bonus.

"Why do you dislike him so much?" Mason asked. "Some of the other prisoners here are truly evil, killing people with no remorse."

"We see those prisoners for what they are." Dr. Jennings walked around the Time chair. "But he's a perfect example of corruption unchecked, a man who uses smoke and mirrors to blind us to his crimes. It's not what he's done that bothers me, it's how he's done it, smiling and pretending he's done nothing wrong."

"Maybe he *has* done nothing wrong, at least nothing to deserve this," Mason motioned towards the chair with his head, remembering the calamity of the first two prisoners.

"You've been deceived like the rest." Dr. Jennings motioned vaguely to the outside of the prison where protests had been growing for the past six weeks. He touched the Time chair. "It's an affordable solution that not only disposes of a harmful element, but does it without the moral implications or debate of the death penalty." Dr. Jennings thought he alone cared whether justice was served or simply placated, hoping time wasn't as forgiving.

NINETEEN

Mike tried to contact Gina without success in hopes of explaining the circumstances of his divorce and daughter. He wasn't sure what to say, but he wanted a chance to say it.

"What do you do when a woman won't return your messages?" Mike asked Stanley. "Or respond to any of your communications?"

"Contact a woman who will."

"But what if you want to talk to her? What if this woman's special?"

"I had a friend," Stanley said, "who felt the same way about a girl, but he was fifteen at the time."

"What happened?"

"She added a twenty-four-hour proximity detector to her BP, designed to give my friend an electrical charge if he came within fifteen feet of her. After the first shock, he felt special, but by the third, he moved on." Stanley put his hand on Mike's shoulder. "I like Gina, but if she doesn't want to talk to you, let it go."

Mike didn't take Stanley's advice and left several more messages before he attempted to confront her with the hope that seeing her face again would make the words come. She was easy to locate electronically, but she became equally

136

aware of Mike's whereabouts which lead to a virtual chase through the city where Mike entered and departed several trains, searched through multiple buildings, ran a half marathon along pathways, and never got closer to the little blinking light that represented Gina on his BP.

Mike stopped his pursuit after he fell for the third time, scraping his chin. He laid on the walkway and didn't care to move as people walked around his sprawled body.

"Don't get near him," a woman said to her friend. "He might be dangerous."

If Mike had turned his head and looked up at the nearby rooftop, he would've seen Gina with tears in her eyes, watching him. Instead Mike sat up and wondered how he had lost control so quickly. The man who had stared down security guards and bluffed some of the most powerful people, became undone within a few weeks in the future, not by advanced technology or foreign concepts, but by a smile.

· · · · ·

Mike woke. Two days had passed. He hadn't seen or heard from Gina nor had he tried to contact her again. He continued with his life, acclimating to Eau Claire—its obsession with fresh food, an over-abundance of information—and the patchwork days of work, hobbies, and volunteering blended together in no particular pattern. He still looked for clues of his past Eau Claire, but they were becoming more irrelevant every day.

He met with Ren often and although their subsequent conversations were as strained as the first, Mike found it to be the toughest and most rewarding con job he ever had. Playing the straight man, he used every form of social manipulation he knew to coax a three-word answer. He understood Ren and saw his own frustrating habits more clearly in her.

On his latest visit, Kali, who was in charge of the house, pulled Mike aside. "You're making a difference," she said.

"It can't be me—we barely speak."

"She monitors who accesses her information and you haven't looked once. That means something to her."

"It means I still haven't figured out how these BPs work." Mike shook his BP arm. Kali gave an approving grin that he found condescending.

· · · · ·

Mike spent an inordinate amount of time studying his BP, not to become a better user, but to find a weakness in its programming. He found the BP's sophistication in regards to authenticity overwhelming, relying on DNA sampling to distinguish users. It was possible to use another person's BP as Mike had done, but it still made a DNA trace which ultimately led back to the individual user.

Mike had nearly given up when he remembered that some of the best social manipulation schemes were the simplest, and he found the BP's soft spot. Energy points were registered using two techniques—proximity and a simple seven-digit code. According to Mike's tests, if he stood within a few feet of another person, something that happened every day on nearly any walkway, he could use a generic code of symbols instead of numbers and intercept another user's energy points before they could register on their own BP. He thought today was perfect for a live test.

Mike chose the busiest walkways and put himself in the middle of the biggest crowds. He felt a familiar excitement of getting something for nothing—a charge from short-circuiting a bit of the societal wiring linking people in unintended ways. Less than an hour later, he checked his energy points for the day: fifty-six, more than two weeks' worth of energy expectations. It took fourteen hours on an energy

138

bike to generate as many points and about seven hours of work to earn the equivalent in work credits.

Mike spent the rest of the week collecting random energy points and contemplated how best to distribute them. There were no cars to buy and no real property to purchase. If citizens wanted to run a business, they didn't need to buy one and everyone already had enough clothes and food.

"Stanley," Mike asked, "what do people do if they have a large excess of energy points?"

"What do they do?" Stanley said, not quite understanding the question. "I don't know. Eventually the city uses them, I guess. If a person really has a lot, that's different."

"Yeah?" Mike said.

"The top three energy point earners are recognized by the city each month. Dave would know more about it. Something to add to your profile, but I'm talking about over a thousand energy points in the month." Mike had 1,214.

"Why do people count and track them?"

"I'm not sure," Stanley said. "They talked about getting rid of the whole point system, calling it outdated, but some people said everyone would get lazy and ask for handouts." Stanley shrugged. The situation threw Mike's whole sense of purpose in the garbage.

He wondered how he could take advantage of a system that he didn't understand. *Why tinker without a way to keep score?* He had no idea who he was anymore. Everything he had measured himself by was gone or obsolete and he still didn't know who to blame—the future or himself. He thought he finally understood what punishment was— spending the rest of his life in a time and place where few excuses existed for his bad behavior.

Mike took second place in energy points earned for the month, but he didn't include it on his profile. He stopped collecting random points and sank into depression, aided by his interpretive performance which wasn't going well either. He didn't know anything about the Outside and even if he did, he didn't know how to show it. After talking his way out of performing at the last Fair, claiming he needed more time, he knew he couldn't avoid the next one.

With a looming deadline, he put together a short piece, hoping he wasn't being too critical and showed it to other holographic performers for their opinions. It turned out he wasn't being critical enough.

"What'd you do?" Lily said. "Spend three whole minutes on it?"

Thomas tried to be more supportive but couldn't pull it off. "The characters look good," he said, "but you have to do something with them."

At the Fair Mike's performance consisted of three full-sized holographic people, each under a different cup. The cups moved slowly at first, then gained speed through the show while the characters popped out from under their cups to tell stories about manipulation, deception, and commercialization. In the end, all three cups were empty as the holographic performers materialized and bowed, as if to say *I told you so.*

The performance failed, but at least the city considered it a performance. Mike kept his job, but didn't emerge unscathed and understood what it meant to be a professional entertainer. Several performers were amateurs, and while many of the performances were exceptional, a few stank almost as badly as Mike's. But no one in the audience criticized amateurs and saved their pent-up commentary for the few professionals who failed to meet expectations, especially Mike. He heard the word *garbage* several times and knew it to be an extremely offensive curse to use in Eau Claire.

A few people even threw produce at him. As a tomato bounced off his shoulder, Mike was reminded of the earlier prediction he received—*Garbage, soon they will be throwing it at you*—and he felt guilty for his part in its culmination. His problems grew as the city cited Mike for wasting food and required him to clean up the mess, followed by five days of volunteer service in Waste Management.

The next day Mike stood inside a nondescript refuse building with fifteen younger people who made Mike feel as conspicuous for his age as for his Outside designation.

"What's the city blaming you for?" asked a fellow volunteer. The question was so similar to the one Lonnie asked on Mike's first day at the Eau Claire prison, he couldn't help but smile.

"Wasting food," Mike said, agitated once again. "But people threw food at me and I had to clean it up, then come down here to volunteer."

"Believe me, I understand," said Mike's new friend. "The city claims I waste energy, fail to volunteer, and neglect my work expectations, as if they have a right to judge."

"What did you do?"

"Nothing," said the man. Mike smiled, thinking that was probably the point and ignored his own minimal effort on his Outside interpretive performance.

Finally a door opened on the platform to Mike's right. Gina stood in the doorway.

"You have all been assigned several tasks," Gina said, walking down the short stairs. "Find your location assignment. Take a vest, complete your assignment, and return the vest here. Any questions?" No one said a word. Mike found his location and assignment on his BP, turning compost piles in the Garden District.

"Why'd we have to come down here to get our assignments and what's the vest for?" Mike whispered to the man next to him.

"That's your badge of shame." The man pointed to the vests. "They don't want us to blend in with the regular volunteers and they make us come down here because they can."

Mike put on his vest as he watched Gina walk back through the door on the platform, not sure if he ever wanted to see her again.

The next four days Mike's hands blistered and his muscles ached, but he smiled every time he saw Gina and left without a word. Gina's once radiant face turned into a sadistic and vengeful one in Mike's mind with each new blister.

"I don't have an assignment," Mike said to no one in particular on his last day. Gina had already left.

"Lucky bastard," said a disgruntled volunteer. Mike waited a moment after everyone departed, and was about to do the same, when Gina walked back into the room.

"Mr. Newhouse," Gina said in a business-like voice so unlike her own. "We have a special assignment for you. Follow me." Mike hesitated. He wanted her to chase him, but he knew that wasn't about to happen. He walked behind her through the narrow hall much as he did on the roof two weeks ago, except they didn't hold hands and his heart pounded for different reasons. They reached a room where a man stood in a hazmat suit. "Put on a suit and follow this man," Gina said.

Mike turned to Gina, "What if I decide not to put on the suit?"

Gina looked at him, her face a mask until she closed her eyes and mouthed, "Please." Mike put on the suit, not knowing exactly why.

"This man will show you what needs to be done." Gina walked away. Mike didn't see the anguish on her face. If he had, he wouldn't have known what it meant. Instead, he followed the man through the city about a quarter mile without saying a word.

"We need to clean this up," the man said with a muffled voice as he talked through his mask when they reached their destination. Mike could barely see his face and held no malice toward the man who worked alongside him. They picked up garbage and put it in metal bins already at the site.

"The Fortune Tellers?" Mike asked, inquiring who was responsible for the mess. The man nodded his head and continued to work. As Mike studied compressed paper wads and decomposed globs of organic matter, he considered how someone could have dumped garbage without the city recording his identity through BP activity. Either he took his BP off before dumping the garbage or he never wore one.

After his last forced volunteer duty, Mike wanted to speak to citizens who didn't wear a BP and he knew of the perfect helper. Ren had talked about people she knew without BPs. It was the only time he saw her animated. Mike hoped to find out more about the Prolong Life Movement while engaging Ren on a topic of interest. He almost felt guilty conning the child he was supposed to mentor, but he figured the system put them together for a reason.

The next day he visited Ren and when she brought up a friend she knew without a BP, Mike jumped in. "Do you know where he is now?"

Ren didn't answer right away. "I think I can find him."

"Lead the way." They searched three places before they located him. It was impossible for Mike to guess the boy's age, somewhere between sixteen and mid-twenties.

"Hi Jeremy."

"Hello Renee."

"It's Ren, remember?"

"Who's this?" He didn't look at Mike.

"He's from the Outside," Ren said. "He wants to meet people who aren't hooked up."

Jeremy looked at Mike for the first time. "What's it like on the Outside?"

Mike appraised the enclosed gap between buildings where they stood. "It's a lot like this, lonely with not much to do." Mike glanced at his BP. It didn't transmit, meaning they were standing in a dead zone which explained why Jeremy chose to hang out in such an isolated area. He didn't sleep or eat there, at least Mike didn't see any sign of either activity—the area contained nothing except a lonely boy, a tree, and a bare patch of dirt where he stood.

"Yeah," Jeremy said, examining the tree, "but you didn't have anyone looking over your shoulder on the Outside."

"No, they were too much in my face." Mike was referring to his recent past life between prison guards and lawyers. He stepped in front of Jeremy. He wanted answers and knew pleasantries weren't going to work. "If you're not going to wear a BP, why not live on the Outside? It's roomier than this."

"What?" The kid looked alarmed. Mike didn't repeat the question, but waited. "It's more of a protest, a statement of freedom," Jeremy said, regaining his confidence. "You wouldn't understand. All hooked up to your little life saver. You can't always play it safe."

Mike wondered if he had ever said anything as stupid and quickly realized he had. "What do you get out of this besides a shorter life, no friends, and people running into you?"

"He has friends," Ren said.

Jeremy didn't look at Ren or Mike. "I get to keep my thoughts as my own."

"Because you have no one to share them with," Mike said softly with empathy.

"Why are you here?" This time Jeremy turned to Ren.

"Is there a group for people that aren't hooked up?" Mike asked in order to diffuse the situation and get the answer he needed before the conversation fell apart.

"This isn't about socializing." Jeremy paid considerable attention to the tree trunk he picked at. "It's about living freer, on our own terms."

They remained for half an hour, talking in a familiar circular fashion that led to no conclusions until Ren finally suggested they leave. Mike had his answer. This kid wasn't part of the PLM. He hoped Ren got something out of it too. He only hoped she was smarter than he was at her age.

"What did you think?" Mike asked on the walk back.

"You should have been nicer."

"Why? He wouldn't even look at me."

"Maybe he was scared."

"Of what?"

"Of not meeting everyone's expectations."

Mike was sure of it—she was definitely smarter than he was at that age, maybe even now. They were quiet the rest of the way.

TWENTY

Mike interacted less with Stanley. He and Sara reminded Mike too much of Gina and their date at Solar Pizza. He spent more time with Paul and Kevin. Mike and Paul visited intensity bars, riding energy bikes in group competition with other bars in Eau Claire and the Region. The drinks tended to be healthier, vegi-protein shakes, while the opportunity to meet women and socialize was ample.

Paul capitalized on Mike's second place Eau Claire energy award and made up increasingly elaborate scenarios which he traded for women's attention. "I know this guy," Paul said, "who got so much action and was so energetic while making love, he put an energy wave converter on his bed and earned enough energy points in a single month to take third place in Eau Claire's energy awards."

The crowd reacted with a roar, the guys pretended Paul referred to them while the women were collectively sympathetic, claiming, "He must have been in bed alone at the time."

Paul let the commentary continue before adding, "Did I mention that my friend, Mike here, took second place that month?" Mike was ready for the line and smiled, bowing for the crowd.

Mike learned more about Eau Claire women, along with dating and relationship customs. Women weren't more aggressive as Mike had originally thought. Sex simply wasn't taboo. Children were treasured, and therefore well-planned, and the planning had more to do with the man. Though it was inappropriate to advertise a person's fertility or the steps taken to prevent it, Mike watched more than one woman casually operate his BP and, after seeing he was fertile, move on to the next guy.

. . . . .

Mike and Kevin spent more time in art studios where Mike discovered how quickly ideas coalesce during a discussion about nature.

"We should paint the Outside," said one person in the group.

"What's so great about sitting in the wind with nothing to do?" said another.

"I don't mean paint in the picnic area. I'm talking about going out beyond the ridge, where we can see nothing but wilderness." Everyone in the studio froze and all nine heads turned towards Mike.

"What?"

"Is it safe?" asked another painter in the group. Nobody moved.

"Sure," Mike said, and with that one-word answer, he became their leader to the Outside.

Mike hadn't been on the Outside for much more than four hours himself, but sometimes being first was all that mattered. Mike remembered Doug, a neighbor and friend in high school who was the first in his group to have had sex. They all wanted to know the details and hung on Doug's every word. But in retrospect Doug had no real insight, offering nothing in the way of new knowledge except to say that Megan wore pink underwear. Mike figured he could do as well and agreed to be their guide.

The group of nine grew to twenty-two the next day, including Mike's unit-mates, Sara, and Ren.

"Isn't this getting out of hand?" Mike asked Kevin.

"We're going to the deep Outside," Kevin said. "We passed *out of hand* long ago." Mike thought about backing out, but a larger group made him feel safer. He didn't know if there was anything to fear on the Outside. He still didn't know if it was safe on the *inside*.

"We'll use the picnic area nearest the ridge," Mike said in a planning session with the growing group. "The ridge represents a dramatic transition between city and wilderness with strong winds and a sweeping view of both sides, before we *plunge* out of sight of the city." Several in the group flinched.

The next day, April fifth, the group of twenty-two had grown to twenty-nine as they gathered between two buildings for a tour of the deep Outside, afraid to walk into the picnic area without their leader. Picnic areas were technically within the city, inside the tracks. They expanded to a seventy-foot buffer zone at twelve designated areas surrounding the city. Mike watched his BP signal disappear as he stepped from garden into matted grass. Unlike the library where his BP simply didn't transmit, here it didn't function at all, meaning the health protection functions ceased to work also.

Mike greeted the few that made eye contact, but most were too excited or nervous. Mike tried to get Ren's attention, but she became fascinated with her friend's water pouch. He wasn't sure how he felt about Ren joining the group, but since the city didn't object, he thought not allowing her to go would cause more problems. Not that he could've stopped her. Besides maybe it would give her insight, adding reality to Jeremy's idealistic view.

Stepping into the wind, Mike pretended to be the expert Outsider they needed, and played the part. "We're going out this way," Mike yelled over the wind and pointed to the ridge to the north. "We'll stop briefly at the top of the ridge, but you won't want to linger. It'll be too windy to talk so we will regroup on the other side. Any questions?"

"Will we be able to find our way back?" asked Ed Brewer, a painter.

Mike suppressed a smile. "The ridge will be visible the entire time as a reference point."

The group looked like they had several questions, but no one asked anything further. Mike turned and headed for the ridge. Most of the original group of nine had easels or sketch pads. Everyone carried enough water in fabric pouches to cross a desert.

When the group reached the top of the ridge, the wind made navigation more difficult and he saw Ren grab her neighbor's arm to stay upright. Mike heard sounds of excitement, not for the view to the north over the ridge, but the view back towards Eau Claire, marveling as Mike had, at the city's brilliance set in contrast with its larger green surroundings.

"Is that the Fairgrounds?"

"I can see our unit."

"Look at the wind catchers."

"Watch the shadows move."

"Beautiful."

They spent more time on the ridge than Mike had expected, whether to admire the view or keep sight of it, Mike wasn't sure. After descending the slope, Mike walked ten more minutes until he reached an area with trees, a stream, and an abandoned building in the distance.

"We'll stop here. This should be a good place to set up easels. Anyone who wants to explore plant life around the area, see Stanley." Stanley raised his hand. "He's our plant expert." Painters unpacked easels and people milled around when Sara walked up to Mike and gave him a kiss on the cheek.

"Thank you," she said.

"What for?"

"Stanley hasn't looked at his BP once since we came out. He turned it off before we left. Oh, I'd better go help him find plants. Thanks again." She bounced over to where a few people gathered to help locate plants, which Stanley had received city permission to bring back for study. A group of twelve approached Mike.

"Now what do we do?" asked Frances Hicks, a friend of Paul's.

"Explore."

Frances gave Mike a bewildered look as more joined her.

"I thought nature was important to you," Mike said, frustrated by their lack of interest.

"Sure, we think nature's great," said Frances with several of her friends nodding their heads in agreement. "We also think water purification is fantastic, but we don't go hang out at the water treatment plant."

"Look at all those trees." Mike pointed towards the forest. "Listen to the stream. Did you see the flock of . . . birds that went by earlier?" Mike had no idea what kind of birds they were.

When Frances and her friends continued to stare at Mike, he tried a new approach.

"Well if you're not interested in plants, Kevin"—he pointed to Kevin—"will talk about painting landscapes." At least Mike hoped. When most of the group still looked at him expectantly, he continued. "Paul will tell stories about the Outside." Mike guessed Paul knew a guy who lived in this field for three years before he learned Eau Claire existed right over the hill. "And I'm going to do a group meditation in a minute."

Mike was surprised when most of the group, including Ren, followed him. He had made up the idea of a group meditation out of desperation.

He walked into a clearing and searched for a good spot to meditate as if there was a science to it. He sat on the ground with nine other people, moving them closer together in a circle until their knees almost touched. He had meditated for years but had never taught it. He remembered what Guru had told him and started with a one-minute meditation, then five minutes, then fifteen.

"If you find your mind wandering, thinking about what you'll do when you get back, that's OK," Mike said. "Acknowledge it and come back to the word I gave you." Mike had given each person a word to say silently to help them focus. He wasn't sure if the word should be significant, using brand names that had no meaning to them such as Corvette and Maytag.

After each short meditation, Mike talked about the process and asked each participant about their experience.

"It was like listening to my BP," said Lucas, a holographic artist. "I kept getting a stream of unrelated messages."

"Time stopped," said Frances. "I kept waiting to hear a time update from my BP, but it never came."

They weren't quite the responses Mike had hoped for, but for his first attempt at teaching meditation, it was better than no reaction at all. After the fifteen-minute meditation Ren spoke for the first time.

"I never felt so peaceful. Alone, but somehow connected to everything." Mike smiled, pleased to get a more positive reaction.

After sitting for an hour on the ground, the group broke up and staggered in different directions. The highlight of the outing came when a red-tailed hawk circled in the sky, then made a loud screech before it swooped down on its prey in the field a hundred feet away. Two people cried out from the startling experience. "There was no warning," said one of the meditators.

"It dropped from the sky."

"It seemed random," said her friend. "It could have gotten any mouse, but bam, it got that one." She shivered. "I never thought death could be so arbitrary."

Mike helped Stanley with plants and admired the artists' work, especially Kevin's, who did an abstract simply called Outside. Most of the other painters had already put away their supplies, uninspired by the wide and sweeping landscape. After less than two hours—shorter than Mike had hoped—many in the group showed signs of restlessness, if not downright anxiety.

"Is it time to go yet?" several asked.

"Start packing up," Mike said. "We'll leave in thirty minutes." But within twenty, the entire group headed back up the slope without him. The only people who seemed to enjoy themselves were Kevin and possibly Ren. As Stanley and Sara walked by, Mike heard Stanley say in a pleading voice, "I only asked the time." Sara walked ahead and didn't look back.

Mike stood and watched until he was alone, his leadership no longer needed as painters and explorers raced each other back to the comforts of the city.

"You're welcome," Mike said to the empty field as he walked several minutes to the east to get a fresh perspective. On the ridge he observed Eau Claire, as Stanley and Sara crossed the magnetic tracks below.

The city looked different than when he first saw it less than a month ago, though nothing had changed. The transformation took place in Mike and his perception of the city. The threatening buildings and perceived barriers were now his home, filled with distractions and connections he had only begun to understand.

He sat down on a flat boulder and turned his back away from the city and any indication that he had traveled 131 years into the future. With the wind whistling in his ears, he wondered who he was and looked to his past, now an open landscape. His present situation, he thought, was much like the place he currently sat—between his past and future, with him facing the wrong direction.

While contemplating his predicament, he noticed a note poking out from under a stone several feet to his left. He could read his name on it from where he sat. He looked around but saw no one. He picked up the note and read the other side: *Too bad about Kevin.*

TWENTY-ONE

"They ripped the thing apart," Dr. Jennings said as he stood in the emptied Time Lab. "Cut the Time chair into pieces and destroyed everything in the process."

It wasn't a complete surprise to Mason who knew of the ongoing campaign by Prisoner Two's daughter, the ACLU lawsuit, and the growing protests. Investors had been fleeing fast, too. He thought the Wisconsin Department of Corrections might have shut down the operation for a year or two and started back up when tensions and attention dwindled. Now, the time manipulation experiments were no longer on hold. They had been permanently canceled. Eight years of work halted with a crowbar and industrial saw.

The audio receiver and transcribing equipment in Dr. Jennings' office and Mason's home went untouched as they had no function in time manipulation. It was unclear if anyone else knew, besides the Time Manipulation team, of the transmitter they sent to the future or the excess of information it provided. Mason and Dr. Jennings never had an opportunity to present their findings.

"I can't believe the DOC caved," Dr. Jennings said, sliding his foot back and forth over the holes in the floor where the Time chair had sat. "I thought this was the solution to our biggest problem, a chance to end the cycle of repeat offenders. Possibly end crime all together some day."

"I'm glad it's over, in a way," Mason glanced into the bare control room. "I wasn't counting on the audio transmitter to actually work or that we'd accumulate so much information about the future via the Bio Pulse."

"This was all you'd worked on. How can you just give it up?"

"This isn't my first government project," Mason said. "You learn to work hard when you have the green light because sooner or later the project ends for the strangest reasons and there's nothing you can do about it. I had three days to get my family out of government-sponsored housing during one project. I'm just glad we still have the audio receivers."

Mason had moved much of his research to his home in response to the growing protests. While he lacked the hardware for time manipulation, the Tapes provided information on everything from advanced theories of water purification to future capabilities of non-invasive medicine. Each day brought new discoveries—information that Mike generally ignored.

"I finally grew a few plants from the Tapes, designed to convert sunlight directly to usable energy." Mason closed an empty drawer. "I've got about twenty of them, in the moss family. I'm no green thumb, but I've kept most of them alive and generated two thousand watts of energy."

Mason also had a scale model of future Eau Claire set up on an old ping pong table in his basement and spent hours adding details to it. He talked back to the audio output, calling people by name. "Stanley, why did you have to ask about the time? You were doing so well." They seemed more real to him than his neighbors, whom he rarely saw.

Mason walked over to where the Time equipment used to be and examined the empty space with Dr. Jennings. "Did you ever think about trying the machine yourself?"

"That's like asking me if I ever thought of using the electric chair. The Time Manipulation machine is a punishment and a fitting one, meant for prisoners."

"I briefly thought about it, but after the mess the first prisoner made, I'm glad it's gone. Besides, you can't get back."

"Time manipulation's finality is what made it powerful in changing behavior," Dr. Jennings said.

"Have you made any changes to your life based on information from the Tapes?" Mason asked. "I started eating healthier after hearing the results of a few scans and I haven't touched a piece of plastic in a week."

"Aren't you overreacting?"

"It's hard to deny the information I'm hearing, knowing its source."

"I stopped eating meat," Dr. Jennings said as casually as possible. "Of course, I've been thinking about it for years. Living in this filthy farming city finally convinced me to do it."

"It's funny. When we started the Time project, I was concerned about how the future would change prisoners." Mason stood right where the chair used to be. "But I never really thought about what effect a prisoner sent to the future would have on us."

TWENTY-TWO

Mike ran the entire way back into the city, his mind shifting among possible catastrophes that could befall Kevin. Once inside Eau Claire, Mike's BP located Kevin at a city studio. Mike raced to the building to find Kevin storing his supplies, looking no different than he had forty minutes ago. Mike's face must have shown concern because Kevin reacted to it with equal alarm.

"What's wrong?" Kevin asked.

"How'd the trip go for the painters?" Mike relaxed and remembered to breathe, then redirected his anxiety to a more reasonable concern. "Some seemed disappointed."

"I guess they expected exotic wildlife packed together like the plants in the city gardens." Kevin dried a brush. "I'm not sure they knew what to do with a larger palette."

"How about you? Was it what you expected?"

"It was breezier and bigger with a loneliness that . . . grabbed me."

Mike couldn't think of what else to say now that he saw Kevin uninjured. "Well, I'm glad you enjoyed it." Mike walked back to his unit vowing to keep a close eye on Kevin.

Not everyone enjoyed the trip to the Outside, as messages Mike received demonstrated. "The Outside is a poor excuse for scenery," said Lucas, a holographic colleague. "It's captured tons better in any simulator a hundred years old."

Mike smiled at the irony, but he still found it puzzling, the lack of appreciation for the expansive world that literally surrounded them.

Mike received more insight when listening to Ed Brewer's message. "I had to use a city Clean Screen to disinfect myself before I dared contaminate my own unit. I can still feel my skin crawling." Mike listened to several other similar messages and began to understand that a deep connection with a person's BP was health-related.

Mike never before had a device that constantly monitored his body for the slightest abnormality. If a cancer cell were to form, the Bio Pulse would detect it and make adjustments. Any infection or physical abnormality was rapidly identified, and in most cases treated by the Bio Pulse. Mike's BP was still learning the intricacies of his body, but he already felt better . . . healthier.

The allure of the Outside, Mike learned, wasn't about majestic landscapes, but the intrigue of walking a tightrope without a net.

Mike confirmed this when he heard Frances Hicks at The Barley Belly tell her friends about her Outside experience.

"It was seriously intense," she said. "You're in your own world and anything can happen."

"How did it feel?" a friend asked.

"Like stepping into nothing, with this cold, contaminated wind blowing on you the whole time."

"Could you breathe?" asked another excited friend.

"Barely. It's almost like you forget how to breathe without knowing the oxygen content or the air purity. Look at this." Frances held out her arm. "I'm still shaking, just thinking about it."

. . . . .

Mike walked his own tightrope between preparations for his next performance and monitoring Kevin's well-being. When Mike walked out of the library, two days after the trip to the Outside, he received the news he'd been dreading.

"Mr. Newhouse," said a man in a hazmat suit, "come with us." Two more people in hazmat suits stood on either side of Mike while his eyes adjusted to the bright sunlight.

"What's going on?" Mike asked.

"We've been searching for you for several hours. All other threats have been accounted for." The man in front turned to a colleague. "Is he clear?" The woman standing to Mike's right ran an instrument up and down Mike's body.

"Clear."

"Come with us," said the man in front.

"Now," said another man when Mike didn't move.

"I don't understand." Mike shuffled his feet forward.

"A unit-mate of yours has become ill," said the person on Mike's left. "We're trying to pinpoint the cause and minimize the city's exposure. The city has been in lockdown emergency mode the last two hours."

"Is Kevin sick?" Mike asked, already knowing the answer.

"How did you know Kevin Wong was ill?" asked the person to Mike's right as he made eye contact with his other two partners.

"I don't know. He said something about not feeling right," Mike lied. "Where is everybody?" The usually busy walkways were deserted.

"We were unable to locate you," said the man in front who talked loudly over his shoulder. "The city quarantine is in effect. All trains in and out of Eau Claire have been halted,

159

portable Steri-Lights have been deployed, and the water supply has been tested and re-purified."

They walked up to a large house in the Park District. "This is our triage center. Anyone Kevin Wong has had more than casual contact with in the past forty-eight hours is here. You're the last subject." The man and woman on either side of Mike grabbed his arms and walked him to the door. Mike's natural reaction was to pull away, but he felt their grips tighten when he hesitated. He walked through the door to rid himself of his escorts.

Inside, health providers in hazmat suits moved Mike to a room on the right side of the house where the equipment and medical personnel were concentrated. Scanners and people filled Mike's room. He asked questions that went ignored, reminding him of his experience in prison. They scanned him multiple times but did not give him any results.

By evening the city released most of the quarantined people who showed no sign of contamination. Paul, Stanley, Mike, and Kevin remained for more tests, housed in separate rooms, the communication features in their BPs disabled. Paul did sit-ups and push-ups to calm himself in a rare display of exertion without capturing energy points. Stanley tried to sleep, twisting and turning until he lay still. Mike meditated, watching over his unit-mates as he hovered between rooms. Meanwhile five people worked on Kevin with another nine overseeing the procedures.

Paul and Stanley left the next day, but Mike remained under observation for twenty-four more hours, until Dave walked into his room. He was the first person Mike had seen in two days without three layers of protective material.

"Hey Mike. You're sure giving Eau Claire some attention," Dave said.

"What did I do?"

"That's exactly what I've been saying. You did nothing. Just a bit of bad luck."

"How's Kevin?" Mike asked.

"He's improving. He should be released in a couple of days, maybe a week."

"What's wrong with him?"

"That's what everyone is still trying to figure out, but his symptoms are mild."

"Now what?"

"Hey, I've been asked to tell you that you're confined within the city. No more trips to the Outside for a while."

Mike was too tired to argue. He had gotten more sleep in prison.

"Does that mean I'm free to go?"

"Sure, but one more question." Dave stepped closer to Mike. "What were you doing venturing Outside?"

"It wasn't even my idea." Mike answered the same question he'd been asked ten different times. "People wanted to experience what was out there."

"Did you see anything unusual?"

"Like what?" Mike thought of the notes and made a conscious effort not to stick his hand in his pocket.

"I don't know, maybe a diseased animal. I heard about the hawk."

"No. Nothing."

Mike learned over the next few days that to call someone sick or contagious was the worst thing to say about them. Some people had always avoided Mike for being an Outsider. After the outbreak, Mike's presence cleared walkways. Beta Carrotene was one of the few health stores that didn't run out of food as he arrived. Kevin's illness remained a mystery for three days after Mike's release, adding to the fear and speculation.

After Kevin's recovery and return, Mike's situation improved marginally.

"They say I contracted a strain of influenza that hadn't been encountered in over a hundred years. Their system couldn't filter it." Kevin looked tired. "They asked me a million questions, but still couldn't determine the origin." Though the threat was minimal, the unexpected and rare nature of the illness created more fear than symptoms.

It wasn't until Kevin walked with Mike to Hops Scotch that citizens' concerns about Mike's contagious status improved and the threat of disease in general subsided. As people viewed Mike with less suspicion, Mike became more worried about his influence on Eau Claire. Mike felt contaminated, as if he might be the Typhoid Mary of the future.

He walked through Clean Screens whenever possible, sometimes five or six times a day. He kept to himself, constantly reviewing his BP, looking for abnormalities. He stopped visiting Ren. He felt vulnerable for the first time since he turned twenty-two and pretended to be other people. Someone knew he was from the past and was using him as a ticking time bomb.

Mike waited for the next note, the one that would expose him completely, but it didn't come, no one else fell ill, and a week later a library patron asked Mike for help re-shelving books. Mike relaxed.

The Fair was scheduled to take place in two days, shifting Mike's attention from self-pity to a plan. He had several ideas to improve his performance, but he implemented only a few. He wanted to avoid the harshest criticism, yet be just bad enough that he might have to volunteer in Waste Management again. He hated the work, but it was the only way he could think to confront Gina. He wasn't even sure he wanted to, but he knew he needed to see her again.

After his performance, the response was less dramatic, with most people uninterested and only a few who had yelled *garbage*. No one threw any.

"It was . . . better," Lucas said.

Lily put it more precisely. "At least you didn't totally suck."

Mike celebrated his success, having created exactly the response he'd wanted—two days of volunteer service in Waste Management. The more he reflected on his accomplishment, the more confident he became. It took talent to put on a good performance, but true skill to perform in that thin layer between good enough to avoid a riot and bad enough to receive the level of desired punishment.

Mike reported to a different building this time, larger than the first, on the edge of the Garden District. He thought he must be early since he was alone.

"Hello? Anyone here?" he said. A cautionary tingle ran up his spine, something he hadn't felt since arriving in the future. He turned to leave just as someone yelled his name.

"Mr. Newhouse?" Mike turned and saw a man holding a door open to the stairway. As Mike approached him, he thought the man might have been the one who assisted him in picking up garbage. "Follow me." The man climbed the stairs to the third floor and entered a room with two chairs and three additional doors. The man took off Mike's Bio Pulse. "We don't want it to get damaged while you work."

Mike didn't know enough to stop him or to understand the threat it implied.

TWENTY-THREE

Mike stood alone in the room and waited. The tingle up his spine intensified.

"Mr. Newhouse, we're glad you could join us," said a voice Mike didn't recognize as it echoed off the high ceiling and distorted slightly. It held no menacing attributes and would have sounded pleasant except for the circumstances. Mike looked around the room for the source of the voice before a mirror blinded him with an intense beam of sunlight. He fell back a step, closed his eyes, then covered them with both hands, and listened to movement along the back wall. "We want to talk with you. Ask a few questions."

"Who are you?" Mike demanded.

"For the time being, let's say we're concerned citizens."

"Not good enough." Mike attempted to sound as if he had some power in this negotiation as he stood with both hands over his eyes.

"I'm afraid it's going to have to be for now." Two people grabbed Mike and pulled his hands away from his face. Mike thought it was an attempt to blind him or identify him, but after a short struggle, they released his arms. Unharmed, he brought his hands back to his face and experienced the tingling sensation of a Bio Pulse on his left wrist. He struggled to remove it, but gave up, knowing instinctively it was designed to stay in place.

"What do you know about the group that calls itself the Fortune Tellers or the Prolong Life Movement?" the voice boomed. Mike remained silent and no longer found the voice pleasant. He didn't mind answering most of their questions, but he knew the ones he couldn't answer were sure to follow and he'd rather have a showdown now than when it really mattered. The room remained quiet.

"Please Mr. Newhouse," the voice said with incredible sympathy. "We don't wish to hurt you, but we do need to know." Mike had been threatened before, but never in such a menacing way. Apologizing for pain that had not yet arrived surely indicated it soon would.

"What makes you think I know anything about the PLM?" Mike said with a hint of indignation to sound believable.

Silence.

"What do you know about the group that calls itself the Fortune Tellers?"

Mike thought of several possible answers. None seemed helpful, so he remained quiet. Twenty seconds later an electrical surge ran through Mike, firing every nerve in his body. After a few seconds, it receded, but not the strange sensation that lingered as a reminder of the consequences for his silence.

He remained standing and shook his left arm where the pain was strongest. After he caught his breath, the voice repeated the question. Mike changed his strategy, if only to lengthen the time before the next shock.

"I don't know anything about the Fortune Tellers," Mike said, "except what I heard, that they want to expand the human lifespan to over two hundred years." Mike's Bio Pulse made a series of soft beeps. "That's the truth," Mike said in response to the beeps, amazed at the sensitivity of the BP on his wrist.

"Thank you, Mr. Newhouse, but there is something you're not telling us."

Mike was about to protest when he remembered the notes from the PLM still in his pocket and grabbed them. "Look at these," he said, holding the notes out as a plausible explanation. "I don't know the PLM. These prove it."

"What are you talking about?"

"They, the PLM, have been harassing me since I first got here. See for yourself." He shook the notes in his hand and explained when and where he found each note. He described how each prediction had come true from the poured beer to thrown garbage to Kevin's illness. Only after the notes were ripped from his hand did he think about the other incriminating comments—*Welcome to the future* and *Not a day over 175*.

"Thank you again, Mr. Newhouse. But if you are not part of the PLM network, where did you come from and how did you get here?" The voice paused. "And before you cause yourself more pain, we know you're not from the Outside. We have been in contact with the few Outsiders in this area. None of them have heard of you and your scans suggest you don't have the survival skills to live alone without resources."

Mike was surprised how quickly they came to the questions he didn't have answers for. Mike remained quiet and waited for the electrical jolt to rip through his body. He anticipated it and the lack of surprise made it manageable, but the after-effects were more intense as if an electrical charge had built up in his cells.

"Let me explain our problem to you in hopes that you will understand the situation we're in, and the measures we will take to find the truth."

"I'd love to hear it." Mike spat out an acidic electrical taste in his mouth.

"We know you're not from the Outside. You didn't exist in any database prior to two months ago, and we've seen your scans." The voice built an argument much like Mike would.

"Your scans indicate a change at the particle level in your cells, the same process Dr. Donavan proposed six years ago with his work in cell regeneration. It is Dr. Donavan's work that is the basis for the Prolong Life Movement. Meanwhile, you have a note in your pocket suggesting you are 175 years old. Keep in mind no one has ever identified a single member of the PLM, even though their popularity grows. And I haven't mentioned Eau Claire's role in this: a small city on the outskirts of an average region, yet it's the center of the PLM attacks with a surge after your arrival." The voice paused to allow Mike to take in the information. "Are you starting to feel the severity of the situation?"

"I felt it with that first jolt." Mike shook his left arm.

"Where did you come from and how did you get here?"

Mike thought about telling the truth and debated its credibility. Yet somewhere in the back of his mind, he believed telling them was a mistake. As he debated, a third jolt brought him to one knee, where he remained, composing himself.

He had barely caught his breath when the fourth shock hit. He thought he might lose consciousness when he heard a different voice, a female voice, screaming "Stop it!" over the dull hiss in his ears. He thought he heard footsteps, then felt hands on his face. "Oh Mike, I'm sorry." He recognized the voice, but it took his mind longer than normal to connect the voice to a person. It was Gina.

She held him, taking much of his weight while he first relaxed, then gained strength. The room remained quiet except Gina saying Mike's name as she gently rocked him.

Five minutes later, she helped him stand and led him to a different door. The sun still reflected off the mirror, making it difficult to find. When they reached the door, it was locked.

"Open. This. Door." Mike felt Gina's body tighten with each word she said. The door clicked open and they went through. No one followed. She laid Mike down on a couch and sat next to him, placing his head on her lap, stroking his forehead.

Once Mike relaxed, he opened his eyes for the first time since the sunlight had blinded him. When his eyes finally focused on Gina's face, her mood shifted.

"Mike, you've got to tell them what you know," Gina said with the same sad face she wore when Mike had told her about his daughter. Mike expected an apology, not that he would've accepted it, but he at least wanted the opportunity to reject it. He didn't think she'd start with more questions.

He tried to get up but lacked the energy to move his body more than a few inches. Gina lowered her face.

"Please Mike, tell them what you know. They only want the truth. They're good people and I have limited influence here. I think I just used it all up." Mike remained quiet so Gina continued. "I can't watch them hurt you again, Mike. Please." Her face softened into the one he recognized best, then it fell completely in on itself as she hung her head and closed her eyes. Mike thought of refusing their questions to cause Gina more pain, but his self-preservation overrode revenge.

After Gina finally opened her eyes, Mike spoke in a voice so weak and distorted that he hardly recognized it himself. "I'll answer your questions. You and me, alone." Gina nodded, unable to speak. "But you have to answer my questions as well."

Gina brushed a strand of hair off Mike's face and mouthed, "thank you."

"What do you want to know?"

"What they wanted to know." Gina took a deep breath. "Where you really came from."

"I'm from the future," Mike said and a long irritating beep emanated from his BP indicating a lie. He looked at the device as if he was disappointed. Mike knew how to avoid the truth. He needed to start with a big lie that closely resembled reality to focus the attention in another direction.

"Nice try," Gina said.

"OK, I'm originally from the Minneapolis Region." The BP gave a series of soft beeps. "Actually, I was born just outside the Minneapolis area." Mike picked up his left arm to show the silent BP, but had to put it back down due to the weakness in his arm. He knew how to hide one lie in another, replacing *when* he was born with *where*.

"Why weren't you in the database?"

"I was born Outside and never properly registered." The BP gave a series of soft beeps again. "I wasn't born in Eau Claire." Again he used the lie within a lie to hide the truth.

"How did you get here?" Gina moved her head closer to Mike's.

"They used some type of particle manipulation contraption. I was the first. It brought me close to Eau Claire." Mike didn't say where or when he came from and no one seemed to care.

"Why were you sent here?"

"It was an experiment to see if it could be done." Mike's BP gave a series of soft beeps. "It was also a punishment for not following their rules."

Gina looked at him with her head cocked slightly as if she were looking for star dust in his hair. "Who sent you?"

"I don't know." Mike's BP gave a series of beeps. "Some doctors with absolutely no connection to the PLM or Dr. Donavan."

"What are you supposed to do here?"

"Survive." Mike stared at Gina.

"What do these notes mean?"

"I'm done. I've been electrocuted and blinded," Mike said. "I've answered the questions you needed to know. Questions you had no right to demand answers for. If you want to talk more, if you ever want to talk to me again, take this off." Mike held up his arm with the BP.

Gina took Mike's arm, but before removing the BP, asked another question.

"Do you hate me?"

"Yes," Mike said and pulled his left arm free to show he was telling the truth by the silent BP. Gina nodded. She looked at him for a moment longer.

"Do you care about me?"

"No," Mike said as the BP beeped, causing Gina to smile.

Gina made a series of intricate movements to release Mike's BP and put it on her free wrist. "Ask me anything."

Mike knew others were listening to their conversation. He stopped caring. "Did we meet by chance?"

"No. It was arranged." Gina sat further back on the couch, but she focused on Mike's face. They looked more like lovers on a romantic evening than participants in an interrogation. "I was supposed to see if I could get to know you better and look for signs of your involvement in the PLM." Mike tried to interrupt, but Gina continued. "I never planned to trick you." The BP made a loud beep. Gina looked at it and frowned. "OK, I never planned to sleep with you." A series of soft beeps came from the BP. "Damn."

"Nice try," Mike said enjoying the change of positions.

"I never planned to fall in love with you." She held up the BP as Mike had done and scowled like an eight-year-old at its silence. "When you told me about your ex-wife and daughter, I fell apart. I didn't want to care about you. I stayed away knowing I was no longer objective. I'm sorry." She touched his forehead and leaned forward as if to kiss him, but sat up straight when Mike asked his next question.

"Why me?"

"We were expecting you," she paused, distracted. "He needs to know, and I need to tell him," she yelled to the empty room. She turned to Mike and continued. "Don't ask me how. I won't tell you."

Mike wanted to give her one good shock out of a primal need for revenge.

"We knew the date you were supposed to arrive in Eau Claire. Finding you was easy once you had a BP."

They talked for another half hour, more in conversation than an interrogation. "Can I remain the group's main contact with you?" Gina asked. "Or do you want someone else?"

"I still don't know what this group is or why I'd want any contact with them or you."

"We're made up of people who are trying to stop Eau Claire from being a pawn in the PLM's quest to extend life. We all have different reasons for being involved, but more than anything, we're tired of being victims."

"How are you a victim? I was the one electrocuted."

"This isn't about any one person. It's about the city. The PLM dumps garbage. They infect people, and we haven't been able to do anything about it. We don't want to move away, and you can't. If there's anyone who should be involved in fighting the PLM, it's you."

"You'll be fine as the contact. Besides I'm afraid of who they'd send next." Mike rested on the couch while Gina brought him a glass of water. She wiped his face and used a clean light on the rest of him. Mike had been in the building for over two hours. He was anxious to leave and wanted to get away from the people who had attacked him.

He was still pondering Gina's role in the group when she helped him to his feet. He had difficulty walking as his brain re-established the electrical pathways to his legs. Gina put her arm around Mike.

"Can you move to my other side?" Mike winced. "My left arm is still pretty sore." She kissed his left arm and moved to his right. They walked out the door and came through the room where he had been electrocuted, empty now. Gina appeared more anxious to get out of the room than Mike, stumbling through the doorway. When they reached the stairs, Mike's ability to walk improved and he became more sure-footed with each step.

On the ground floor, Mike's BP sat on a shelf by the door. Gina put it on Mike and kissed his cheek before he turned away. Gina stood in silence, but she didn't look away, not like before. As he left, Mike struggled to figure out what he was feeling, but his left leg collapsed slightly and he decided to hurry back to his unit while his body still functioned. He would think about Gina and the PLM after his left arm stopped tingling.

TWENTY-FOUR

"He had it coming," Dr. Jennings said to annoy Mason and get him talking. "I'm sorry I couldn't see his face. I remember the smug look he had when he sat across from me and asked for proof of time travel, as if he could understand the concept."

"I thought you'd be more concerned about losing the audio connection," Mason said. "That electrical surge nearly overloaded the audio transmitter. Then we'd have nothing."

Mason met with Dr. Jennings once a week. The other researchers had moved on to other projects, making Dr. Jennings the only other person Mason could talk to about the Tapes. He knew Dr. Jennings listened as religiously as he did, even if they had completely different perspectives. Mason saw Eau Claire as a paradise, blinding him to its imperfections while Dr. Jennings saw only the imperfections.

They were each aware of the other's obsession, seeing more clearly in the other what they couldn't see in themselves. Mason found their meetings annoying at first, similar to discussing religion or politics with someone who held an opposing view, but he saw the benefit as well. He simply needed to calibrate Dr. Jennings' responses, like converting Celsius to Fahrenheit, to get the full value of his comments.

"He was still able to lie his way out of it," Dr. Jennings said. "I thought in the future they'd be better able to detect deception." Dr. Jennings enjoyed their meetings, finding them therapeutic. He relished debating theories of retribution and expressing what he really thought, without consequences, to a man as isolated as he was.

"Think about it," Mason said. "Profit, marketing, manipulation, those things don't exist. They don't need deception. Therefore they're not good at detecting it."

"That's one way of looking at it. Or they've been so stripped of personal freedoms, it's impossible to deceive each other."

"Personal freedoms? These were ordinary citizens, electrocuting an Outsider. It doesn't get any freer than that as long as you're not the Outsider."

. . . . .

They met once at Mason's house, but it was too intimate for both of them. Mason didn't like being on display with pictures of his kids on the mantel, dirty dishes in the sink, and his blood pressure medication in the bathroom vanity.

"We should meet at my office," Dr. Jennings offered. He didn't like being away from his sphere of influence at the prison and with the protesters gone, he found it an oddly peaceful place. "I'll have them bring in lunch. Whatever you like."

Mason refused. He never liked the prison and hated the idea of using prisoners for his experiments. He had envisioned employing explorers, hand-picking the best and brightest. After the Department of Corrections removed the equipment, he decided never to enter the prison or its grounds again. He didn't even know the protesters had left.

"I finally see what you like about Ms. Elliot," Dr. Jennings said. "She has terrible taste in men, but she's a crafty one."

"The most intriguing aspect was that they expected him. They knew when he would be there, maybe from another city, but they knew to watch for him."

They finally decided to meet on neutral ground at an upscale chain restaurant built on the edge of town which offered five choices of potato instead of just French fries. The building wasn't part of future Eau Claire, and it wouldn't last. Its mass-produced booths and fake-wood bar would decompose as nature reclaimed its territory. Mason knew no one would miss the lonely building perched on a sea of asphalt with the constant buzz of highway traffic.

"Could they have detected the arrival of some particle signature?" Dr. Jennings asked. The sophistication of the question surprised Mason, and he remembered why he made time for these meetings.

"It's possible. Their knowledge of particles is far superior. I hypothesize, over time, their science transformed from one of outward exploration to inward investigation." Mason talked passionately about his field in particle science. "I've seen no evidence of air travel, much less space exploration. Their communities, politics, and religion suggest an inward influence. Exploration of an atom is much like that of a galaxy, filled with mostly empty space, but instead of traversing light years to explore that space, a particle requires only insight. They've explored a much-smaller space and have gained a greater understanding of the billions of worlds in each of us."

"What about the notes he received?" Dr. Jennings asked. "It seemed as if someone knew where he would be. How do you explain that?"

"I don't know. Perhaps time will tell," Mason smiled to himself. He loved that joke. "Material Transfer is possible, change the Location particle to make a note appear in another place, or use of advanced analytics, determine his next location by analyzing past positions. They have an incredible supply of background data. It wouldn't surprise me."

"Perhaps the prisoner lied about the notes like he does about everything else."

The waitress arrived and took their order. She appeared as bland as the food in her slightly smudged, black, buttoned-down shirt and vacant smile. Dr. Jennings ordered the trout almandine with au gratin potatoes and a mineral water. Mason chose the vegetable stir fry, the closest meal to one available in future Eau Claire.

"It's interesting. I never thought of the possibility of contaminating the future with a dormant virus, but I don't know how it was avoidable." Mason let his mind drift, as it did, to the pandemics. "It's still hard to believe fifty years from now the world's population will be cut in more than half. I keep thinking we can do something to stop it."

"We talk about this every time." Dr. Jennings didn't attempt to hide his feelings about the subject. "We signed non-disclosure clauses. There's nothing more we can do." When it looked like Mason might continue talking about pandemics, he redirected, going to Mason's other favorite topic.

"What do you think of your Bio Pulse now?" Dr. Jennings rubbed his hands together. "The Department of Corrections must be kicking themselves. Its ability to inflict pain and detect lies on an intimate level is impressive."

"Like any good tool, it can be used for a variety of purposes," Mason said to defend the device he thought was key to a successful high-density community. "When the prisoner reprogrammed his Bio Pulse, I received a wealth of new data. I can't wait to see if I can build one that works more closely to their level of functionality."

Their lunch arrived and they ate in silence. They didn't discuss personal matters, even the weather. When the bill arrived, they split it as usual with Dr. Jennings supplementing Mason's fifty-cent tip.

"I find this aversion to garbage compelling." Dr. Jennings pushed away his half-eaten lunch and leaned back in his chair. "Almost as if the whole city is afflicted with OCD."

Mason was familiar with his colleague's tactics of confrontation. He ignored the comment. "See you next week?"

Dr. Jennings remained seated after Mason left and thought about their conversation. He enjoyed frustrating Mason. It often led to the most revealing information. He knew Mason was working on a Bio Pulse but had no idea he was so close to building a prototype.

The most compelling aspect of the conversation involved what wasn't discussed—doubled longevity through particle manipulation. Mason hadn't mentioned it at all, meaning one thing. He had started work on the procedure. That crazy, crafty old coot.

TWENTY-FIVE

"We really need to stop at City Office." Stanley shook his Bio Pulse. "Dave keeps programming reminders for your thirty-day checkup. I was trying to place an order at Beta Carotene and all I heard was his voice giving me advice on every item. It was creepy."

"That's why I keep getting information about City Office," Mike said. "I thought something was wrong with my BP."

When they entered City Office, Dave was waiting for them. "Hey Mike, how's Eau Claire been treating you?"

"It could be better."

Dave walked back to his office, and Mike and Stanley followed. "I'm glad to hear it's gone smoothly," Dave said as they entered his office. "The reports I've received on you have been mostly positive."

"What reports?" Mike and Stanley said together.

"Hey, we get a daily report from your BP feedback." Dave rearranged report icons floating in the air. "Your mentoring with Florence has been stellar, and your artistic endeavors have been going well. But that evening on top of the city's water building went to Review. Fortunately, the information from our Observers has all been good."

"What Observers?" Mike and Stanley said together again.

"It's a volunteer position," Dave said. "A handful of people to keep an eye on anyone with suspicious BP behavior or, in Mike's case, a lack of any BP history. Standard stuff, nothing to worry about."

"How did I not know about this?" Stanley moved in front of Dave. "I never knew we even had Observers."

"Remember when I used to point out possible Observers at bars?" Dave asked.

"I thought you were kidding—part of your city espionage fantasies."

Mike stepped in between Dave and Stanley. "How do you and your Observers decide which behavior is bad and good?"

"We don't. The Review Team does." Mike wanted to interrupt, but Dave held up his hand and continued. "Made up of citizens who have lived in Eau Claire for at least twenty years or were raised in Eau Claire, and then selected randomly for a two-year term. It's like the Council you were on once Stanley."

Mike turned to look at Stanley.

"There were twenty-five of us. We discussed procedures and expectations," Stanley said. "We didn't spy on people."

"Neither does the Review Team. They simply look over data and determine if a violation has been committed."

"What if the Review Team makes a mistake or acts maliciously?" Mike enjoyed discussing politics, looking for a conspiracy. Plus it took the scrutiny off of him.

"It happens, but then there's an appeal if necessary. Besides it's only a two-year appointment, then it might be them up for review and they all know it. These aren't secret meetings. See?" Dave brought up images and selected one.

"A liaison on a roof?" said the recorded voice of a Review Team member. "This shouldn't have even been brought to us, or everyone in this room would be up for review."

179

"See? Anyone can pull up that information," Dave said. "We've got nothing to hide."

"Now everyone in the city knows I had sex with Gina Elliot on the Water Relay roof?"

"Of course. All information is public. I, for one, find it comforting to know that eighty-nine percent of the people in Eau Claire have kenophobia, the fear of the Outside, or that nine percent have solemumbrashphobia, the fear of sun collectors. I thought I was the only one afraid of those creepy panels that enclose the city in the summer." Mike and Stanley watched Dave as he put his hands up to cover his face before he regained his business-like composure.

"Enough about me. Hey, let's get back to Mike. Everything looks good except for three things. Your work evaluation is rated poor by both your peers and the public, but I'm sure that will change." Dave sent the evaluations to Mike in case he hadn't seen them. "Then there's the incident the other day when our Observers were unable to locate you."

"I didn't know I had any Observers until two minutes ago," Mike said, knowing Dave referred to Mike's interrogation by Gina's group. Mike wanted to keep that experience private, feeling violated, embarrassed, and partially guilty. "What do you want me to do, walk more slowly so it's easier for your henchmen to follow me?"

"Sounds great."

"Wait a second," Mike said. "You collect all this data and have people observe me. What do you do with the data? What gives you the right to control people's lives?"

"We're not controlling anyone's life. Like I said, the information is available to everyone." Dave nodded towards Stanley. "Stanley will tell you we have far more people watching us, than the other way around. Data is only powerful if it's tightly controlled. If everyone can access it, the power fades."

"That's it?" Mike asked.

"We've already talked about the infectious incident—not your best work," Dave said. "Perform better, don't lose the Observers, and stay healthy."

"Go on with my life and don't mind the people watching me?"

"Hey, you're all set. In the meantime, keep up the good work. Your Bio Pulse has been recalibrated." Dave ushered them to the door.

"What about the Observers? Are people going to be hanging around our unit?" Stanley said as he stepped in front of Dave again, his face bright red. "I feel like I'm being spied on. I've had enough. I'm done with this Office and I'm done sharing information."

Dave and Mike looked at Stanley. "You're not going to wear a BP?" Dave said, expressing surprise for the first time.

"No, of course I'm going to wear my BP!" Stanley said and looked equally shocked. "But if you want to know my favorite ice cream flavor, you're going to have to ask for it." Stanley stormed out of the building.

Mike caught up with Stanley outside and smiled for the first time in a week. "You sure told him."

. . . . .

For the next few days, Mike kept glancing around, looking for Observers. He felt guilty and important at the same time, like when the FBI had him followed. With Gina's group hovering and city Observers watching him, Mike decided he needed to proceed on more than instinct alone and worked to increase his capabilities.

He enhanced his BP with Stanley's help and made his own modifications while he incorporated his growing knowledge of holograms. Sara unknowingly gave Mike the idea of carrying a knife as she took hers from the pocket of her tailored shirt.

Mike researched the Prolong Life Movement and found their presence in Eau Claire started five years ago, a year after Dr. Donavan's cell regeneration research became public. He also found a sharp spike in PLM activity with his arrival.

Eau Claire, with a population of ninety-two thousand, had capacity for nearly twenty-five thousand more as guests, mostly in spare bedrooms like the one Mike occupied, but Eau Claire rarely had more than ten thousand guests at a time. Currently, they were near capacity.

. . . . .

Gina's first visit with Mike after the interrogation started out awkwardly. Neither knew how to act. Their relationship felt different, knowing about Gina's assignment. While making conversation, Gina pointed to her BP and put her finger to her lips. Mike understood and talked as if they were being listened to, which amplified their awkwardness.

Gina pulled the conversation in a different direction. "That feels good when you brush my hair back like that," she said as she brushed her own hair back. Mike sat on the couch five feet away, shrugged his shoulders. "Mmmm." Gina moaned as if Mike kissed her neck and ran his hand down her body, but he hadn't moved from the couch. "There's something I've always wanted to try," Gina purred. "And I heard you guys from the Outside were pretty kinky and into this kind of thing. What do you say we have sex without our BPs? I hear it's incredible."

Gina put her finger to her lips again as she looked at Mike's BP and shook her head at his active fertility status. She attempted to take off Mike's BP, but he grabbed her hand, remembering the last time someone took off his BP. She looked around the room to show him they were alone. He took hers off first, then his own, and laid their BPs on the couch.

She took his hand and led him into his bedroom and closed the door. "Sorry about that," she whispered close to his ear, "but I needed to talk with you, and I didn't know how else to prevent people from listening without the trouble of leaving your unit."

"Who's listening?"

Gina shrugged. "Who isn't listening?" They sat on his bed, the only place to sit in his small bedroom—which felt much smaller with Gina in it. "Our group needs your help," Gina spoke softly, leaning towards Mike.

He stood and stepped away from her. "After what you and your friends did to me, do you really think I'd help?" Mike whispered loud enough to carry across the entire unit. Gina stood, but didn't approach Mike, telling him to be quieter with her hands.

"They were sure you were part of the PLM, perhaps the top leader." Gina looked down. "I can understand why you don't want to help. Why you hate me." She paused, but Mike didn't refute her statement. "We're convinced there'll be more attacks like the one on your friend Kevin, except next time it might include all of Eau Claire and other cities. And it might be deadly."

"How do you know this?"

"I don't have all the answers. I only know you're involved, whether you want to be or not." She looked at Mike with that strong, determined look he found both irritating and appealing. "The PLM has made sure of it. Your presence here in Eau Claire is the catalyst."

"How do I know your group didn't send me those notes?" Mike stepped closer to Gina. "Dump the garbage? Infect Kevin? How do I know you aren't the PLM?"

Gina sat back down on the bed. "Sit down," Gina said, but Mike didn't move. "Please sit down." She patted the area next to her. "I really want to help."

Mike sat. "What?" Anger and sympathy battled within him. Gina had a way of breaking down his wall of self-preservation.

"I don't know how to convince you and maybe I don't have to. We want to exchange information. The city is nearing capacity. People have been arriving from other regions. Many are young thrill-seekers who want to be where the action is. We've been analyzing manifests for the last month and the number of specialists trickling in is alarming, from all areas of discipline, including infectious diseases. Whatever is going to happen, we suspect it will take place soon, within the next month."

"First prove you're not part of the PLM."

"Can you?" Gina asked. They stared back at each other until Mike found it arousing instead of confrontational.

"What do you want from me?" he asked.

"If you receive any more notes or strange interactions of any kind, let us know. Send me a message and we'll agree on a place to meet. Of course, if you want to just get together, that might keep suspicion down from whoever's watching." She smiled and looked directly at him. "But more urgently, we need to know what makes you special. Why you are the focal point? I know there's something you're not telling me."

"Why are you involved in all of this?"

"Because of you." She looked at Mike before continuing. "I was vocal about Dr. Donavan's work. Many people were. We saw it as an attack on our way of life and a return to the Poly Plagues. I found out that Dr. Donavan wasn't even in favor of using his discovery. But once he published his findings, the threat was out there."

"What's to stop anyone from extending life?"

"It's a theory that only a handful of people could put into action," Gina said, "and none of them could proceed with even the preliminary work without everyone in the country knowing about it instantly."

"And your role?"

"I volunteered for a few minor missions, but it seemed pointless. I hadn't been involved in several years, but then you arrived and changed everything."

"How?"

"We knew someone from the Outside would arrive in Eau Claire at roughly the time you did," Gina said. "We believed that person would have some connection to the PLM. We just didn't know what type of connection."

"How did you know this?" Mike said.

"You tell me your secrets," Gina said, "and I'll tell you mine."

"Why you? Why were you the one to seduce me?"

"I didn't seduce you," Gina said. "At least not on purpose. All I can say is that it was my choice to meet you, but I didn't think it would hurt so much."

"What? The electrical charge?"

Gina pinched the ridge of her nose and shook her head. "After we met, I did some research and we're nearly a perfect match."

"What does that mean, nearly a perfect match?"

"I ran an analysis the next day, and match isn't the right word. It's more like we're the perfect blend."

Mike looked at her and almost laughed except for the serious look on her face.

"Based on our brain scans, chemistry make-up, pheromones, hormones, preferences, skills, habits, and even annoyances, we match in key areas, which isn't that rare, although hormonally we have some pretty interesting connections. But we also have incredible pairings. I'm not an expert in erotology, but I'm told it's a pretty rare match."

"I still don't buy it." Mike said. "It sounds like you're making this up."

"I didn't simply want to sleep with you when we first met." Gina studied the cuff on her shirt. "I wanted to rip your clothes off and rub my whole body against yours. I felt safe and comfortable and I loved the way you worked to keep your face neutral. You looked at me like you'd found a rainforest, but at the same time pretended you didn't care. You're always hiding something, and there's nothing more exciting to me than finding what most people never see."

"If this connection is so strong, why did you run from me?" Mike didn't plead, but he wanted to know the truth. "Why didn't you let me explain? And why did you electrocute me?" Mike stood up to get as far away from Gina as possible in his small bedroom.

"You were ready to explain? To tell me the truth?"

"Maybe," Mike said, knowing neither of them believed it.

"When you told me about your wife and daughter, I knew I had underestimated my feelings for you and sooner or later someone would get hurt or worse. I stayed away, but somehow we kept coming together, and finally what I feared the most happened."

"You electrocuted me."

"Yes, I electrocuted you," Gina said. "I didn't activate the electrical charge, and I was told the effects would be less severe, but I didn't stop it either." Gina stood and took a step towards Mike. "I fought to stop them after the second shock, but by the time I got to you, you were nearly unconscious."

"Then you stepped in as my *savior*, but all you really wanted was more information."

"I couldn't watch you in pain anymore." Gina walked closer to Mike. "But yes, I still wanted information. I needed to know if you were involved with the PLM."

"Why?" Mike sat on the bed solely to get more space.

"I needed to know if I was in love with the enemy."

"Am I the enemy?"

"No." Gina sat on the bed next to Mike. "Am I?"

"Where do we go from here?" Mike wanted greater clarity and less emotion.

"We don't know why the PLM has focused on you, but we can help each other. And I don't mind having an excuse to see you again." Gina held out her hand and laid it next to Mike's on the bed. Mike didn't take her hand, but he didn't move away either. They both looked straight ahead at his white walls, each caught in their own thoughts.

He wanted to take her hand, but the tingling in his left arm remained, reminding him of his imminent danger and Gina's role in it. In the back of his mind something didn't add up and Mike knew he needed to continue on his path alone. Gina could be the ally he needed or his destruction. He'd be patient and find out which.

They left Mike's room together. Gina gave Mike a quick kiss on the cheek before she put on her BP. "That was incredible," Gina moaned. "I never felt so vulnerable and powerful before. We have to try that again." She smiled and Mike instantly became aroused by her perverted grin and the way she experienced the words as she said them. She looked down, saw Mike's excitement, and her smile broadened, reaching her eyebrows before she walked out.

. . . . .

"Mike," Sara said in a frantic voice unlike her warm demeanor, "come to Beta Carrotene. Now." Mike suspected another disease outbreak and ran to Beta Carrotene.

She hadn't been able to reach Stanley or locate him for several hours. "His last BP reading puts him in his lab, but he's not wearing it." She grabbed Mike by his shirt and shook him. "He's not wearing it. I don't think he's ever willingly taken off his BP."

At the word *willingly* Mike panicked, thinking about how his BP was taken a few days ago and what happened after. He couldn't explain his fears to Sara, so left her standing at Beta Carrotene with the terrible task of waiting for Stanley.

Mike ran to Stanley's lab and paused when he noticed the door propped open. Inside he saw Stanley's BP on the counter next to a tray of plants. He looked around for some indication of where to go next, his brain envisioning several brutal scenarios. When he found Stanley sitting on a black metal garden bench thirty feet away, he relaxed a little.

Mike took a deep breath and informed Sara. "He's fine. Clearly a problem with his BP," Mike said. "We'll be at Beta Carrotene shortly." Stanley sat on the bench and stared at pepper plants as Mike approached.

"I have no idea what the temperature is or the person's name who just walked by," Stanley said to the peppers. "I didn't even know you were here until I saw you."

"Sara was worried about you." Mike sat beside Stanley.

"Can I see your BP?" Stanley finally looked at Mike. Mike held out his arm, but Stanley shook his head. "No, can I have your BP?"

Mike figured Stanley was in withdrawals and gave him his BP. Stanley weighed it in his hands before he threw it across the garden, where it landed near a compost pile.

Mike half stood to retrieve it but sat back down. "Here we are, you and me, roughing it out here in the garden." Mike picked up a handful of dirt from a raised bed and poured the black soil from hand to hand. "Untethered from the world. What should we do now?"

"What color is the sky?" Stanley asked, his head tilted up.

Mike followed his gaze. "I don't know." He dropped the dirt and put his hand up to block out the sun. "I'd call it a medium blue."

"I never gave the color of the sky much thought," Stanley said. "I receive information about the weather, sunrise, sunset, but not the color of the sky, so I stopped noticing it."

"I've gone years, decades, my whole life without a BP, but I've seldom noticed the color of the sky." Mike grabbed another handful of dirt from the garden. "Life is filled with distractions."

"When I was little, my friends and I used to see who could go the longest without our BPs." Stanley looked straight ahead. "I never won. I was too afraid. Everyone in the city told us how sickness and disease can strike in a flash. Anything can happen."

Mike thought of different things to say—that the BP was only a tool or Stanley had a choice—but decided it wasn't more words Stanley needed. It was time, time to think without the world whispering in his ear.

"Do you know what they call people who don't wear BPs?" Stanley asked.

Mike wasn't sure if this was a question or the beginning of a joke. "No. What?"

"They're called ghosts. Not quite in this world, and not in the other. Neither in the city nor Outside."

Mike reflected on his life, his lack of adjectives for the sky color, and his own fears. Growing up, he didn't want to be used or fought over like a pawn as part of his parents' divorce strategy, so he tried to control his situation, all situations. Now he sat on a bench with a man who had thought he had control from a watch-like device only to learn he was misled. Mike nearly laughed at the ridiculousness of it, finally seeing in others what he couldn't see in himself.

"There is no control," Mike said, "just little tricks to distract us from the fact that we are part of a bigger whole, a gear, a balance, a transfer wheel." Mike turned to Stanley to see if he was listening. "The question isn't who flips the levers, but where we fit in." Was he simply a man out of time, Mike wondered, or a timely man here to reset the machine?

Ten minutes later as Mike ran his hand across the black dirt, he looked up at the sky again. "Do you think it's more periwinkle or lavender?"

"Definitely periwinkle. Mike, are you really from the Outside?"

"Not quite," Mike said.

"I didn't think so." Stanley stood and retrieved Mike's BP. "Do you think I over-reacted?"

"Not at all." Mike put on his BP. "With the sound turned down, you can almost forget you're wearing one."

TWENTY-SIX

Mike was tired of waiting for the next note, wondering when the PLM would intrude on his life, implicating him again. He needed to be one step ahead. To do that he needed to know what they wanted from him, to find them before they struck again.

In five years, no one had been able to identify a single member of the PLM, much less locate one. He and Ren had visited several people who weren't *hooked up*, but Mike needed a more systematic approach. Stanley's latest meltdown with his BP made him a potential accomplice.

"Ren and I have been talking to people who don't wear BPs, to understand them better," Mike told Stanley. "Do you want to join us?" With Dave's help, Stanley easily gathered a list of all 123 Eau Claire residents who didn't wear BPs—ghosts.

The first person they met was Betty Manderfield, 111 years old. She still volunteered at the Child Center every day, worked at a food market, and repaired metal. She was born in Chippewa Falls, a smaller town north of Eau Claire that no longer existed.

"My family moved to Eau Claire not long after the first plague started. Eau Claire was pretty isolated and had bio filters. We didn't see the worst of the Poly Plagues, but it was bad enough."

"How old were you?" Ren asked.

"I must have been about your age." She looked at Ren. "Eau Claire was bigger then, with more houses and plenty of people living outside the city, on the other side of the major roads then. The population had to be more than one hundred fifty thousand. As people got sick, the city set up medical centers in the houses and old shops to the east and north to isolate and comfort the infected. When people died, the city left the dead where they were and burned the houses and shops."

The stories and the woman telling them fascinated Stanley, Ren, and Mike. "I go in for an annual scan and we have a personal scanner, but I don't use it as much as I used to, my husband even less. We've both lived longer than expected without a Bio Pulse. Some information we just don't want to know any more."

Betty recorded her volunteer time on a system interface at the Child Center, but the food market didn't have an interface so she had to use one in the square a few blocks over. She had an energy bike which she and her husband used to meet the city's energy expectations. "It's inconvenient, but nothing like when I was young and we had to carry water halfway across the city."

Her husband, Harvey, joined them in their small first floor unit filled with big, bright metallic flowers that drooped from long metal stems. "I'm a youngster, a year younger than my wife. Never felt better." He didn't wear a BP either, and remained the city's algae expert, working mostly in water purification.

"We married young. I was thirty-nine and Betty forty. People married younger back then. Even after the Poly

Plagues ended, it took years, close to a decade, before people traveled."

"Eau Claire felt isolated until the travel ban was lifted," Betty said. "Then we traveled everywhere like the young kids do today." She touched Ren's knee. "But we came back to Eau Claire. It protected us when so many people weren't as lucky."

"Why don't you wear a BP?" Ren asked.

Betty and Harvey looked at each other before Betty spoke. "We had a few devices like a Bio Pulse when we were kids and of course, once the plagues hit full force, everyone wore one, but they weren't reliable and couldn't stop the Poly Plagues." She looked at her husband again before continuing. "We saw enough people die, all wearing an early version of the Bio Pulse. The appeal wasn't there."

"By the time reliable BPs were available, we had gotten married." Harvey picked up the conversation where Betty left off. "When we thought about the other wearing a BP, it reminded us of death." He grabbed Betty's hand and gave it a tight squeeze. "The worst part is that people don't see us."

"Most of our friends still can't believe we don't wear one." Betty patted Harvey's hand.

"But we're happy," Harvey said.

"What do you think of the PLM?" Mike asked. "And extending life?"

"They make me sick," Betty said. "Dumping garbage and hiding."

"After the Poly Plagues, everyone worked for years to clean up the wreckage." Harvey made a fist. "To think someone is causing a health hazard on purpose, we'd like to get our hands on them."

Betty nodded vigorously in agreement. "They're selfish people, only thinking about themselves, wanting to extend their own lives. What do they think is going to happen with zero population growth and a life expectancy of 240 years? They don't care if any more babies are born. *I* couldn't show my face at the Furnace without any babies to celebrate because *I* wanted to live twice as long."

"And we sure as hell aren't going to go back to the way things used to be," Harvey said, "slowly poisoning ourselves, living in the filth of overpopulation."

After two weeks of talking with various people about why they didn't wear BPs, Mike was exhausted, but Stanley bubbled with excitement. He enjoyed talking with ghosts and hearing their stories. Stanley looked for a greater understanding while Mike sought a connection, a lead to the PLM, and Ren simply liked conversations that didn't focus on her.

They had met with slightly more than half of the 123 ghosts. Ren accompanied them on many visits, hearing stories that differed from the young people she knew. Many were older like Betty and Harvey with similar histories while others were ghosts because they had a deep mistrust of the city. Some sought the thrill the younger people talked about while a few wished to abuse their bodies without a Bio Pulse stopping them.

Mike read the ghost's faces while Stanley or Ren asked questions, but none were likely PLM candidates. Mike was more interested in the fifty-nine people they couldn't locate. They didn't seem to exist, didn't show up for scans or record work duties. They were the true ghosts.

Mike and Stanley talked with Dave about it.

"The city doesn't spend much time on ghosts," Dave said. "It's a poor use of resources. Each year we lose track of a few."

"Why don't you put your Observers on them instead of following us around?" Stanley pointed to himself and Mike.

"Hey, we're only following Mike and, like I said, ghosts are too hard to track. Some are probably dead. Their numbers are low and the effort to verify is enormous, so we ignore them."

. . . . .

Mike began his own surveillance, watching the units of ghosts they hadn't found. While he sat for an hour staring at a door seldom used, it occurred to him it might not be ghosts he sought, but anyone in Eau Claire who simply took off their BP. The more he thought about it, the more it made sense that a few isolated individuals didn't make up the PLM, but a highly connected group did. "They simply know how to disappear," Mike said to himself. He needed to find out who wasn't broadcasting when the garbage was scattered. He walked away from the lonely door with a new purpose.

Recreating the timeline of events, Mike started with the garbage incident outside the library and moved to the garbage he picked up. Before he could do anything else, he needed data—BP data on everyone in Eau Claire. He could access the billions of transactions, but he knew someone who was much better at it. Mike didn't want to reveal his plan for tracking down the PLM, knowing he was already a suspect. Fortunately, Mike excelled at obtaining information people were reluctant to give.

At City Office, Mike explained to Dave his idea for a performance in which he would correlate BP use with different times of the day. "I need to know how many people were in a health store on March ninth."

"Hey, I sent you the data," Dave said a second later. "I look forward to your performance."

"I also need to know how many people were in Child Centers on March thirtieth."

195

"Done." Dave turned to walk away.

"I also need all the—"

"Hey, give me the range of dates and the data's yours."

"I'm looking at March ninth through the thirtieth, but I'm not sure I want everything," Mike said. "We can work the details out in less than an hour."

"I sent you all transactions for the month of March." Dave walked away from the tall table in the lobby, escaping to his office.

"But . . ." Mike smiled.

Back at his unit, Mike spent hours looking over the new data, overwhelmed with billions of transactions until he noticed a pattern and simply selected all people with *No Status* during the dates and times he knew. He had over two thousand *No Status* inputs during the first garbage incident and six thousand for the second, but only 586 for both. It was still too many. He needed another event to narrow it down.

Entries were broken down by day, then time. Each event had a short description and a location like Beta Carrotene. Inquiries were listed along with meetings and any conversation longer than thirty seconds. Each event included biological measurements creating an overwhelming list of data. "Think what marketers would do with this," Mike said.

He looked up Gina's data, intrigued to see how they met from an electronic standpoint. He didn't think he'd find fireworks, but something more than his name and the word *excited*. It proved two things—Gina knew about him before they met because he was in her proximity file and she was interested in him.

He was about to move on when he noticed her many *No Status* entries. With his mind on high alert, he thought it must mean something, until he looked at his own log and noticed several *No Status* entries as well, correlating to time he spent in the library. Gina spent time in libraries also and with all the shortcuts and hidden spots she knew, it wasn't hard to imagine interruptions in her connection. Mike wanted to take a closer look at the rest of Gina's entries, but it became an impossible task of reviewing details without context. Still, he continued to look at it in hopes of learning more about her.

· · · · ·

Mike eventually returned to work on his next performance. He changed it once again, this time tailoring it to meet his needs. He made thirty holographic Mikes. Each moved in towards the center as they morphed together along the way to form one perfect Mike, only to fall apart, back into the thirty Mikes again.

He had just finished the logic for selecting the right Mike for each potential audience question when a holographic Mike walked up to him. Mike looked up at the image of himself as it stopped three feet away. Mike thought he must have made a mistake in the programming when the holographic Mike spoke.

"Mr. Newhouse, it's time we had a conversation." Mike froze, mesmerized by the holographic image of himself as it spoke in his voice. The image even leaned forward as Mike would have, to create a closer bond. "We need to discuss your future," the holographic Mike said. Mike shut down his program. All of the other holographic Mikes disappeared except the one in front of him. Mike sent a message to Gina. "You shouldn't have involved her," said the holographic Mike.

"How did you—?" Mike said as the holographic Mike cut him off.

"You are predictable. You're also putting Ms. Elliot in danger."

"What do you mean?"

"Our grievance is with you, but if you continue to involve others, we don't particularly care who we hurt as long as we get what we want."

Mike saw his winning smile on the holographic Mike, the same grin he had flashed to numerous people, and he hated how his brown eyes appeared sincere and his face warm and believable.

"What do you want?" Mike asked. "What problem do you have with me?"

"We want all lives extended, Dr. Donavan's work fully implemented, and for you to go away," holographic Mike said with Mike's familiar facial expressions and voice that grew mellower as it became angrier.

"Why me? Go where?"

"You jump through time while the rest of us are limited to a short existence, trudging through every single day. You are an affront to our cause and an annoyance that will soon disappear. How many people do you want to take with you?" The holographic Mike finished with a smile and a short familiar nod before it disappeared. Mike ran outside. The pathways appeared normal, and people walked by as usual. A blur of motion through the arched walkway made him jump. It was Gina, out of breath.

"What's wrong?" she said, looking around as Mike continued to scan the area.

"I'm sorry," he said. "I must have activated your name by mistake."

Gina gave him a look to indicate it was the worst lie she had ever heard, then continued on a new topic. "While I'm here, can we at least have dinner together?"

"Sure. Let me put some things away first." Mike glanced at his BP and lead Gina into the studio. Using hand signals, he directed her to the right.

He went in the opposite direction. He knew the range of a hologram was less than fifty feet, but all Mike found was a spot a person could have stood to control the holographic image. It didn't tell him much, other than someone from the PLM had been so close to him, close enough to catch.

Mike met Gina back in the studio and put a finger to his lips. Gina understood.

"Stop stalling and let's get something to eat," she said. "You choose since you contacted me. But I really need to go through a Clean Screen on the way."

Mike agreed, thinking Gina must have worked up a sweat while running over. Gina walked closely to Mike with a tight grasp on his arm, steering them toward a Clean Screen a block away.

"What happened?" Gina whispered to Mike as they entered. Mike put a finger to his lips again. "Clean Screens interrupt transmissions. Your BP works." Gina took Mike's arm and operated his BP. "But it can't transmit in here." Mike looked around before he whispered in Gina's ear and explained the rogue hologram, its interactive ability, the threats made about her, and even his attempt to locate PLM members.

They walked back and forth several times in the Clean Screen. Gina nearly tripped when he told her the details of his search for ghosts and his latest idea about tracking BP status.

"Why didn't we think of that?" she said. "We've spent weeks trying to connect people who were at several PLM-related events. We didn't think to look for a pattern of who *wasn't* there." She tightened her grip on him. "Here." She handed Mike a grease pencil and held out her other arm. "When we exit, write down the exact time you saw the hologram. We can determine the dates and times for the garbage, but your numbers will be helpful."

Mike grabbed the pencil, but hesitated. "I'll give you the information, but only if you tell me what you find as soon as you find it."

Gina looked at him and nodded with her arm still outstretched as they stepped out of the Clean Screen. "We can do the work without your information, but I want to see if I can duplicate your results."

"Remember it was my idea," Mike said, before he wrote on her arm. The pencil glided over her skin in dark brown numbers.

"Come to my unit in an hour." She took the pencil. "And we're still having dinner together."

Mike paced through the city, too anxious to sit still and walked down random paths, his mind assessing threats. An hour later as Gina opened her door, Mike's anxiety didn't subside. Her unit was much like his without the elaborately painted walls or a kitchen.

"What did you find out?" Mike asked.

"I found out you think I'm irresistible," Gina said, taking the conversation on an unexpected detour. "Aren't we supposed to eat dinner first?" Gina threw her BP on the table and walked to her room. Mike did the same to discover Gina lying on her bed in a sea of orange.

Her room was larger than his, with walls covered in big bold blotches of color. Mike lay next to her and stared at her orange ceiling, feeling as if he was in a tree fort planning a big adventure.

"The two garbage events narrowed down the numbers a bit," Gina said still looking up at the ceiling. "But the incident with the rogue hologram helped considerably, allowing us to narrow the list to eighty-four."

"I want to track them down," Mike said.

"We're already working on it." Gina reached for Mike's hand, but he pulled it away. Mike realized he'd made a mistake in sharing the information with Gina and understood the reason for his growing anxiety during the past hour.

"This isn't about longevity or garbage for me." Mike leaned on one elbow. "I need to find them because if I don't, they'll find me and I don't think I'll like the result."

"But why are they looking for you?"

"I don't know—the same reason you were looking for me."

"I'm not even sure myself."

"I'm not equipped to deal with them on their terms."

"I understand, more than you know. This has been about much more than the PLM." Gina sat up on her bed. "We have many more resources and *we're* not being followed by three different Observers. Let us do the legwork and I promise I'll include you on anything we find."

Mike thought she might have a point and he didn't have much left to bargain with. "I can't sit and do nothing, waiting for them to surprise me again."

"Good. We have an assignment for you."

TWENTY-SEVEN

"You were right about Gina," Mason said at their weekly meeting. "There's something unexpected about her."

"I only found her interesting, one of the few people able to see through the prisoner's lies." Dr. Jennings sipped his coffee. "Although, I like her more and more. She's not afraid to inflict a little pain."

"When I analyzed the Eau Claire-wide BP data the prisoner obtained, her entries described a much more robust involvement in a wide range of activities. I can't figure her out." Mason reviewed the data in his head. "While nearly every resident in Eau Claire had occasional No Status reports, Gina's were prolific at times and statistically significant." Gina became his newest obsession. The more complex she became, the more he wanted to know.

"What are you saying, *she* dumped the garbage?" Dr. Jennings asked.

"I don't think so, but she's more . . . involved. She knows the guts of the city better than anyone and her knowledge about the prisoner is odd."

"Why? Because she electrocuted him?" Dr. Jennings smiled, remembering the moment. "It simply shows she has good judgment."

"Gina's data might be an anomaly. It may have more to do with the city," Mason pulled a piece of paper from his briefcase. "The interrelatedness of Eau Claire makes reading the data more complex. The patterns in the social structure are almost mathematical. Did you know seventy-four percent of the people in Eau Claire were born in Eau Claire?"

"No, but I'm beginning to appreciate Eau Claire now that I know they're monitoring the prisoner," Dr. Jennings said. "For a while I thought it was one big hippie commune."

"It's funny you said commune. The one thing I couldn't find in the BP data is a strong connection between parents and child. It appears children belong more to the city than to the parents who conceived them, although each parent has defined responsibilities."

"That's another thing they got right. Get rid of the parents. Most of them aren't qualified to own a dog." Dr. Jennings pulled his computer from his pocket. "You look like you haven't been sleeping. Do you need me to prescribe a sedative?"

"It's Dr. Donavan's work. It keeps me up at night. He sees cells in galactic terms. I can bully particles to a different time, but altering the aging of cells takes finesse. Let me show you." Mason took two small plates from the table and sprinkled them with pepper. "Each of these plates represents a cell in the body and the pepper is the enzyme telomerase. Telomerase is the material required for cells to replicate and replication is how cells age."

"I know." Dr. Jennings looked up from his screen. "I am a doctor."

"Sorry, but I need to say it out loud. It helps me think." He paused. Dr. Jennings nodded and Mason continued with a plate in either hand. "In a healthy person each cell replicates about fifty times in a lifetime. Dr. Donavan has been able to double that by increasing the amount of enzymes available. The more enzymes for replication, the longer a cell survives, which means the longer we survive with healthy cells." Mason shook both plates until the pepper danced. "By altering the Aging particle, Dr. Donavan is able to siphon away unused telomerase in flawed and precancerous cells and add it to healthy cells." Mason poured pepper from one plate to the other.

"Using what's already in the body, Dr. Donavan feeds healthy cells with the extra telomerase, allowing those cells to replicate twice as many times as normal, extending the human lifespan by twofold. The flawed cell, which has been drained of its telomerase, fades away." Mason waved the empty plate and set it on the chair under the table. "He's not only extending life, but cleaning up as he goes."

"Does it work?" Dr. Jennings moved his cup out of the cellular mayhem on the table.

"In theory, but the elegance of the process is more compelling." Mason had no wish to live longer, empathizing with his many friends in future Eau Claire. He had never met any of them, except for Mike, yet he felt closer to his future Eau Claire friends than nearly anyone in his time. The only exceptions were his family—his daughter Cindy and son Matt—who lived in different states. Half the time he didn't know which time he was in, his own or Mike's. He understood Mike's better, hearing dangers Mike never noticed—up to seven people following him, aggressive anti-Outside sentiments, and Gina's elaborate investigation into Mike's activities.

Dr. Jennings was lost in time as well, tallying Mike's sentence in a series of pluses and minuses to measure time's influence on the prisoner. He thought of it as research, but his need to continually update responses and keep score bordered on compulsive behavior.

"Do you think you'll ever leave Eau Claire?" Dr. Jennings asked.

"Not as long as the transmitter keeps working." Mason wanted to move into the heart of Eau Claire, an area still vital 131 years later, but he also liked the idea of Eau Claire sloughing off his existence like a dead skin cell, his house decaying outside of Eau Claire.

TWENTY-EIGHT

Mike and Gina had dinner in a noisy health store called The Mill where they filled specially milled tortillas with roasted vegetables, beans, sundried peppers, salsas, and sauces. They sat in the back of the room at the edge of activity.

They each constructed ten tortillas in a friendly competition to see who could create the tastiest combination with the winner allowed to ask one question and the loser required to answer honestly. They both understood the seriousness of the wager. They each had secrets and needed to trust the other without the use of gadgets or coercion.

"You go first," Mike said. "Pick your best tortilla combination. Let's see what you got."

Gina proudly grabbed one topped with artichoke and celery salad, took a big bite and handed it to Mike. "Try to top that," she said with her mouth full.

Mike hoped to grow a new relationship with Gina from the debris of the first. They had laid on Gina's bed for an hour, quiet most of the time, getting used to the presence of the other. Mike had finally taken Gina's hand and felt a new sensation nearly as strong as the electrical charge that had raced through his same arm several weeks before. He hadn't forgotten the pain or loss of control he'd experienced and

Gina's shadowy role in it. He remembered, too, the look on her face when he told her about his wife and daughter.

"Not bad," Mike said, handing Gina's tortilla back to her, but not before taking another bite. She pulled it from his hands.

"I take it you've given up already," she said.

"I haven't even started." Mike picked up one with hot peppers. "Wait until you try this." He took a messy bite and handed it to Gina. She licked the smoky sauce from Mike's hand before taking the tortilla. She didn't return it.

"Not bad, for an Outsider."

Maybe, Mike thought, their relationship had already suffered too much pain to salvage. Perhaps they were better off as acquaintances. But then he saw her smile across the table, more intimate than their evening on the roof, and he wanted to hold her, protect her, knowing that he might be the one who needed protection.

"This one's the winner," Gina said, before they swapped half-eaten tortillas, each finishing the other's. Mike wiped dressing off Gina's chin.

She was his equal, not only in temperament, but in deception as well. Mike had always treated every relationship like a questionable entrepreneurial opportunity. He had loved his wife, but he told her only what she needed to know. His daughter, who he loved as unselfishly as he could, was an object he admired without ever exposing himself to her critique as he watched her from a parking lot or across the street with binoculars.

Gina knew his nature and understood his character. Mike thought his relationship with Gina might be the most honest one he'd ever had, even in the midst of their mutual deception.

After eating more of each other's food than their own, finding pleasure in what the other had created, they agreed to a tie, allowing each to ask a question and requiring both to answer honestly. They left The Mill in their usual tight formation, their hands still slippery from the oils and sauces of dinner.

Gina led the way saying she knew of a quiet place. Mike gave her a quizzical look. He had decided not to sleep with her again until all threats had passed and he understood how she fit into this mess. As she leaned into him, he hoped disaster would strike quickly so he'd have his answer.

They sat on a few large stones in what might have been an old riverbed in a portion of the city that few Eau Claire citizens knew existed. Gina explained that the elevation and minerals in the stones interrupted BP signals.

"Who's going first?" she asked.

"Since I was the one kidnapped and electrocuted," Mike said, "I'll go first." Gina bowed her head and separated herself from Mike.

Mike had thought about his question as they walked, wanting to be the first to ask in hopes of setting the tone. He wanted to know how she knew about him, where she got her information, and who was in her group. Instead he asked what he needed to know. "How much can I trust you?"

Gina smiled. "More than you know, but only as much as I can trust you." She slid closer to Mike. "I didn't take your arrival here seriously enough. I didn't treat our relationship with the care it deserved. So much of this is an act of faith for me." She put her hand to his face. "You are connected to me in a way even I don't understand."

"What connection? What are you talking about?"

"I know I'm not making sense, but I love you and that's what scares me." Gina stood and pulled Mike with her. "I had originally hoped to protect Eau Claire from the PLM and now all I want to do is protect you. But I don't know if I can keep either safe." She took Mike's arm again. "You have no reason to trust me and I could as easily suspect you. Which I've done. Twice. I turned my back on you when you told me about your past, and I let others hurt you to learn even more. I don't want to know anything else."

She brought Mike's wrist up to her cheek and rubbed it against her skin. "I have no questions to ask. You and Eau Claire are one in the same to me, save one and I've saved you both. I can't expect to know any more about you than I know about this city."

"But you know everything about this city, every sun collector and secret passageway."

"There's so much I don't know. The PLM has proven that. And I know plenty about you."

"Like what this says?" Mike tapped his BP.

"Every time you lie, your face becomes unnaturally calm. You never had a dog, you hate spinach, you rarely listen to your BP, and you like to test boundaries, always looking for a weakness."

They didn't move, standing inches from each other as Mike put his hand on her chin, sucking in every bit of information from the dewy wisps of hair along the sides of her face to her plump earlobes free of holes. They remained in the same position, holding on to the moment when they were simply two people attracted to one another without a thought of what else it might mean, like two teenagers on the porch with the light flicking on and off, signaling that it was time to come in.

. . . . .

Gina's assignment for Mike was to act as bait, to attract PLM attention and force them to respond in hopes her group could identify or apprehend PLM members.

"Who's in your group again?" Mike asked when he received his assignment.

"I told you, mostly Eau Claire residents, everyday people who are tired of the PLM using Eau Claire as their dumping ground."

Gina's group enhanced Mike's BP to detect people, not merely their BP, but their body heat and carbon dioxide signature. It also had a DNA identifier, allowing him to determine who had been at a location up to five minutes prior. It was a tight window, but if he had had the capability earlier, he could have identified the person who had manipulated the Mike hologram.

Acting as bait wasn't a particularly difficult job, giving Mike the opportunity to wander. He didn't know who the eighty-four people on the No Status report were, but he did know the ghosts. With Ren's assistance, he took a new approach and talked with neighbors of ghosts.

"Excuse me, do you know where I can find Stuart Moser?" Mike asked.

"Listen garbage heap, don't you have any manners?" said the lady Mike had approached. The exchange was common. Mike still forgot it was impolite to engage people in conversation without the proper electronic handshake.

In bars or health stores people sought conversation by broadcasting a general greeting. But many people turned off their greeting when relaxing near their unit. It was a subtle technique for creating privacy in a densely populated city and one faux pas Mike continually made because he still hadn't learned to rely solely on BP data. He found Ren on a bench two gardens away.

"You have to be the most embarrassing person in the city," she said when Mike sat down next to her. "Let me do the talking from now on and save us both some time."

"OK, Ms. BP etiquette." Ren talked less but got better results. "How come nobody calls you names?" Mike asked.

"Because I don't barge into people's private space like an Outsider."

With Ren's help, a neighbor introduced them to Chester Jones, a ghost.

"You really from the Outside?" Chester asked.

"See?" Mike showed him the region on his BP.

"He doesn't look like an Outsider," Chester said to Ren.

"Well, I am," Mike said. "How about you? Are you an Outsider?"

"No, I was born right here in Eau Claire. I never cared for that cow pie pulse. I don't need any more voices in my head." Chester turned to Ren and smiled. "Do you even know what a cow pie is? Or a cow for that matter?"

"I've got to go." Ren whacked Mike in the gut with her scrawny arm. "My services are no longer needed. Offend away."

"Kids," Mike said as Ren departed. He examined his BP to determine if he could locate Chester by body heat and other signatures.

"What are you doing?" Chester asked.

"Just checking your position on my BP."

"Who said you could do that?" Chester walked away grabbing his head. "I can't believe I trusted someone wearing a cow pie."

"I was only checking to see if . . ." Mike stopped yelling as Chester walked out of sight.

Mike continued to scan the immediate area, finding six people—five with BPs and one without—confirming Chester's location. Mike monitored his BP display, waiting for Chester to move out of range, when he discovered another ghost, one much closer.

Mike walked for fifty feet and the new ghost followed. He thought about contacting Gina, but what would he say? He had found someone not using a BP?

Mike changed course and followed the ghost, but he had difficulty keeping up with the ghost's progress. He never made visual contact, instead tracking the ghost electronically. The ghost appeared to walk through walls at times, which forced Mike to double back and run around an entire block to keep the ghost in range. Mike jumped over a bench and cut through a park, shaking his head, wondering how he ended up doing exactly what he'd tried to avoid.

The electronic image of the ghost finally stopped in what appeared to be a lab. As Mike walked towards the lab, he stepped into a dead zone, losing his signal and his ability to monitor the ghost. He didn't like his current situation, but given few options, he continued forward and opened the lab door.

His mission involved being bait and he embraced it. "Hello? Is anyone here?" He grew tired of waiting for bad things to happen and wanted to help them along. The room looked like a standard lab with sturdy tables, labeled solar sensors, and not much else. He saw no one.

The lab contained one other door. He thought again about leaving, but it would only be another day and another door he must walk through. He proceeded through the back door.

Nothing happened. He expected weapons and threats, but then remembered the year. *They don't use guns. They use* . . . and he saw it, a rough piece of paper laid on a petal of a flower. Lifting the paper, he read his name on one side, and, *Thank you for showing us the way* on the other, along with a mark in the right corner, possibly a name or a word too small to read. Mike thought there had to be more. He searched the lab and found nothing, not even a DNA signature. Defeated, he left.

He walked, turning the note over in his hand. He'd wanted to end this feeling of vulnerability, to take the initiative, but he ended up right back where he started, looking over his shoulder.

He contacted Gina and sent a cryptic message, suggesting they meet at the stones in the ravine. He had been heading in that direction without realizing it. Gina was already there, pacing when he arrived. He immediately handed her the note, and attempted to explain how he got it, but she cut in.

"What happened? Did you find anything? Did they hurt you?" She examined Mike, checking for signs of damage. Mike grabbed her hands to calm her before he explained how he found the note.

"We knew something was wrong when you ran." Gina pulled her hands free. "We had three people trailing you. One wound up following a false reading while the other two lost you through a few dead zones. We only learned that the PLM is always three steps ahead of us."

"Welcome to my life," Mike said. "I can take you back to the lab, but it was all a set-up."

"Could you get a DNA read?"

"No, nothing. There wasn't even another exit, meaning the note had been left there long before I arrived."

"What do you think it means?" Gina looked at both sides of the note.

"I don't know," Mike said. "I think they're taunting me—knowing I can't find them, but they can find me—but I don't know why. I think the mark on the corner might be significant."

"I'll have some people take a look at this," Gina held up the note. "It's like they're trying to tell us something." They looked at each other, not sure what to do next and walked back towards their two units. "I've got to go, but be careful," Gina said. "I know you want this to be over, but not at any cost." Her smile was gone.

In less than twenty minutes, before Mike could get back to his unit, he received a frantic message from Gina telling him not to touch anything and meet her outside City Office. When he arrived, Gina stood with seven other people. Mike recognized two, but not by name. He had seen one man several times throughout the city, but never paid any attention to him. The woman often volunteered at Juiced, the bar closest to his unit.

"You were right," Gina said, "that mark on the corner of the note was a word—norovirus."

"What?" Mike said. He'd heard Gina but needed to give his brain a three-second window to absorb the information.

"The note was contaminated with norovirus. It's a virus that causes nausea and—"

"Like on cruise ships?"

"On what?"

"Can't someone in your group treat it?"

"Nobody has any experience with it. We did some research and in the last seventy years no one has seen or been treated for a case of norovirus. I'm surprised you've heard of it and what's a crew strip?"

"I must have heard something about it on my BP," Mike said. He tried not to make his face unnaturally calm, as Gina had mentioned, but he saw a small crinkle at the bridge of her nose. She detected his lie. "I don't get it. There are easier ways to infect you or me. They've already shown that. Why go through all this work?"

"Everyone who touched the note is here," Gina said. "We need to report it to City Office. On the bright side, now we know what the message meant." She gave a weak smile.

Mike was confused, but after a pause, he understood the purpose of the note too. "I revealed seven members of your group. That must have been what the PLM intended, knowing I'd involve you, you'd show it to your people, and we'd all end up standing here where anyone can identify us. I'm sorry."

"It wasn't your fault. Someone went to a lot of work. Let's get this over with."

. . . . .

Four days later Dave visited Mike to release him from quarantine. Dave looked efficient, but he showed the first signs of exhaustion. Mike had never developed any symptoms, but Gina experienced severe stomach pain for a day.

"Hey, Mike," Dave said, "I don't care what happened. I'm here to tell you that if you're involved in one more contamination, you will be the first person the city has ever banished to the Outside." He didn't look at Mike, but at his BP. "Most people have you set up on a fifty-foot proximity alarm. The city's energy expectations have gone up to thirty points a month with the city-wide use of Steri-Lights. Do us all a favor and make yourself scarce."

Mike had been ready to protest his treatment, which had been more grueling than before, but Dave's redress erased his desire. Mike simply wanted to leave.

"What did you have in mind, Dave?"

"Hey, you're still welcome in Eau Claire, if not by the people, then by the city's expectations." Dave finally looked up from his BP. "Your unit-mates have agreed you can stay with them. I suggest you stay in your unit for a while. Keep out of sight and proximity range. Your ban to the Outside has also been lifted if you want to stretch your legs."

"Thanks," Mike said, not meaning it. He didn't see a single person on the way to his unit. He opened the door, expecting it to be empty, and was surprised to see Stanley making dinner. Kevin painted Mike's room to look like a library, and Paul arranged for an energy bike challenge after dinner.

Gina visited the next day to cheer Mike up.

"I just want to be left alone."

"Why?" Gina said, "I'm the one who got sick."

Mike felt dirty and responsible and, for the first time in his life, like a criminal. He had always felt a certain righteousness in his actions, but now he felt worthless. He was a victim, a reminder of everyone's vulnerabilities. Guilt was a new emotion for Mike. He had deserved it at other times, but he wallowed in it now. This novel sentiment didn't bring about a new sense of responsibility, just a robust feeling of helplessness.

He was the city's burden, their infection, and he bathed in his own self pity. In the past, Mike had moved money around, but no one feared him. A few people who he had taken advantage of didn't press charges, but laughed about the incident, bought him a beer, and called him gutsy. Now he was a prisoner, the thief who had stolen Eau Claire's innocence.

"OK, you big baby," Gina said on her second visit. "I've got the perfect solution to get a rise out of you." She smiled and reached into her shirt.

"I'm not in the mood," Mike said. She froze and turned toward him.

"You would be in the mood if I was offering, but I'm not." She pointed a brown grease pencil at him. "I've found a way to deal with the PLM and you're the solution. Do you want to help me or would you prefer to sit here and feel sorry for yourself?" Before Mike answered, she jumped on the bed, landing next to him. She took off both their BPs and wrote on her arm for Mike to read while she talked about food and the city's water retrieval system.

She wrote in blocky letters like a five-year-old unfamiliar with writing. She scribbled a few words, then rubbed them into her skin once Mike had read them, then she started the process over again. Mike pieced together sentences until he understood their full meaning and was shocked into silence.

TWENTY-NINE

The next four days Mike and Gina continued to make plans, meeting in Mike's room. Gina's visits became a highlight for Mike, who hadn't left his unit since he returned from the norovirus contamination. With Gina's plan, Mike's mood improved, but he still felt like a prisoner.

Stanley had offered to take Mike to the library, a gesture Mike appreciated, but still declined. Kevin suggested a midnight trip to the potter's wheels.

"Come on. We can lose ourselves in the spinning clay." Mike lay on his bed and shook his head.

"Mike and I are going to the busiest bar in Eau Claire and watch the frightened and uninformed run," Paul announced. He turned to Mike. "Leaving the most adventurous women for us." Mike smiled at the offers of kindness, but he didn't want to cause more difficulties for the people who had stood by him as few had ever done.

Mike did agree to one offer and left early the next morning to meet Gina near his unit for a day Outside. Mike carried food and Gina brought entertainment in the form of a book borrowed from the library.

"Do you know what I went through to get this book?" Gina said. "I threatened to run out the door with it. I finally

218

told them I had a dying mentor who wanted to hear one story read out loud from a book with actual pages."

They walked west, crossing over the ridge much further from Eau Claire as the ridge gradually curved southward. They selected a flat spot near trees, under a sky so blue Mike didn't have a name for the color. He laid out a blanket and lunch, but they sat on nearby boulders to discuss their plan first. They drew in the dirt, using stones and forest debris to map out a plan that varied from their words.

"Do you really think Dr. Donavan will be able to convince enough people of the hazards of extending life?" Mike asked for the fiftieth time for the benefit of anyone who could possibly be listening in on their conversation. "Do you think what he says in Eau Claire can make a difference elsewhere?"

"It's about time we spoke up and who better than the man who developed the disastrous method? Besides, Eau Claire has become the lightning rod for the longevity movement." Gina absent-mindedly placed her hand on her stomach. "We've been filled to capacity for weeks despite the norovirus and earlier disease scare."

"How do you know he'll be safe?" Mike asked.

"Mike." Gina continued the charade and pretended to be frustrated. "Only a handful of people know Dr. Donavan is coming to Eau Claire. He'll be here for a few hours and vulnerable briefly when he's in the lab prior to his speech. And his speech won't be made public until an hour before he gives it."

They wiped their drawings clean and moved to the blanket where Mike took a nap, sleeping deeply for the first time in a week. Gina fell asleep beside him while stroking his arm.

It was a gorgeous day-long vacation topped off with Gina reading out loud from a book of short stories. She read beautifully, adding drama with long pauses and perfect in-flection. He had his head in her lap, his ear against her dia-phragm and felt the words as much as heard them. In the shade of a majestic maple tree, out of the wind, with Gina's voice blending with the chatter in the woods, Mike was con-tent, maybe for the first time in his life.

Hours later they took their time walking back to Eau Claire, Gina close to Mike and shielded from the wind. "I had a great time," Mike said. "Thanks for making me leave my unit. I was a little self-absorbed."

"A little? You were one big Mike sponge." Gina squeezed his arm. "It was nice. When this is over, we should come out here more often, just the two of us." Mike smiled until he remembered what had to happen first and remained quiet.

Mike turned and, with his hands on either side of Gina's face, kissed her. He didn't know if it was a goodbye kiss or a reuniting kiss—so much depended on Dr. Donavan's fake visit in seven days.

Mike kept his distance from Gina once they cleared the ridge, holding her hand occasionally. He wanted to wean himself from her, before they had to separate. They wouldn't see each other until after they announced Dr. Do-navan's speech and it was all over. They had discussed it for hours, writing on each other's skin, and finally decided the best way to ensure the security of everyone involved was complete silence and no contact between them.

In the picnic area Mike pleaded with Gina to go into the city without him. "It's easier if I'm alone. I can ignore peo-ple's reactions better."

"Then ignore me too." She walked pressed against him. When people cleared the sidewalk ahead of Mike, Gina commented, "Isn't that sweet? People are making room for us." Mike appreciated her show of support, but Gina's closeness reignited his bond to her, making their final goodbye at his door more agonizing.

Gina and her group made preparations leading up to the announcement of Dr. Donavan's speech, but Mike played no role in them. Mike's job was a familiar one, that of bait and disruptor. He was perfect for the role, still causing a commotion whenever he left his unit. He needed to attract the PLM's attention and keep them busy as long as possible. Meanwhile, members of Gina's group would track and identify any suspicious people Mike attracted.

Mike decided to start with a splash and took Paul up on his offer to visit the busiest bars and see who remained when they entered. Stanley and Kevin loved the idea and came along, inviting a few of their own friends. Their first stop was Twisted, a bar with a younger clientele, and Paul's favorite. Walking to the bar, a few people left the path entirely to avoid Mike, but many simply diverted their course casually. When Mike first noticed this less anxious reaction to him, he looked at Stanley.

"People's attention spans are pretty short," Stanley said. "Like I told you, nobody cares anymore."

Paul heard their conversation and glided in between them, putting his arms around both their shoulders. "We should have done this last week. It would've been so much better. Did you see those three guys trip over themselves struggling to get out of your way?"

Stanley looked at Mike, but Mike smiled. He decided maybe it was time to see the humor in his situation.

They reached the bar and found it quieter than they expected considering the unusual number of visitors currently in Eau Claire. Many people had left prior to their arrival and a few more departed as they walked in. Mike had to admit,

Paul was right. Women made up the majority of remaining patrons. Mike's group took over a large table, swelling with mutual friends. It didn't take long before three women approached Mike.

"What's it like on the Outside?" one asked.

"You must be exhausted from all your close calls with death," said another.

None of the women kept their distance as one ran her hands through Mike's hair and another gently stroked his arm, Mike guessed, as an attempt to see his fertility status. Paul had to assist, escorting the three women away.

"Let me tell you about the challenges of living with someone from the Outside. You have to keep alert. It's a constant battle for survival. I know a guy . . ."

Mike enjoyed the attention, but he wanted an opportunity to scan the room even though he knew it was someone else's task.

They visited several other bars with similar results, meeting up with Sara at the last. "Did you hear Dr. Donavan is coming to Eau Claire?" Sara asked Stanley. Mike nearly spit out his beer at the question and listened.

"I'm not really surprised," Stanley said. "I've never seen Eau Claire so crowded. Dave said they've kept an extra regional train here for overflow." Stanley saw Mike listening. "And let's not forget Mike, who seems to be a growing fascination."

"I thought Eau Claire would be nearly empty by now with the two outbreaks," Mike said. "I thought I'd be the most hated person in Eau Claire."

"People love excitement." Stanley put his hand on Mike's shoulder. "See? I told you this would turn around."

"What other rumors have you heard, Sara?" Mike wanted to know more about what had happened in Eau

Claire while he was under his self-imposed unit arrest. He and Gina had planned on Dr. Donavan's visit not staying secret, not in a city of 125,000 BPs, but he still wondered how the story had grown and mutated.

"I heard people are camped out in the Garden and Park Districts," she said. "I also heard Eau Claire might host a national cooking competition."

"I heard it was a plant expo," Stanley said.

Kevin dropped off drinks and joined the conversation. "I heard some women talking a few tables over. They were comparing their conquests of other Outsiders." Kevin put his hand on Mike's shoulder. "You might want to consider that."

Mike wasn't sure if Kevin meant this could be Mike's lucky night or that Mike had better start thinking about crowd control.

Mike decided not to push his luck, having caused enough disruption for one day, and returned to his unit. Stanley and Kevin came with him while Paul remained to console any women disappointed by Mike's early departure. As Mike left he saw a man and woman nod to him from across the bar. He thought they must be part of Gina's group there to scan the room, but when he looked again, they were gone.

Eau Claire swelled with people, overflowing every venue. Mike became the focus of attention, even while getting a vegi-shake.

"Wait until I tell my friends," said a woman next to Mike who made sure to bump into him at least once. "I had my morning shake with the Outsider. They'll be jealous."

It became impossible for Mike to scan for the PLM or continue his work to track down ghosts. He wondered if this was another of the PLM's plans, instead of ostracizing him with disease, were they now overwhelming him with attention, to make it difficult to stick to his plan?

Mike visited bars each night of the week. Paul didn't miss a night and rallied the largest group on the last night before Dr. Donavan's *secret* speech the following day. All of Eau Claire seemed to know the importance of the night as the crowds and intensity swelled beyond a sustainable level.

"Who's going to join me in the Clean Screen?" said a younger man before he took off his shirt and headed for the door, followed by a sizable group of half-dressed men and women.

Mike became calmer as Eau Claire spiraled into excessiveness. It was orderly by Mike's standards, ranking far below a riotous basketball championship celebration and somewhere along the lines of a Black Friday shopping spree. He relaxed and listened to conversations around him. Though the number of theories about Eau Claire multiplied, most people agreed whatever was going to happen, would take place tomorrow.

"I was slow getting out here and barely made the last train in," said a young man. "They moved our train onto the interior tracks, and it's become party central."

"My friend and I have spent the last year travelling hot spots throughout the country," said a young woman, sitting with her equally young friend. "We came from the DC Region. The cherry blooms were intense, but not nearly as life-altering as this."

"How long have you two been here?" asked the young man.

"About a month, but we're leaving in a few days. These things build slow but die fast. We were in the Medford Region a few months back, when an ancient redwood fell."

"You were there? I heard you could feel the earth shake a mile away."

"It took two weeks for the tree to finally collapse. It was tragic, but the best party ever. Once it fell, the place emptied the next day."

Mike didn't mind the thrill seekers, but when he thought of the dangers of an infectious disease, he had a difficult time feeling the same excitement as the people around him.

He wanted to get drunk on his last night as bait, but it would take huge amounts of beer to reach the kind of drunk he wanted to be, if his BP didn't interfere first, and he needed to be clear-headed tomorrow. He drank tea instead. Though he was the center of attention in the early evening, by midnight his presence went mostly unnoticed. The celebration had a life of its own and Mike's sober demeanor was in sharp contrast.

. . . . .

At 8:00 the next morning, Mike left his room and walked to the library for no particular reason other than it was near where he received his first note from the PLM.

"Hi Nova," he said to a volunteer. "I'm just looking." Mike liked how greetings were more genuine in the library without electronic interference. He absent-mindedly paged through a few books before leaving. Mike's job was to act natural as if he expected nothing to happen.

As he walked to the studio, several people bumped into him and many barely avoided a collision. He wore a fake BP that he'd created. It did nothing but register energy points to a blind account and shield him from scans, making him electronically invisible. He was only detectable by visual contact and therefore generally not seen.

He struggled against the crowd and finally reached his empty studio where he worked unenthusiastically, his mind

225

on other tasks. He put his hand in his shirt pocket and felt a surge of adrenalin. Inside was a note.

He read his name on one side, then read the other side. "Shit," he said as he ran for the door, but before he reached it, someone grabbed him. With a second rush of adrenalin, Mike bucked his body and nearly escaped his attacker's grasp. Instead of breaking free, he sent himself and his captor flying through the air.

Mike landed on his head, knocking himself out, and didn't feel the impact of the bigger man falling on him. He woke up some time later sore and gagged. He attempted to talk, making a muffled sound that drew his captors' attention. He sat on the floor in the studio and saw four men he didn't recognize. Two moved in his direction. There were things Mike wanted to tell them, but he doubted they would listen.

THIRTY

Dr. Jennings paced in his office with an untouched thermos of coffee sitting on a silver tray. He was already too anxious for caffeine. The tension in the transmissions had been increasing all week, leaving him as exhausted as he was during his medical residency.

He had heard the commotion and the orders to tie up the prisoner. Looking out his window, he waited to hear voices again and smiled, thinking his day had come, that the future had finally caught up with the prisoner.

"Try talking your way out of this one," he said to the window with a tiny part of him hoping the prisoner would escape so he could relive the capture. He turned to the audio receiver and willed it to make a sound. To his surprise, the speakers erupted with noise.

· · · · ·

Mason sat at home and listened at his desk while shuffling through piles of papers which occupied every horizontal surface including the floor. Printouts, calculations, and diagrams, Mason hoped to understand them all. He was a problem solver and needed to untangle the events of the past week. He laid a sheet of paper on his desk and worked on another of his many hypotheses.

With the speaker quiet except for background noise, Mason picked up a plate of dried cheese and several cups of liquid he didn't recognize and brought them to the kitchen to gain more desk space. The kitchen, like the rest of the house during the past week, was a wreck, papers among the dishes. He set the plate on a pile in the sink as voices erupted over the speaker and he ran back to the other room to listen.

He heard what sounded like a dog growling.

"Look who's awake," said one of the captors. The growling continued. "Mr. Newhouse, we have a few simple questions for you and we want simple answers. If you try to tell us anything other than what we ask, you'll be gagged again and punished." The captor paused. "Is that clear?" A short grunt followed. "What is your mission?"

"I have a note," Mike said in a raspy voice. "Read the note. Read the—" The growl escalated.

"Mr. Newhouse, I asked a simple question," said the captor, "but you didn't give a simple answer. In fact, you gave me no answer at all." The growling grew louder as the captor spoke. "Mr. Newhouse, you have one choice, one thing you can control, and that is how much pain you receive today." A pause preceded a deep thud and a grunt. "I will ask you again. What is your mission? Think before you answer."

"My mission is not to answer any of your questions."

"Mr. Newhouse, your mission is not completely unknown and certainly not important enough to die for. I will ask you again, what is your mission?"

"Kill me already," Mike yelled.

"If he doesn't start talking in the next fifteen seconds, shoot him in the arm."

Mason and Dr. Jennings froze and listened to silence until an explosion ripped through the stillness followed by dead air. Dr. Jennings stopped pacing, stood perfectly still, and stared at the speaker on his side table. He smiled, but when the silence continued, his smile faded. He walked to the receiver, confirmed the signal was dead, picked up the speaker, and threw it against the far wall.

He looked out his window at prisoners loitering in the yard below and slowly realized the signal was lost forever. He didn't think he'd miss the transmissions from prisoner fifty-eight, but he would miss the unique perspective and status it gave him. Without the Tapes, he was a prison warden in a small town in the middle of nowhere—no longer the keeper of time.

He sat at his desk for several minutes and studied the broken speaker along with the three folders of information he had on the prisoner. He tidied up his office, returned the folders to his private storage, and replaced his cup on the tray. When he left his office, it was immaculate except for the broken speaker, left where it came to rest on the floor, a dent in the wall.

. . . . .

Mason tried with shaky hands to reestablish the signal and finally froze with his hand still on the tuner. He verified he still had all of his recordings and transcripts of future Eau Claire. He hadn't anticipated anything happening to them, but after losing the audio feed so unexpectedly, he wasn't taking chances.

He gathered the data he had accumulated over the last week and hugged the piles to his chest, unable to set them down. He stood in the same spot, continuing the tapes in his head, making up conversations. He eventually walked through the house, the papers still firmly held to his chest. The house looked different, lonelier, too quiet.

While staring at his model of Eau Claire, Mason wondered if his current Eau Claire would feel the same without a connection to future Eau Claire and his own personal tour guide. Mike was his sole connection to Eau Claire and the reason Mason remained in the shadow of the prison that once held his entire life.

He felt as if his best friend had moved away in the middle of the night, leaving him to play catch alone. He kicked the leg of the ping-pong table. He wondered if Mike survived, what Gina would do next, if Stanley would get a new roommate, how Sara would react. All these things ran in his head in a jumbled mess, but one thought pulled him out of his ruminations—he had glimpsed the future and gathered enough data to study for the rest of his life.

THIRTY-ONE

Five people stood still in Mike's studio without making a sound after the cacophony of noise a moment earlier. They waited a tense thirty seconds for a man holding a flat metal box.

"We're clear," he said. "The audio signal has been terminated." Everyone moved at once. Gina ran into the room, threw herself on Mike, still on the floor. Three people cleaned up while others ran to and from the studio to take on other duties.

"Get the note out of my pocket," Mike said in a tired voice, unable to move his arm. Gina gave him a kiss.

"How's your arm?" Gina asked before pulling out the note and untying the simple knot around his hands.

"The note first," Mike said.

Gina read it: *It starts with Gina. Welcome to my future.* She looked at Mike and scrambled away from him.

"You let me kiss you," she moaned as she shook the note in Mike's direction, "after you read the note and knew I'm most likely infected."

"I've always had a weakness for tall muscular women," Mike said and gave a weak smile. "Call back anyone who's left and test the room."

231

"Bring in a Bio Scan. Sweep the room for any pathogens and start with me." Gina didn't move, yelling her order across the room. A man and woman walked over to Gina, but before they got too close she yelled, "Don't come any closer. I'm probably infected with something deadly. Let me know when the equipment gets here and keep me isolated." They backed away and set up barriers around her and Mike. "Now how's your arm?" Gina asked, standing fifteen feet away from Mike. They had used a high frequency pulse to destroy the transmitter in his arm.

"It makes the electric shock you gave me feel like a handshake. Why didn't you tell me that blast would also light up every nerve ending? Look, I still can't move it." Mike moved his shoulder and his right arm laid limp in its wake.

"Did you really want to know how it would feel?"

"Probably not, but why is everything so painful with you?" Gina shrugged. "Love hurts."

Mike slowly stood, balanced himself, and walked towards Gina.

"Don't," she said, closing her eyes in a plea for him to stay away and to hold her at the same time. Mike never broke stride in his unsteady state and nearly knocked Gina over as he took her into his one good arm.

"You already kissed me," Mike said. "What more can you do?"

"Plenty, now that we're not performing for whoever has been listening to us." Gina kissed him, then apologized for the kiss, wiping it away.

Using his left arm, Mike grabbed Gina tightly and kissed her, making as much body contact as possible. In the room, people moved around purposefully, attending to a multitude of tasks. Mike had no other job than to appear dead after first pretending to be tortured to death.

"Did it work?" Mike asked, wanting to change the subject. "Did the PLM believe Dr. Donavan was really coming? What happened over the last week? Did you catch anyone? What are people going to do when they find out Dr. Donavan isn't really coming to Eau Claire?"

"It's nice to see you, too," Gina said looking at Mike as if she hadn't seen him in months. "It kind of worked. We identified four people we thought were PLM. We captured one and questioned him, but we're convinced he doesn't know anything. He's a repairman who was asked to install a holographic mechanism in the lab we've been monitoring, the one we said Dr. Donavan was going to be in. The repairman's not even sure who ordered the installation."

"What about the other three?" Mike asked.

"We haven't learned much except it appears the PLM use local people to carry out legitimate services to fulfill their plan."

Mike stroked Gina's short hair. "Any other leads? We may need them."

"We came across some interesting traffic patterns and a few relationships to follow up on, but with the extra people visiting Eau Claire, it isn't going to be easy." Gina moved her head against Mike's hand. "The scary thing is, they knew what we were going to do before we did."

"What do you mean?" Mike stepped back while taking her hand.

"After we questioned the guy who installed the hologram generator, we searched the lab again and found evidence the PLM had already been there. We didn't notice it the first time because we weren't looking for it, but someone had already scanned the room and installed two sensors. As far as we can tell, it was done two weeks earlier, days before any of us even had the idea to use the lab."

"We planned carefully," Mike said. "We never said anything out loud except what we wanted them to hear."

"I know," Gina said. "It was my idea."

"We eliminated any BP contamination in the signal. Whoever had been listening to the transmitter in my arm, had to think it was real."

"They did. They did exactly what we thought they'd do by going to the lab. But they did it two weeks too soon."

"At least we stopped the signal." Mike looked at his right arm.

"When I first accessed your scans and saw the FB—"

"The what?"

"Foreign Body, the transmitter." Gina touched Mike's right arm. "I didn't think anything of it. Implantable solutions were common not long ago."

"What changed your mind?"

"Once we detected an audio signal and found it coming from the same implant, I knew you had to be part of the PLM." Gina traced around the disabled audio transmitter in Mike's arm with her finger. "It wasn't until after we questioned you," Gina said, letting go of Mike, "that we thought you might not know about the transmitter."

"You could've asked."

Gina ignored him. "The type of transmitter strengthened our PLM theory. It's meant more for stealth than performance because of its short range. But by the look you gave me in your bedroom when I wrote that you have an audio transmitter in your arm, I knew without a doubt it was placed without your knowledge."

"I was reacting to that scribble you call writing." Mike wrote in the air with big block letters. "I could barely read it." Mike took Gina's hand. "It's nice to be able to finally talk

234

again. It was hard saying one thing and writing another, like rubbing your stomach and patting your head."

"I was sure we could trace the signal from the audio transmitter right to the PLM, but it wasn't even protected. Anyone within a couple hundred feet could pick it up, which only told us whoever had been receiving the signal was in Eau Claire."

"I'm just glad it no longer works."

"I thought we could at least use the knowledge of the transmitter to our advantage, set up this false plan. It *should* have worked. We should have found the PLM."

"Do you mind if we sit?" Mike was exhausted from a day that still wasn't half over. He squirmed in an attempt to find a comfortable position before he gave up and lay on the floor. Gina joined him with her head next to his and their bodies pointing in different directions.

"I heard you panicked," Gina said.

"I saw the note right before your guys came in." Mike turned to Gina. "I needed to warn you. I almost blew it. Luckily the guy interrogating me—what's his name?"

"Randy."

"Luckily Randy kept the plan on track. How do you feel?" Mike asked. "Have you noticed any symptoms?"

"I've been tired lately," Gina said, "but so has everyone with our busy schedule." She closed her eyes for a moment and they both remained quiet.

The equipment arrived and people in hazmat suits separated Gina and Mike. They scanned Gina for twenty minutes, using every setting.

"Clear," said the lead scan operator.

Before he could take off his hazmat suit, Gina grabbed his arm. "Keep looking. Whatever I'm infected with will be designed to fool your scanner and be immune to bio filters."

Ten minutes later they all heard the high-pitched squeal of the scanner and everyone in the room stopped and looked at the machine as if it swore.

"I'll kill them," Mike said loudly to himself as he stomped towards the exit. Three people tackled him.

"Where were you going to go?" Gina asked a few minutes later. "Who were you going to kill?" Mike didn't answer because he didn't have a good reply. The PLM members still remained a mystery.

Once they knew how to scan for the contaminate, Gina lit up like the Furnace on Fair Day. Everyone in the studio including the people in the hazmat suits was contaminated.

"Ms. Elliot has been infected for seven or eight days and is probably the origin of the virus," said the lead infectious disease specialist on-site. "Based on my projections, I'd say at least ninety-five percent, if not the entire city, has already been infected." Mike displayed the lowest level of infection, due in part to his isolation from Gina over the past week.

City Office analyzed the information along with eight independent sources throughout the country and confirmed the city-wide epidemic within the hour. They put away the hazmat suits since there was nothing left to contain. Holding hands, Mike and Gina waited with the rest of the city and the entire country to hear the predicted fatality rate.

"The virus, tentatively named Eau Claire Zero, appears to be an altered bacteriophage, or bacteria-attacking virus, used widely for treating the common cold and allergies," said Gina's voice as they listened to her BP. "Designed to be highly infectious with a latent period, time from infection to infectiousness of four hours, Eau Claire Zero is slow-developing, taking up to fifteen days for symptoms and at least twenty-eight days before irreversible damage, followed by death. Currently no known cure exists, but resources have been diverted to this epidemic."

Her voice continued talking about Eau Claire's travel ban along with greater details on the epidemiology of the virus, but Mike had heard what he needed. The virus kills. He took Gina's hand and turned down the audio to get her attention.

"The PLM wants to extend life," Mike said. "They probably already have a cure for whatever's in you . . . us. It's the only answer that makes sense."

"The one I'm worried about is you," Gina said. "You're likely to get blamed for this, if not by the city directly, then by the citizens, and their response won't be pleasant."

Mike hadn't thought of that. There might be a cure for the disease, but no cure for an angry mob beating him to death. "Maybe I should dress as a woman," Mike said.

"Are you trying to tell me something?"

"As a disguise."

"You already have the best disguise. You're dead, or you soon will be, if Eau Claire citizens don't kill you first. After a few more days without BP activity, the city will declare you inactive and schedule your death to be acknowledged at the next Fair." Gina reached to kiss Mike but stopped herself.

"Stop that," he said, kissing her before she pulled away. "You'll make me think I've lost my Outside magnetism."

THIRTY-TWO

Several hours after the infectious disease specialist ran every test available, Mike and Gina snuck out of the studio. With no BP activity, Mike technically didn't exist and could have left sooner, but he waited for Gina. He wanted to visit his unit first.

"You're in no condition to walk that far with me," Mike said, already treating Gina differently due to her infection, but his argument proved inaccurate when he needed Gina's help. He hadn't fully recovered from the pulse that disabled the transmitter in his arm and he felt its effects with every step.

The walkways were slightly less crowded than normal, but quiet and calm for a city that recently received a death sentence. Couples walked closer, friends talked louder, and every person who came near the flowering lilac trees slowed to smell the scent in the air.

Mike and Gina walked slower and closer for other reasons, utility being the main one, but they stopped at the lilac trees and Mike noticed the subtle red highlights in Gina's hair as the sun bounced off her head. He wanted to tell Gina how comfortable he felt with her and what she meant to him, but there had already been too much drama. He settled on a simple compliment.

"You look beautiful." He tucked her hair behind her ear and they continued walking.

Traffic thickened as they neared Mike's unit. A mass of people filled the square outside his building. Hundreds chanted, sung, and sat in protest. The crowd began to react to Gina's presence as she came within range. Mike responded instantly, regaining some use of his right hand as he took off Gina's BP and slid it into a passing woman's pocket. Gina gave Mike a puzzled look as he said, "Ms. Elliot is here. Can you see her?"

"No," Gina said, understanding the situation. "Let's get closer to the building in case she comes out."

Lost in the crowd, they heard people scream, "Grab her" and "leave her alone" to the confused woman with Gina's BP in her pocket. The crowd pushed while Mike and Gina escaped around the next building.

"Sorry, I wasn't thinking," Gina said. "I can't believe I wore my BP. Will that woman be all right?"

"She'll be fine," Mike said. "She's still wearing her own BP. It won't take them long to figure it out."

Gina and Mike continued in the opposite direction until each of Gina's steps made the familiar sound of breaking glass. Luckily, they had already reached a large park on the other side of the gardens.

"Beta Carrotene isn't far from here," Gina said. "We can hide in the kitchen."

"I thought without our BPs we're basically invisible."

"We are except for the energy relay alarm on the walkway, and that big crowd around your unit has me scared."

They walked through the kitchen door of the quiet health store as Sara chopped vegetables and dropped them into a

239

big pot of soup. Too engrossed in her activities to notice them, she turned, knife first, when Mike said her name.

"What are you two doing here?"

Sara's anger surprised Mike. "My unit was mobbed. We had to get out of the crowds." Mike grabbed Gina's hand. "Don't worry. We'll leave."

"I'm sorry, Sara," Gina said. "We probably contaminated your whole store."

Sara put her knife back in its protective sleeve. "I mean, why aren't you in a safer place and what were you thinking returning to your unit? You could have . . ." Sara stopped and held out her arms to give them both a big hug, but Mike and Gina hesitated.

"We're contagious," Mike said.

"So am I," Sara said as she closed the distance between them, "so is everyone in the city." They hugged without saying another word, letting their emotions catch up.

"Stanley can't get out of his unit," Sara finally said. "He's been trapped inside since the announcement. I wanted to start a rumor that you were in the Garden District so he could get out, but then I thought maybe you *were* in the Garden District. It's safer than your unit."

"We need some time to think and then maybe we'll go to the Garden District," Mike said.

"Oh no, you don't. You aren't going anywhere. You aren't wearing BPs, are you?"

Mike held out his arm. "Mine's a fake."

"We left mine in some poor woman's pocket outside of Mike's unit," Gina said. "I wasn't thinking. I should've taken it off long ago."

"We've all been given a lot to think about." Sara turned and resumed chopping vegetables. "Besides, when I'm nervous I cook and I need someone to feed. Until you have a better place to go, you're both staying here."

"Can we help with anything?" Mike asked.

"No, I've already made too much. Keep me company. It's been hard without Stanley."

"I'm sorry, Sara," Mike said. "This is my fault."

"If I hear you say you're sorry one more time—" Sara pointed her knife at Mike. "This has nothing to do with you. The damned PLM wants it to be about you so it's not about them."

Mike wasn't about to give up. "But Gina has already been infected for eight days. The closer anyone gets to me the more infected they become."

Gina took Mike's hand. "It's not how close they get to you. It's how close they *got* to me."

"This isn't a contest, and there isn't any award for being the most infected." Sara stirred her soup. "Eau Claire was a PLM hot spot before you got here, Mike. It's fuller than it's ever been, with people thinking this is either the place where life will be extended or extinguished. Both are a good reason to stay away, but they came, and it has nothing to do with you."

"Why did they come?" Mike asked. He never understood the appeal.

"Some think the PLM have it right by extending life and they want to be part of it." Sara looked into her soup. "Others want to experience the possibility of death and the heightened sense of living that comes from it."

"What?"

"Every person is nearly guaranteed a long healthy life of at least 115 years." Sara stood with her spoon in hand. "While most people celebrate that, some bristle at the predictability, looking for more risk, a bit more randomness."

"Yeah, and maybe I'm infected longer by chance," Gina said.

"It wasn't random," Mike said. "We have the note to prove it."

"It also ensured that every person you two knew best became infected first," Sara said. Mike and Gina both looked at her. "Stanley, Paul, and Kevin have been infected for seven days, same as me."

"I'm—" Mike stopped apologizing when Sara pointed her knife at him.

"If you want to do me a favor, eat," Sara said. "I feel better when people are eating." Mike and Gina put Sara in a very good mood, eating nonstop for an hour. Neither of them had had a meal since early morning.

Stanley arrived at the health store two hours later. "I had to climb on the roof and come down the back-exit ladder to get out. I left my BP in the unit." Stanley waved his bare wrist in the air smiling. "I felt naked walking down here." Sara canceled her two volunteer cooks for the night, as the four of them prepared for a slow evening at Beta Carrotene that never came.

Like every evening for the past several weeks, Beta Carrotene overflowed. Mike, Gina, Sara and Stanley worked continuously for five hours. Mike still ached, but cooking created a needed distraction instead of worrying or blaming himself. These were new emotions for Mike who normally snuck out of town in the middle of the night to avoid complications. Now he had nowhere to go, and no place else he wanted to be.

"What really happened?" Stanley asked Mike as they cleaned up. "You and Gina had been running around like a . . . a couple of Outsiders and every time I asked, you just smiled. What do you know about Dr. Donavan?"

"He was never coming," Gina said. "We started the rumor by trying to keep it secret, so everyone knew about it."

"But why?" Sara asked.

"To lure the PLM to a place, Dr. Donavan's staging area, where we could catch or at least identify them," Mike said. "I'm sorry we didn't tell you but I had a listening device embedded in my arm and every word we said went straight to the PLM."

"Did it work?" Sara asked.

"No. It backfired. Instead they used us to spread their virus." Gina put her hand on Mike's shoulder. "Mike's dead by the way." They all looked at Mike. "We faked his death as part of our PLM ploy."

Stanley picked up his glass of wine and they all did the same. "To Mike. The best Outsider I've ever known. May he roam in peace."

An hour later, after making Mike and Gina comfortable at Beta Carrotene, Stanley and Sara left for the night. "Too bad the couch isn't bigger, but it's better than sleeping in the park."

Mike and Gina relaxed on the couch, given their first opportunity to discuss plans. "What do you think we should do tomorrow?" Gina said. "I need to get in contact with some people and . . ."

The conversation lasted less than a minute before Mike began talking in his sleep.

"Guaranteed cure. Ten thousand credits. Meet the future in catastrophic care," Mike whispered to no one.

Sara arrived early the next day with a sack of food to find them both sleeping on the couch with their heads at opposite ends and their feet at each other's shoulders. She unloaded food and moved metal pans until the noise woke them.

Stanley arrived while they ate and brought disguises in the form of new BPs with alternative identities. "These will work for a couple of weeks until they've generated too much data and connect you to your old identities in the database," Stanley handed Mike and Gina each a new BP. "And they're only made possible because the city's desperate. I told them Gina wouldn't cooperate otherwise."

"Good thinking," Gina said.

"Dave also agreed to speed up Mike's death notification from his inactive BP. I've already told Kevin and Paul what's happened."

"Thank Dave for me," Mike said. "But he was getting on my nerves."

"He can do that," Stanley said. "I met with him this morning and made a deal. He agreed to the new identities, but I had to promise to bring you to City Office if, as Dave put it, 'there's anyone still alive when this is over.'"

Mike laughed at the deal, reminding himself of the true life or death nature of the situation, unlike the hundreds of previous imitations he either created to accelerate a deal, or imagined, in his own false sense of importance.

"And Gina needs to report to City Office as soon as a cure is found."

Gina became Bridget Davis and Mike became Philip Sanders, both from the Denver Region. They blended into Eau Claire easily with all its new visitors. When they left Beta Carrotene, Gina checked in with her group and Mike investigated the crowds that had formed at the Fairground. He was reluctant to leave Gina with their lives changing so fast, but he still didn't feel comfortable around Gina's acquaintances, some of whom had electrocuted him.

Several factions for and against Dr. Donavan's work divided the Fairground crowds, each debating and proselytizing. Mike heard his name mentioned several times and had the impression of being at his own funeral.

Mike mingled with the different factions, but he felt most comfortable with the contingent who believed 120 years was long enough to live, but who thought forty-eight or - thirty-six, or whatever age they happened to be, was too short. They had no agenda or personal truths to convey, only a battle with reality to understand. *This sucks* was a phrase he heard most often.

One man in particular fascinated Mike. The man sat in the middle of the crowd, remained perfectly still, and meditated. People bumped into him, but the man didn't move or open his eyes. After watching him awhile longer, Mike sat down beside the man and meditated too. It was the most sensible thing he could think to do amidst the chaos.

With each breath, he took in the energy from the crowd, turning worry, rage, fear, excitement, and anxiety into strength. He didn't know how long he sat or how many people ran into him. As he floated over the mass of people, he noticed a man and woman on the edge of the crowd giving off a different kind of energy, like the smell of garlic at a chocolate tasting. They were spectators like him, separate from the collective emotions of the crowd, with their own brand of disappointment. After talking to a few people around them, they wandered into the health store across the walkway.

Mike stood and bowed to the meditating man before he walked toward the same health store. He contacted Gina through her new Bridget BP.

"I think I found two members of the PLM."

Mike located the couple in the health store when Gina arrived with four other people. Mike explained what had happened and made it sound as if he'd overheard them talking and suggested he lure them out of the building.

"Bring them to Step On It," Gina said. "We have access to that lab."

"Where?" Mike pointed to his BP.

"The door with the pretty rose bricks above it," Gina said with a smile, pointing with her head.

"On one condition." Mike tried to stand taller than Gina. "I get to ask the questions. You guys are too rough for me."

Gina shrugged.

Mike approached the couple. "We need to talk." He looked around.

"Who the hell are—?"

"Not here," Mike interrupted. "Someone might hear us."

The couple looked at each other. "We don't know you," said the woman, glancing at her BP.

"And I don't know you," Mike said. "If you two have this under control, I'll leave, but from what I can tell, something isn't right." He gave them one more look and walked out the door, knowing they would follow. Once in the lab, Gina's companions easily apprehended them in a BP dead zone.

The couple panicked and Mike knew they wouldn't know much, clearly not the master-mind types. The lie detector feature of their BPs confirmed what they said. "We were asked to keep the crowd nervous and even violent," said the woman. "In exchange, our lives would be extended twice as long."

"Who asked you to do this?"

"We don't know," the woman said. "The person wasn't wearing a BP."

"And you believed this ghost?"

"We figured it was worth the risk." The woman counted the six people that surrounded her. "Besides, we came here for some excitement."

"Did this person make a prediction?" Mike asked.

"We were told the exact time," said the man, "within minutes of when the announcement about the infection would be made."

They were both young and from the Chicago Region. Mike asked for a description of the person they talked to, but the couple looked confused, giving Mike a useless general account that didn't even specify if the person was a man or woman.

"I think the risks got a lot higher for you two," Mike said. "I suggest you keep your mouths shut while you're here or you might end up cleaning out the sewage recycling ponds."

As Mike and Gina left, he turned to Gina and smiled. "See? You don't have to hurt someone to get the truth."

Gina twisted his ear while kissing him. "No, but it gets their attention."

THIRTY-THREE

Time passed differently for Mason and Dr. Jennings. Without the audio transmissions to mark time, future Eau Claire faded as the doctors moved toward the future they knew so well. When to go to the office or buy groceries no longer depended on Eau Claire 131 years in the future. They both wondered where the time had gone and, like most people, they couldn't reconstruct a meaningful timeline, but marveled how important events of each day, week, and year faded so rapidly and blended so completely.

Five years later, Mason still lived in Eau Claire. Dr. Jennings had moved to the Minneapolis area. He drove to Eau Claire a few times a year to visit Mason.

"Remember when Sara went berserk about women being unpredictable?" Mason said, stabbing a potato in his frittata. Future Eau Claire was like a lake cabin he had vacationed at years ago. He clung to his souvenirs—his model city collecting dust on its garden roofs and the pencil sketches still pinned to his wall, curled and yellowed.

"I thought she was finally going to stab someone with that knife of hers," Dr. Jennings said, seated at the same table in the same bland restaurant where they had always met. Dr. Jennings had stayed at the prison for one year after the

Tapes ended, creating separation between the protests and his departure in an effort to rebuild his reputation.

He and Mason grew more comfortable with each other once the audio connection to future Eau Claire was severed, no longer emphasizing their differences. Dr. Jennings never brought up Mike, but he talked about Eau Claire, having gained an appreciation for the city over the years.

"I hoped you could show me the parts of Eau Claire that survived," Dr. Jennings said as he sipped his coffee.

After lunch they walked downtown for a mini tour. "I'm convinced nearly every building in this downtown survived in future Eau Claire." Mason rubbed the outside brick wall of the salon on the corner. "This is a shoe repair shop in the future with four living units above it."

After the tour they even visited Mason's home. Dr. Jennings was interested in the model of Eau Claire, and they spent hours comparing the two cities.

"Energy Squared is what today?" Dr. Jennings asked.

"The Grand Avenue Cafe." Mason pointed to the same building on a current map of Eau Claire taped to the wall. "And the Furnace is in the Lakeview Cemetery."

When Dr. Jennings saw the nearly complete Clean Screen in the backyard, he walked through it.

"It's not finished yet." Mason waved his arms, but when he got closer, he looked at Dr. Jennings' shirt and felt the fabric. "Not bad."

Mason still lived in the same house, on the edge of the city. He couldn't pack his notebooks, abandon his city replica, leave the Clean Screen unfinished, throw away his vials of untested life-extending serum, or put away any of his future Eau Claire paraphernalia. Even a move to Eau Claire's downtown was too much change for a man who had worked so hard to preserve a piece of his past which happened to be in the distant future.

At sixty-three, with twice as many notebooks stuffed with questions and ideas, and a make-shift lab filled with hand-me-down equipment, Mason knew he wasn't going anywhere.

The doctors reminisced about their favorite moments in the Tapes, and Dr. Jennings took a much more neutral view seated in Mason's living room.

"Remember the first person we met in the future?" Dr. Jennings said. "What was his name?"

"Stanley," Mason replied, priding himself on answering any question his companion had.

"Remember when Stanley rebelled against wearing a Bio Pulse? I liked Stanley." Dr. Jennings raised his glass of water. He had stopped drinking alcohol. "A toast to Stanley."

Mason raised his glass as well. "To Stanley and Eau Claire."

"I never understood the appeal of the Bio Pulse," Dr. Jennings said. "They sounded practical, but never very fashionable."

Mason smiled at the comment. "Eau Claire citizens didn't care much about fashion, but I think the Bio Pulse was the one stylish possession they owned. Let me show you." Mason retrieved his latest BP. "This is a prototype." He handed it to Dr. Jennings. "I think Stanley's was about the same size, but with greater capabilities."

"It looks fancier than I'd expected." Dr. Jennings put on the BP which wrapped around his wrist like an incredibly decorative piece of tape and became a part of his skin, eliciting a light electrical tingle. He admired the iridescent shine. "Even attractive."

"It's plant-based with a few metals, no synthetics of any kind. The biggest limitation is the lack of comparison data to create a reliable baseline. That and it doesn't have the same computer power." Mason touched a button on the BP. "This one needs to be downloaded to another computer in order to compile data."

"Why not make it bigger?"

"I wanted to capture the feel of the whole apparatus," Mason said. "Make it practical while still functional."

"I've looked at the commercial market." Dr. Jennings played with the BP. "I was surprised to see the first attempts at health bands."

"This is exponentially more functional than anything on today's market."

"I didn't mean to imply an equivalence," Dr. Jennings said, looking down at the BP on his wrist. "It'd be like comparing a toy microscope kids get at Christmas to the electron microscope we used in the lab. This is incredible."

"Keep it as a souvenir. I have plenty."

"Thank you."

"Are you still running?" Mason asked.

"Four days a week. Never felt better." Dr. Jennings tapped his stomach in a universal sign for fitness. At fifty-two, he was in better shape than at any other time of his life. He had started running while still at the prison, utilizing their extensive exercise facilities.

"How's your psychiatric practice going?" Mason asked.

"It's part-time, working with rich families of expelled high school students. You should visit." Dr. Jennings knew Mason would never leave Eau Claire.

· · · · ·

The only other visitors Mason had were his daughter, who visited twice a year, and his son, who came every year or two.

251

When they visited, typically with their spouses and Cindy's three children or Matt's two, Mason dropped everything to see his grandkids and catch up on soccer games and science fairs. They generally stayed at the hotel along the freeway with a pool instead of the motel near downtown that Mason recommended. Staying at his house was impossible due to the accumulation of Eau Claire paraphernalia.

Cindy worried about her father and wanted to clean the entire house whenever she visited. "Dad, I can get a dumpster in here and get rid of some of this big stuff," Cindy blew dust off a metal cylinder which spun around on a pole. "Look. It's collecting dust."

"This is ground-breaking stuff," he said, cleaning off the wind catcher and showing her how it worked.

She knew the passion he had for his work and forgave him long ago because she shared that same passion in science. She connected with him when they talked about her work in battery chemistry.

"Did you try algae?" he asked. "The regenerative properties are incredible. I think it'll be what they use a hundred years from now."

"Daaad," she said, whining like she had when she was a kid, "I already told you, no one is interested. It can't be mass marketed."

If she feared her father becoming a frail recluse, she only needed to see that he was in the best shape in decades, and that more people on the street waved and called to him by name than in the neighborhood where she grew up. He remained secretive about his work, but that was normal. Unlike her mother, she didn't take it personally, understanding the proprietary nature of scientific discovery.

Their phone conversations had changed lately, with her father spending more time trying to convince her to move away from Florida and live in the Midwest as sea levels began to rise.

"You know it's a matter of time before most of Florida is under water."

"Dad, we're not moving. We like it here. They're telling us to prepare for a drought next year."

He had found a company that made clear bags from plant material and kept giving Cindy samples to take home when she visited. "Here, use these. Do you know how much plastic is in our cells, slowly poisoning us?"

"Thanks, Dad," Cindy said, thinking this must be what happens when people get old and believe the garbage people tell them.

Every time a home came on the market near downtown Eau Claire, he sent messages to Cindy, offering to help pay for it.

"Dad, we don't need the money," she said over the phone, "but thank you for thinking of us." Through the years she found herself actually taking a closer look at a few of the homes, and she wasn't surprised when her daughter, Ellen, decided to move to Eau Claire after college, eight years later.

Matt's visits were more strained, filled with awkward quiet moments only relieved when a grandson made a farting noise or claimed he could fly.

"Don't lecture me on the environment," Matt said. "You used to sit in your car with the engine running for hours, thinking about things no one else could see instead of interacting with your own kids."

Mason judged his son equally harshly. He loved him and thought his two grandsons would take over the world, if they survived the plagues, but found his son insensitive to anyone's struggles but his own, with an unhealthy attitude towards money.

"How can you continue to work for an oil company, eking out a few more years of profits before the market implodes?"

Mason couldn't change his son or himself, or eliminate disappointment, but when he held his grandson who asked, "Can I be a scientist when I grow up?" he understood what he could do. He knew the plagues were coming, including the times and places most affected. More importantly, he had the information needed to develop a vaccine to protect his family in his absence. He regretted that he hadn't thought of it sooner, having fixated instead on less-useful curiosities.

He debated whether to give the information to the city, state, or federal government, to prevent the plagues from happening, but he didn't think anyone would believe him, nor did he have a good explanation for how he acquired the knowledge. He knew the disaster was unavoidable. He could postpone it at best, until an even worse pandemic replaced it and put his family in greater danger.

His routine remained the same after his latest visit from his son, but his work took on a new purpose. He began constructing survival kits for each grandchild with enough resources for their potential children, including vaccines, Bio Pulses, and a timeline of events with places to avoid. He included enough of everything for his son and daughter as well, but knew they'd be the hardest to convince given their histories and biases. He put his faith and hope in his grandchildren, that they might convince their parents of the things he couldn't.

He used the most durable air-tight containers to hold his precious work. He'd wait for the world to begin to fall apart and hope the next generation would see more clearly.

· · · · ·

Mason knew he would finally have a sympathetic ear eight years later, in 2033, when his granddaughter, Ellen, moved into a loft apartment in the brick building he owned in downtown Eau Claire. Evacuations had escalated along many coastlines. His daughter had moved from Florida while the housing market was still strong and the weather predictable, finding a job in Chicago six years earlier.

At seventy-one with the plagues nineteen years away, Mason began to slow down, walking four miles a day instead of five. His granddaughter lived a short walk away and loved her grandfather's tours of the city, meandering through areas she never knew existed. She worked as a scientist for a large food company developing drought-resistant crops.

He visited her on Sundays when they walked down to The Farm restaurant for lunch—never breakfast—in case she was out late the night before. They talked about her job, Eau Claire, her mother, and the strange weather. He didn't talk about the plagues, but he hinted about how the planet was overdue for a pandemic. The best conversations occurred while he showed her around Eau Claire, still amazing her with his information about buildings, rock formations, and traffic flow.

"How long do you think you'll live in Eau Claire?" Mason asked.

"I don't know." Ellen examined the soil along the side of the road. "Are you trying to get rid of me?"

"You know I love having you here. It's the best thing that's ever happened to me. You've heard they evacuated another county in Florida, right? I've done some research and Eau Claire is one of the safest places to live right now."

"Grandpa, you don't have to sell me on Eau Claire. I love it here. Besides, I got a promotion. You can't get rid of me."

"Here." He gave her a small box. "It's like the health bands they sell, but this one's better. I made it myself."

"Oh, Grandpa." She gave him a hug.

Twelve years later, in 2045, seven years before the plagues began, he finally gave Ellen the containers for all five grandchildren. At eighty-three he had it written in his will, but he felt better seeing the cases sitting in his granddaughter's basement. Ellen was married now with two children and lived in a house near the brick building.

"Thanks for the survival kits, Grandpa. You're so sweet."

"Remember to open them by 2052."

"You can help me do it."

The world had been changing fast. The United States had banned fossil fuels two years prior as the upper Midwest, and central Canada grew in population. The United States was over six hundred million people, and the world population reached eleven billion. Mason continued to update the containers for the next five years, making improvements to Bio Pulses, discovering new gadgets, and updating the vaccine. His granddaughter let him tinker with the containers whenever he liked, happy to have him visit.

THIRTY-FOUR

Time didn't change for Mike and Gina. The day after the virus's discovery, they were eating lunch at Stone Soup when they heard the news announced on their BPs.

"Reports are coming in that a cure has been found for Eau Claire Zero." Mike grabbed Gina's hand and stood, about to hug her when the next announcement came. "It appears the cure for Eau Claire Zero is Dr. Donavan's age-extending therapy, which has reignited the debate over this already-controversial discovery."

Neither Mike nor Gina moved, waiting for more. "It has been acknowledged that several adjustments need to be made to the formulation and findings are currently theoretical, but the age-extending therapy, now being called Eau Claire 84, has been confirmed as a viable solution." Mike sat back down, knowing this wasn't the cure Gina had wanted.

Secretly Mike was thrilled, more concerned about a cure for Gina and himself than the implications involved in extending life. He looked at Gina to gauge her reaction as the announcement continued. "Though a solution has been found, both Regional and National Councils have determined no remedy will be produced or distributed while the

PLM is still at large, for fear of additional terrorist attacks on other cities."

It made sense to Mike, even if he didn't like it. If the city administered Dr. Donavan's life-extending formula, the PLM would infect every city in the country within the week, drastically changing the delicate balance between sustainability and survival.

They sat in Stone Soup as Philip and Bridget, prodding vegetables around their bowls with spoons.

"I told you they'd find a cure," Mike said, "and in less than twenty-four hours."

"How can you be excited about this?" Gina threw her spoon in her bowl. "Either we all die, or we accept the *cure* and the PLM gets exactly what they want—life extended. And I couldn't stop them."

"*None* of us could." Mike grabbed Gina's arm.

"Yeah, but . . ." Gina pulled her arm free of Mike, picked up her spoon, and stared at her bowl.

Mike wanted to push, to find out what Gina meant, but knew she was already upset. "When they infected you," Mike said, "I wanted to tie each member of the PLM up to solar collectors and watch them fry."

Gina turned to Mike. "You're sweet . . . I think? But look at what they did to you." Gina touched the bruise on his arm from the high frequency pulse, then kissed the same spot.

. . . . .

The next day Mike woke frustrated. Gina slept next to him in a unit they shared as Philip and Bridget with two other couples they didn't know. Death slept with them, hovering in the corner, creeping into the darkness under Gina's eyes.

Mike thought he had come closest to finding the PLM when he worked towards narrowing the list of people who weren't transmitting at key times. During the planning for

Dr. Donavan's fake arrival, he had forgotten about the list, sure their plan would work. Now he reached for the list like a life raft, hoping to save himself and everyone he knew from sinking to the bottom.

"What about the list?" Mike asked as they ate breakfast in their otherwise empty unit.

"What list?" Gina said half listening.

"Remember the information I gave you several weeks ago?" Mike looked for comprehension. "I located people with No Status entries?" Mike looked at Gina's blank face. "No Status entries that took place during the two garbage incidents and the spooky holographic encounter?"

"Oh that. I don't know. Someone was supposed to check on it, but I have to admit, none of us put much hope in the list once we looked into it further. If you took any series of events, you'd find a number of people who weren't transmitting at the time. Maybe they live near a dead zone or enjoyed visiting the library."

"Either you can get me the list and the information I need," Mike said, "or I'll continue asking questions."

Gina looked at Mike to see if he was serious. He looked back intently. "Give me twenty minutes." She learned the list had barely been touched, leaving seventy-six people to check, not including fifty-six remaining ghosts.

"I got you everything you asked for and more," Gina said an hour later, "including the latest BP transactions for the whole city. Now what?"

"I thought I'd see what the BP logs for the past four days tell me and then compare the results with the names on the list."

"Why? What do you hope to find?" Gina shut her eyes.

"I'm not sure. That's the point."

"What about the ghosts?" Gina asked.

"I don't know what to do about them." Mike had already begun manipulating large amounts of holographic data. "I can't see how someone without a BP could get so many steps ahead of us."

Gina left Mike with his data and inquired into the city's efforts to analyze the manifest of new arrivals over the past three months. A few city volunteers in applied mathematics who specialized in pattern recognition had determined the escalation of PLM activity started then.

It wasn't until the afternoon when Mike and Gina finally had a chance to talk again. "They thought they'd get more information from the infectious disease specialists who arrived in the last few months," Gina said, "but they each told them the same thing—Eau Claire was the natural place to go if you were interested in infectious diseases."

"They have a point," Mike watched Gina's hand shake slightly. "If I were a young infectious disease specialist, with the two outbreaks we had and the PLM threatening more, I'd come here too. It might be the only place where there's any actual disease to study."

"I know. It makes sense, but I hoped for some greater rationale."

"What about the other people? You said there were close to thirty thousand visitors here."

"Some didn't even know why they came." Gina covered her shaking hand. "A few think they'll live longer and the youngest are here because they heard the city might close and they wanted to be a part of the excitement."

"What?"

"I don't know anymore." Gina stretched her neck. "I can't think. I need a break."

With the free time of a dead man, Mike continued to analyze data, applying search parameters he designed based on a world he knew best, one of want and acquisition. He reminded himself of a government spy, snooping into things he wouldn't have tolerated a lifetime ago. For that reason he kept his findings to himself. He didn't trust anyone to treat his data with the care he thought it deserved.

He narrowed the list of seventy-six down to five people he thought were most likely involved with the PLM, based on the No Status report and other suspicious behavior. Mike reviewed the data three times and came up with the same results. He picked the first name on the list, Jeff Weber, who had two unit-mates. Even though Mike's information was several days old, no one was usually in Jeff's unit from one in the afternoon until at least five.

At 2:06 Mike arrived at Jeff's building and timed his walk to enter the main door behind a young man. Heading straight for the stairs and up to the third floor, Mike acted as if he belonged. At Jeff's unit door, Mike reprogrammed his BP to send out a series of randomly changing signals until the door opened.

The unit looked similar to any other, smaller for three people with no kitchen, nothing on the walls, and—luckily for Mike—nobody home. He searched the main room which didn't take long. Mike had seen prison cells with more in them.

The first bedroom contained no clothes or other signs that anyone used it. The second bedroom held only slightly more. Going through the drawers of the built-in dresser, he found a few spare BP parts and an occasional seed stuck in the corner.

Mike assumed the third bedroom was Jeff's, though little evidence identified the resident. The room looked the way Mike had expected, lonely. Even Jeff's few items were crammed into two drawers with the third completely empty.

Mike lay on the bed, searching for another angle. "What am I missing?" he said to himself, putting his hands behind his head. He nearly fell asleep, exhausted from his long nights of searching through data. He thought about the empty drawer and saw it was out of place. It didn't fit the pattern.

He pulled the empty drawer out, flipped it over, and looked behind it. Nothing. He was sure he'd find something. Sitting on the floor with the drawer in his hand, he thought about how he had broken into a stranger's unit and searched through it like the righteous. He laughed as he heard the front door open and didn't attempt to move when a man walked into the bedroom.

"Who the hell are you?" asked the man. Mike had turned his BP off before he broke in. He saw the man was more nervous than angry.

"Jeff," Mike said with an exasperated tone. He shook his head and secretly hoped he had the name right. "Where is it?"

"What? I don't know what you're . . . Who are you?" Jeff stammered.

"I'm the Clean Up Man," Mike said, making it up as he went along. "I clean up loose ends. Now where is it?"

"I don't have it," Jeff said. Mike looked at him and maintained his silence. "I hid it on the Outside." Jeff sat on the bed while Mike remained on the floor and leaned against the dresser. "I got nervous when city representatives asked me some questions. I thought sooner or later they might search units looking for a connection."

Mike repressed a smile with the drawer still in his hands, but he didn't want to lose the tension. "Aren't you supposed to be performing some type of assignment about now?" Mike asked. "What are you doing back here?"

"I sometimes . . ."

Mike saw that Jeff wasn't wearing a BP and let the tension build, thinking this kid wouldn't last a day in prison. "You thought you'd come back here and take a nap," Mike said, as he changed to a friendlier tone, having already established his dominance. "Gets boring sometimes, doesn't it?"

"Yeah, it's been days without any transmissions," Jeff said tentatively. "And he hasn't been to his unit."

Mike realized Jeff was talking about him. "I think he's dead," Mike said. "Our efforts to find him might be a waste of time, but I don't think a nap is the way to go. How about you show me where you hid it and we'll forget we ever saw each other." Jeff appeared to be thinking about it. "That wasn't a question," Mike said with more force as he held out his hand for Jeff to help him up.

They walked through the Garden District. Jeff avoided the walkways, taking a series of shortcuts and acrobatic routes along garden ledges. "What do you do, simply leave your BP behind?"

"Sure," Jeff said as he balanced on bricks next to a building. "With a few adjustments it records the same information whether it's on my wrist or perched in a tree branch."

It also wouldn't transmit long without a DNA signature, Mike thought, playing with the possibilities.

Jeff relaxed outside of his unit and became less anxious and less suspicious as well. "You're the first person in the group I've met. It's kind of neat. With all this great stuff happening, I had nobody to talk to about it."

"You never mentioned anything to a friend?" Mike asked.

"They know what's going to happen before it happens." Jeff looked around as if Mike's question was a trick. "I'd probably get chicken pox if I even thought about telling someone."

"Good point. What prediction did they make for you?"

"They told me some dirty Outsider would come to Eau Claire and try to spread disease at least twice, but that the Fortune Tellers would stop him. After the first incident, I joined the next day."

"Can you believe the city's blaming the Fortune Tellers for this disease?" Mike said.

"We know it's really that slimy Outsider's fault." Jeff shook his head. "Why else would we spend all this time trying to find him?"

As they reached the outskirts of the Garden District, Mike followed Jeff around a few buildings to a long, narrow field of prairie grass that filled the space between the buildings and the magnetic track.

"I hate even going to the Outside," Mike said.

"I know, but it's the best place to find greasy Outsiders."

Mike didn't like Jeff's tone or their isolation and needed to change their relationship. "All right, back to business. Where did you hide it? I need to get this cleaned up so we can move on." They crossed the tracks and walked into the trees.

"Here it is." Jeff reached inside a hole in a tree. Mike took a defensive step back as Jeff turned to show him a light brown shirt, Mike's light brown shirt, the one he wore the day he time traveled. "I kept it in this container the whole time to ensure the DNA wouldn't get contaminated." Jeff held the lid open.

"I'll be glad when we finally get rid of this." Mike held out his hands for the container.

"If he isn't dead," Jeff said, fiddling with the container before he gave it to Mike, "I can still put this shirt anywhere you want."

"You'll be the first one we call." Mike reopened the container, wanting to know more. "Everything looks in order, but how do I know you're the best person to contact if we need help?"

"I was able to run a hologram for five minutes without being detected," Jeff said. "And I placed a few notes in tight quarters. I know how to be invisible."

"We'll keep in contact." Mike walked away with the container under his arm, but after a few steps he stopped and turned towards Jeff. "What's the best way to contact you?"

Jeff looked confused. "They've always left me a note under that rock."

Mike saw a group of rocks along the edge of the trees and the suspicion on Jeff's face. "Between you and me," Mike said, as he walked closer to Jeff to create a more intimate atmosphere, "everyone communicates differently, and they're not the greatest on documentation. You know what I mean? It's a real pain in the ass."

Jeff smiled, apparently enjoying the shared secret. Mike took the opportunity to make an exit before his luck ran out. He thought about walking back with Jeff or following him, but he wanted to be on his own to think, and he already knew where Jeff lived.

He paid close attention to his surroundings to make sure he could find the tree and rocks again. Once he reached familiar territory, he let his brain wander over the implications of his shirt and Jeff's hatred towards Outsiders. He initially wanted to keep the information about his list to himself and work alone as he had done for so many years. But the weight of over 125,000 lives changed his perspective.

Gina noticed the container in Mike's hands when he entered their unit and grew curious about its contents. Mike showed her his shirt and explained how he found it, including his unique selection process.

"I built a matrix based on suspicious behavior."

"And this Jeff is the only one you found?" Gina looked amazed and tired.

"I found four others, plus your name kept popping up."

"I . . . If you think I'm part of the PLM, we have a serious problem."

"You're as much a part of the PLM as I am, but you have some unusual BP patterns. I don't know what it means, but I know suspicious behavior when I see it."

"Tell me about Jeff and the list."

He told her he found the shirt behind the drawer and kept the tree, rocks, and messages to himself, not trusting Gina or her friends with the information. Gina made some contacts and within a few hours the twenty-five City Supervisors gave approval to search the four other units Mike had identified.

Searches were unique in a city that had little to hide, but people were frantic for a solution. In one unit, they found Mike's pants, in another a DNA scanner, and in the other two they found nothing. His shoes and socks were still missing. Each suspect told a similar story—they had joined the PLM in the last three months or less, they'd never met anyone in the PLM, and they received notes stashed in different locations which they burned immediately.

Mike attempted to identify Outside-haters, but the group was too diverse. After the city searched his unit two days later along with everyone in Gina's group, Mike's passion to identify people on questionable criteria faded. He hit another dead end.

Gina grew more tired each day. Mike slept next to her and in the morning woke to watch her sleep, often times curled in a ball with a light blanket wrapped around her like a straitjacket. When she woke, saw the time, and Mike perched on a chair watching her, she panicked. "Why didn't you wake me?" she said before her eyes closed again for a short nap.

As the disease progressed and days continued, Mike had one person he needed to see. Ren was on the porch when he walked up behind her and gently touched her arm. She pulled back ready to strike but stopped when she saw Mike's face. She glared at him with a look that made every word in Mike's head disappear.

They stood that way for half a minute until Ren, the smarter one, flung her arms around him and held on tight with her head near his heart. Mike panicked for a second without words to help him, before he let go of control and put everything he had into that one hug. He held his daughter. He held his great-great-great granddaughter. He held the girl in front of him, the only one who mattered at that moment.

After a minute Ren pulled away and kicked him in the shin. "That's for not telling me you weren't dead." The look she gave him was more painful, but she kicked him in the other shin to make her point clear. "Why did you let me believe it?"

Mike stood still, afraid if he moved he might cause another painful reaction. "With this deadly virus, I needed to disappear or I would really be dead."

"I understand why, I'm not stupid, but why didn't you tell me?"

"I wanted to tell you . . . It happened so fast. There was no way I could electronically, and it's been difficult moving through the city. I shouldn't even be here." He took a different approach. "I wanted to see how you were doing. I miss lying to you."

"You've got to be the worst mentor I've ever had." She smiled in spite of herself. "I knew you were looking for the PLM the whole time we were visiting ghosts. I thought if I said anything, you wouldn't take me along anymore. And it was better than working on another stupid art project."

"I just hope I haven't warped you for life." Mike wished he hadn't said those exact words *for life*. "Don't worry. You'll have a long life. I need to see how you grow up." Mike couldn't think of what else to say, treading into areas he knew little about. He looked at Ren, imagining her younger and older at the same time. "I have to go. I'll show you how to hotwire a BP when this is over."

"You'll take me to the Outside again, just the two of us, when you're done making a mess of everything."

· · · · ·

Mike didn't have much contact with Stanley, Sara, Kevin, or Paul, seeing them in unplanned places and then only for a short time. He noted the changes in their bodies—drawn faces, shaking limbs, stooped postures.

"I was hoping I'd see you here," Mike said to Stanley at Beta Carrotene. "I saw Kevin and Paul a couple of days ago."

"They told me." Stanley sat down, too tired to stand. "They say they miss your cooking. Paul is telling anyone who will listen about a guy he knows who is so old he can't remember if he still likes sex."

"I'd stop by if I could."

"I know. I've probably reduced the effectiveness of your Philip's BP by three days, talking to you for this long. If you

268

stay here much longer there'll be enough information in the database to link you back to your old identity."

"I don't care."

"Well, I do. I spent too much time showing you around Eau Claire, the city I grew up in, to see anything bad happen to you in it." Stanley stood to leave and Mike hugged him, the first man he had hugged in his entire life. His first real friend.

Mike, whose timing was usually perfect when giving his straight-faced lies without hesitation, had picked the worst time to develop friendships. He painfully watched his friends decline, the changes most noticeable in the ones he didn't see every day. But it was excruciating watching Gina, who he read like a favorite novel, eagerly turning the pages and still trying to prolong the ending.

THIRTY-FIVE

The disease that ran through Mike's body produced blurred vision and a craving for naps, but his symptoms were less pronounced than his friends who had a six- or seven-day head start. The solution to Mike's illness, his friends' and the 126,583 people in Eau Claire was simple. They had found seven members of the PLM, the two from the Chicago region and the five whose units they searched. Eau Claire citizens needed one to confess. They needed the leader. No threat was necessary beyond the truth—without a leader they all died. The region wouldn't produce the cure with the PLM still at large.

"I am the leader of the Fortune Tellers," Brad, the oldest at eighty-two, said on a message sent throughout the country. "I'm solely responsible for the PLM's activities. I want to set the world free from the limitations of age. We should have no limits."

He knew no crucial information or had any valuable data, but he made for the perfect PLM leader with his long hair, defiant approach, and, as a life-long Eau Claire resident, inside knowledge of the city that had been at the center of

PLM activity. No one in Eau Claire believed Brad was actually the leader of the PLM, but they were all happy to accept his confession.

With PLM leadership "identified," addressing the region's fears of further PLM attacks on other cities, minimal production of the Patch began. Behind the scenes, regional and country supervisors watched closely, along with everyone in Eau Claire.

The Patch was the preferred delivery method of Dr. Donavan's age-extending treatment. Gina received the first trial of the untested remedy and required seven days of monitoring in isolation. Mike saw her only once, not long after she received the treatment.

"How do you feel?" he asked with his hand on her forehead, even though her temperature floated clearly in large numbers over her bed.

"No better, but no worse either. I think it's too early to tell. I only received the Patch an hour ago. Not that I had any choice."

Gina sat in bed while Mike stood beside her, holding her hand. Gravity pulled on her face with little resistance and lines sprouted around her eyes and mouth. Mike could see how she'd look in old age, giving him the impression that he'd jumped another fifty years forward in time.

"I love you," Mike said as he held her hand tighter. He and Gina remained quiet, wondering if there was anything more to say, until medical staff escorted Mike out.

After Gina survived the first day without complications, testing continued with other individuals, consisting mostly of Mike's closest friends, to determine the Patch's widespread effectiveness. The initial results appeared positive until Kevin fell unconscious with a high fever.

Isolation of the test patients became stricter, leaving Mike no one to discuss his ideas with, so he proceeded on his own. He gathered what he needed with the understanding that he had three, maybe four days before the Patch was either distributed to the rest of Eau Claire, including unidentified members of the PLM, or denied based on any number of criteria, the failure to identify the actual PLM leader being the most prominent.

If the Patch didn't work, Mike's actions wouldn't matter, but he couldn't let the PLM receive the cure and walk away—not because of some greater goal, but for his own sanity. He thought about camping out by the rock where Jeff, the PLM member, received notes, but he didn't want to sit still.

With a fever and no idea what to do next, Mike met with his group of nine holographic advisors, characters he had created for his next performance as entertainer. It might have seemed silly to talk with nine holographic people he'd created, but he found it to be a unique and innovative way to free his mind. Instead of contemplating a few ideas, he garnered nine different perspectives ranging from narcissistic to strategic.

"I say we poison anyone with even the slightest connection to the PLM, all 586 of them," Elroy said, suggesting an aggressive plan because that's how Mike had programmed him.

"That's the stupidest idea I've ever heard," Cynthia said. "We should enlist the city and go unit by unit, interviewing everyone in Eau Claire."

Bickering ensued until Dick Lee proposed his own plan. "I suggest Mike go to any bar, get drunk, and spend the night in an admirer's unit where he can wait until the Patch is released, then sneak out of town when visitors leave."

"I have a better idea," Kirk said. "We lure the PLM together in one area for a celebratory party, then turn them over to an angry Eau Claire crowd to rip them apart."

The team discussed several other colorful solutions, including the introduction of a smoking campaign to help lower the soon-to-be extended life expectancy.

The unconventional suggestions by his holograms didn't surprise Mike since they were all his creation, but he was surprised that when he left his studio, he had a plan.

Mike's plan, like those of his holographic friends, was neither completely thought out nor well-reasoned, but he had to do something. If his plan didn't work, he most likely would end up dead, for real this time. Mike walked into Squeezed Dry, a popular bar in the area, sat in the middle of the crowd, and reattached his own BP to his wrist.

He had nobody to protect him or convince bar patrons of his innocence. With the threat of a deadly epidemic and Mike's history of infecting others, he knew it was a big risk. The patrons might rip him apart as Kirk suggested or admire him as Dick Lee alluded. One thing was certain: they would not ignore him. It took about ten seconds for him to go from dead to the center of attention.

The bar exploded as three angry men approached from the right. Mike saw four younger women coming from the other direction and instinctively moved towards the women, hoping he had found his fan club. It was his first mistake.

As Mike neared the women, one launched herself at him, knocking him to the ground. A man grabbed Mike by the shoulders while the woman punched him in the gut. The man pulled Mike to his feet and stepped in between them, stopping her progress.

"None of us will ever be able to have children," the woman who punched Mike said, "if we're lucky enough to survive this disease you gave us." Mike saw the bags under her eyes and the sweat on her forehead and hoped the disease would slow her down, but she still took another swing at him.

"Are you really Mike Newhouse?" said the man who picked him up. Mike nodded his head. "The Outsider who caused this disease?" Mike thought of giving an explanation, but simply nodded again. "I thought you were dead." The man let go of Mike as if he no longer wanted to touch him.

"Severely injured." Mike grabbed his arm.

"Not injured enough," yelled someone. Mike braced for impact, but nobody moved.

"I'm sorry. I didn't have anything to do with the disease," Mike said. He formed his words carefully and swore to himself for not being better prepared. "I have it myself. I simply want to find the PLM and make them pay for this." Mike built his argument as he looked for a hook and found it. "To ensure we all get the Patch."

"What do you mean?" yelled a woman near the front of the crowd. "They're testing it right now. They're supposed to release it in a few days."

Mike knew he needed to build fear of the disease to displace the anger towards him. "Has anyone here gotten the Patch?" Mike asked without waiting for an answer. "Do you really think they found all of the PLM members? Seven people who never met each other and have no idea where they got their information?"

"Don't listen to him. He's an Outsider," said an old man. Mike remained silent and knew he had reached the critical moment.

"The Outsider's right," said a woman in the first group of four. "Everyone knows there are more members in the PLM. I say we find them and make sure we get the Patch. Then I can go back to hating this guy," she motioned with her head to Mike.

"Does anybody know anything about the PLM?" said a voice in the crowd. After a short hesitation everyone in the bar sent hundreds of messages in seconds. Mike worked his own BP, not to send a message, but to monitor the room for ghosts. Nothing. He captured BP signatures in the area and attempted to match them with the 116 names on his updated Suspicious Persons list.

He found a name, though it wasn't on his list. It only stood out because it was the name of his mom's favorite movie star, Gary Cooper. She'd seen all his movies.

Mike did a quick database search on Gary Cooper and found no one with that name in Eau Claire even though the individual stood in the same room. Mike didn't have time to investigate this anomaly, but he knew he needed to meet Gary Cooper.

He didn't know what to do next. It didn't matter. The room erupted again as leads about the PLM came pouring in, nearly every patron sure they had the missing information to lead them all directly to PLM headquarters.

"A group of people in Raspberry Park are bragging they're part of the PLM," yelled someone from the crowd.

"I think it's the people at City Office," yelled another.

"I have 278 people telling me it's Mike Newhouse," said someone else as several people nodded in agreement.

Mike had enjoyed the lapse in attention, but when the crowd turned back to him, he was again unprepared.

"Look, I understand I'm the most likely candidate," Mike said as he automatically shifted into his entrepreneurial persona, sounding more friendly and convincing. "I get it, but why would I come down here alone? Most of the people in Eau Claire already hate me more than the PLM. Why would I be looking for PLM members if I was one of them?"

"To screw with us," one person yelled.

"'Cause you're an Outsider."

"Everything started when you arrived."

"Grab him."

Mike closed his eyes, but nobody moved, each person looking to his or her neighbor for action. Eau Claire residents had lived close together for so long that the flame of mob mentality was hard to reignite. Community and cooperation were driving forces, not suspicion and accusations, which left the residents ill-equipped to properly crucify Mike. Even the woman who had punched Mike didn't move, uncomfortable to act for the crowd.

A loose plan formed in Mike's mind. He wanted to talk to one person, not because he was on Mike's list, but because he wasn't on any list.

"There is one person I'd like to talk to in this bar." Mike watched his BP and thought maybe he could get Gary Cooper to incriminate himself by turning the spotlight on him. "He has some odd BP activity that brings into question his involvement with the PLM." Mike watched as Gary Cooper moved out of range, giving him his answer.

"You accuse *us* now?" someone said.

As Mike determined what to do next, four people entered the bar out of breath, a mixture of Observers and security. They headed straight for Mike.

"Mr. Newhouse, please come with us," said the nearest one. Mike didn't hesitate, glad for the escape. He moved towards the door, ahead of the Observers and worked his BP as he walked. He didn't have time for questions and worried about their motives after the city had threatened to throw him out of Eau Claire. He waited for the right moment, then activated the preprogrammed setting on his BP and apologized quietly. The Observers, security members, and two people standing too close, fell to the ground in pain from the electric shock running through their BPs.

With his would-be captors on their knees, Mike headed for the library. Thirty feet away from the building, he used another custom-designed feature on his BP that transferred his BP signature to all BP wearers in the vicinity. He entered the library where his signal disappeared while roughly twenty Mike Newhouses gave ample cover outside.

Mike waited in the library, then slipped out another door. He had both BPs turned off, remembering the city's awareness of the Philip BP. After both shocking and fleeing city representatives, Mike concluded the city's attitude towards him might have further deteriorated.

He searched for Gary Cooper, using Philip's BP for short, fifteen-second bursts. He didn't locate Mr. Cooper, but he found one ghost and worked his way in that direction. Checking Philip's BP again, Mike immediately picked up the ghost travelling on a parallel walkway and watched the ghost walk into a shop.

Surveying the shop, Mike had time to think as he sat on a nearby bench and researched Gary Cooper. He confirmed no Gary Cooper currently occupied Eau Claire while only 137 Gary Coopers existed throughout all the regions.

Mike finally used the manual entry on his BP, not trusting what he had found, and stumbled upon Gary Cooper, not in Eau Claire, but in a misspelling of the city name. Gary Cooper was the only resident of *Eau Clare* without an *i*, making Gary Cooper the sole resident of a city that didn't exist, a true electronic ghost. No one would have found Gary Cooper of Eau Claire, unless the person doing the search was a horrendous speller like Mike, and hadn't grown up using a BP, forced to use the old manual entry method.

Gary Cooper had never been a part of any of Mike's prior searches nor the city's because he didn't exist in any known database. Mike was aware of his presence because of his proximity to Gary Cooper. If Mike hadn't been standing near him and recognized the famous name, he wouldn't have known Gary Cooper existed in Eau Claire because he was really in Eau *Clare*.

Mike saw the ghost walk out of the shop as he considered the brilliance of the concept, a bit jealous he hadn't thought of the idea first. Mike's street sense told him the ghost was Gary Cooper.

He remained seated long enough for the ghost to progress comfortably forward. The shops ended at the large square ahead where the train tracks cut through the city, signifying a transition from the Art District to the Garden District. Beyond the square, the walkway turned either left or right. The ghost turned left. Mike used a shortcut and climbed over a compost pile in the process to avoid the wide expanse and noisy walkway.

Without the ghost in sight, Mike turned on his BP, but he found himself in a dead zone. To maintain visual contact, Mike climbed a nearby tree to achieve a better vantage point, settling himself on a comfortable branch not far from the ground. He saw the ghost walk at the same comfortable pace and enjoyed his elevated position as the ghost entered what looked to be a lab.

When no one emerged from the lab after twenty minutes, Mike climbed down and walked towards the building. He traveled the length of the block in both directions and ended up back in front of the lab again, surprised he couldn't find a signal anywhere along the square, which helped explain the lack of bars and people.

Mike thought about leaving. It was late and he was tired—terminally ill to be exact. He wanted to spend a week to learn more about the area, the lab, and the building, then devise a plan with many options. Mike didn't have a week or a plan. He saw one option. He made a deal with himself. *If the lab door doesn't open, I'm out of here.* Even as he said the words in his head, he knew he would ignore them.

The door didn't budge, but when he tried to activate the program he needed to unlock it, he discovered his BP was inoperable. Unlike a dead zone where a BP didn't broadcast but still functioned locally, now it didn't function at all. Why his BP didn't work was as big a mystery to Mike as how he was going to enter the lab.

He could pick a lock, but the door offered nothing to pick and he had no tools. Then he remembered the small knife he carried like Sara in a tailored pocket. Mike knew Eau Claire took a lax view of security and guessed correctly that the latched door acted more as a symbolic gesture than a true physical barrier. He slid the knife through the gap in the door, and it opened.

The front room loomed twice as big as Stanley's lab with half of the plants. Mike stuck his hand in the dirt of a random tray and pulled back a dry finger. The front room lacked the slight dishevelment of work—spilled soil, a few loose leaves—some indication that the labor was sincere. Mike had created enough false fronts to recognize one. He wanted to leave, but when he thought about his options, he remembered he was on his own. His friends were quarantined and dying, and the city wanted to confine him or throw him out.

He continued on his journey through the open doorway to the back of the building. He expected a sparse room, but the room in back expanded and contained wooden boxes and covered items. The room was bare by Mike's standards six months ago, but in the Eau Claire Mike knew now, it represented the biggest cache of unused items he had seen. The other curiosity was an indoor stairway leading up to the next two floors, making those floors accessible only from the back room and the largest private space in Eau Claire.

"Hello? Is anybody here?" Mike called out as he climbed the stairs, not going for stealth, but camaraderie. The second floor looked like a traditional house Mike might have rented a room in as a college student, with oak floors, wide wood trim, and light switches. He attempted to turn off the lights, but the switch did nothing except make a clicking sound that Mike found comforting. He flipped the light switch several more times simply to hear the familiar click.

When he grew bored of the clicking sound, he looked through the rooms on the second floor, amazed by the old furniture and the number of useless items lying around— lamps, a wastepaper basket, a china hutch filled with dishes and figurines.

He eventually walked up to the third floor, calling out again. The third floor resembled the second, except for wall-paper—ancient wallpaper which Mike ran his hand across to feel the embossed flowers. He searched rooms calling out a greeting. "Hello? Is anyone here?" He entered the dining room and froze. It took his entire concentration to understand what he saw and still stay upright.

THIRTY-SIX

Twenty-eight years had passed since the Tapes ended. Mason, at eighty-six, still puttered at his work, taking a much less disciplined approach to science—starting in the middle of projects, picking topics at random, and making wild assumptions. He enjoyed his new haphazard methodology, which led to new discoveries. He created new plant cultivars, fixed his neighbor's electric car, and constructed the most comfortable shoes he had ever owned. Most recently he used it to perfect Sara's recipe for squash casserole.

Gina was a favorite topic of his. He sketched what he thought she looked like as he imagined whether she would have enjoyed baseball or how she acted as a child.

Mysteries also intrigued Mason as he searched for clues to the identity of PLM members. He had studied the Fortune Teller notes and predictions years ago, but he never discovered how the group knew events ahead of time.

Recently he had indulged himself and delved into questions and incidents the way others attempted crossword puzzles to keep their minds sharp. He laid out each PLM event on the floor in chronological order.

Shuffling from file to file, he became sidetracked by new thoughts and ideas. What influence did the Beatles have on

Eau Claire's music? Did anyone make a hologram of the Beatles? How programmable were holographic images? What would a hologram say?

Mason's playful brain jumped to other conversations and, consequently, a particular conversation he'd heard involving a hologram on an afternoon many years ago, when Mike was threatened by his own holograms.

Mason stepped around piles of paper on the floor to the file marked Holographic Threat and pulled out the text— *You jump through time while the rest of us are limited to a short existence, trudging through every single day.* He remembered someone else saying a similar expression, and his playful brain juggled the possibilities.

The files on the floor and the items they contained came together in Mason's head, leading to one simple solution to the mystery of the PLM's identity. It seemed too easy, so logical once he saw the connections. He smiled and enjoyed the exquisite rapture of discovery before he walked into his den.

On the bookcase where odd things had accumulated sat a box covered with dust, forgotten on top of books he had not read in decades. He gently lifted the box from its humble location and opened the lid to discover what he, a man who has spent years studying the future, already knew. One of his vials of life-extending serum he created based upon Dr. Donavan's theories was missing. As the dust attested, the box hadn't been disturbed in years, perhaps decades.

Mason started from the beginning. He walked through his papers and re-analyzed every piece of data he had on the PLM against his latest discovery and saw for the first time the whole picture. He wondered if anything else was missing from his house and knew it was impossible to tell, but he did remember a time, years ago, when he thought he had misplaced several vaccines for the impending plagues. Now he wasn't so sure they had been misplaced.

Driven by a passion for the truth, he questioned every assumption he had ever made. He re-read notes while eating lunch and fell asleep under piles of papers covering him like blankets. He recalibrated his research and looked for other missing pieces. He woke early one morning as sleep washed away the debris of the previous day and saw the other obvious truth with clarity regarding Gina and her knowledge of Mike's arrival into her Eau Claire. He smiled at the thought of it.

. . . . .

When Mason died in 2050 at the age of eighty-eight, two years before the plagues began, his family gathered to say goodbye. The service took place in the gardens of his granddaughter Ellen's house in Eau Claire on a beautiful June day, with chairs facing an urn made of clay. He requested to have his ashes scattered around the large rock formation not far from Ellen's house, to which guests walked, creating a small parade.

A surprising number of people showed up to a funeral for a man his family thought was a hermit. The gathering included many regulars from The Farm, gracious neighbors, and an assortment of city personalities who told stories of a man they had wanted to know better. A few others lingered in the background, wanting to be a part of the experience, including a man who looked like he could have been Dr. Jennings' son, if he had had one.

THIRTY-SEVEN

"Mr. Newhouse, how nice of you to join me," Dr. Jennings said as he sat in an old upholstered Queen Anne chair looking as comfortable, in control, and healthy as he did in his office 131 years ago, or three months, depending on a prisoner's perspective. Mike experienced a range of emotions, starting with shock to see a person in what he thought was an empty house, followed by horror when he recognized the seated man as the warden, and vague disbelief that Dr. Jennings could still be alive.

Before he knew what else to think, his body had already gone into motion, lunging towards Dr. Jennings. When he came within three feet, he hit a wall of electricity and collapsed on the floor.

"Proximity sensor," Dr. Jennings said, pointing to the instrument on his arm. Mike lay on the floor and shook his head before he regained his senses and stood. He tried to activate his own safety features, when he remembered his BP didn't work. "As I was saying Mr. Newhouse, I've been looking forward—"

"How are you still alive?" Mike asked. "How is that even possible?"

"I could ask you the same thing. Your death was broadcast two weeks ago, but something told me you'd even lie about that."

"But how are you here?"

"You, who have traveled through time, are asking *me* how it's possible?"

"You simply time travelled as well. Got here before me."

"Never," Dr. Jennings said. "I didn't take the easy way out. I experienced every one of those 131 years, from the massive migration, through the Poly Plagues, to my life here in Eau Claire. I watched more people die than you've ever seen alive. I suffered the slow and inevitable changes of time up to this very moment. I am prepared because I didn't take the easy way out. I didn't cut corners like criminals often do. I didn't jump through time. I lived it."

The warden's voice instantly transported Mike to their first conversation over three months ago where every sentence was a threat, each word a challenge.

"I didn't choose to be hurtled through time," Mike said, agitated by the doctor's calm and condescending comments. "You sent me forward in time, as an experiment, a punishment. Spare me the lecture." Mike stared at the warden, feeling blood pumping through his veins. He took a deep breath. The warden was manipulating him, pushing him to react, a technique Mike had used often. He took three deep breaths from his diaphragm and let the air escape through his nose while the warden talked.

"You are a prisoner, Mr. Newhouse. As such, you have been treated like one." The warden spoke calmly, completely unrushed. "As a criminal, you're accustomed to taking shortcuts, never understanding what you've missed in the process."

Mike finally adjusted to his shock and gained some control over himself and attempted to get control of the conversation. "Were you the one I followed here?"

"No." The warden barely moved in his chair. "I was the one who led you here."

"Are you a member of the PLM?"

"No," the warden said with a smile that had no other purpose than to annoy. "I am *the* PLM, *the* Fortune Teller. The seven people the city thinks are Fortune Teller members are errand runners. I'm the one who has looked into the future, with your help of course."

"Are you also Gary Cooper?" Mike continued his questions, afraid of the silence, hoping to have time later to think about what he heard.

"Very good, Mr. Newhouse. I hoped the name would catch your attention."

Mike vaguely thought of hundreds of details he wanted to know about the prison, the warden, how and why he ended up in Eau Claire—or was it Eau Clare? These ideas flipped through his brain and he was unable to slow them down, much less stop on any one thought.

"You don't look well, Mr. Newhouse. Perhaps you caught that bug that's been going around?"

"Times have changed," Mike said. "You're no longer in charge, and I'm no longer your prisoner." Mike decided it was time to leave and lurched back the way he came.

"I wouldn't do that if—"

As Mike approached the stairway in the next room, another electric shock knocked him to the floor.

"Proximity sensors have been located along the third floor," the warden said from the other room. "You see Mr. Newhouse, I *am* in charge, and you are *still* my prisoner."

Mike remained on the floor, exhausted, thinking if he didn't move, didn't say a word, he'd deny the warden any further pleasure. After a minute of figuratively holding his breath, he began to analyze his situation. Still on the floor, he looked at the room and found it familiar, with what appeared to be sheetrock walls he could break through.

He moved to a seated position and meditated, centering himself as he surveyed his surroundings. He moved through the rooms he had already seen before and continued into unknown spaces, finding closets, bedrooms, a small library. He saw additional proximity sensors on the windows and staircase and examined the thick stone outer wall of the building.

He stayed in meditation a while longer and examined the warden, seeing in his eyes the years that didn't show up on his face, noting the calm demeanor of a confident man in complete control.

He opened his eyes and thought his surroundings might look different based upon his relaxed state of mind and was surprised to find he really didn't like the wallpaper. He had a plan. He needed to get rid of the warden first, but he also wanted to know what he was escaping from.

Mike stood and strode casually back into the room where Dr. Jennings sat without the slightest change in position or expression. Making sure not to get too close, Mike walked past the warden, grabbed an antique dining room chair, and sat.

"I'm your prisoner once again," Mike said. "Surely you didn't live through 131 years of challenges and difficulty merely to teach me a lesson in consequences?"

Neither the question nor the prisoner's calm appearance surprised Dr. Jennings. He had seen thousands of men in every situation and studied how they reacted. He had also programmed his BP to detect the physical status of anyone within a short radius, which revealed Mike's near normal heart rate and blood pressure. As a citizen of Eau *Clare*, Dr. Jennings' BP worked in his own city.

"No, this meeting is an added benefit, a reward to myself. You, Mr. Newhouse, are a distraction, entertainment while I wait for the Patch to be administered." Dr. Jennings shifted a leg and turned his head towards Mike. He moved gracefully, no longer a pacer, having learned to calm his body over time.

"I experienced the rewards of Dr. Donavan's research many years ago in a serum." He held his arms out as if to present himself as evidence. "Which is how I'm able to be here today. But the effects last only so long, and it's time for my booster application, the Patch. You've provided me not only the perfect scapegoat, but also insider information." Dr. Jennings tapped his arm to indicate the audio transmitter that had been inside Mike, and he received the response he sought in Mike's raised heart rate and adrenaline.

"I was there with you during your first few months in Eau Claire. I know your secrets. I shared your most intimate moments." The doctor saw the prisoner's stress indicators fall and was disappointed. He reacted more to the numbers than the man.

"Why am I here, in this house?" Mike said. "The Patch will be released, and I'll most likely be kicked out of the city. What could be a better punishment?"

"I've lived too long to take anything for granted, including getting the Patch." Dr. Jennings looked down at his BP. "When I'm ready, I'll leave here. You unfortunately won't be as lucky. You'll die a painful death alone in this house from a disease you would have contracted if I had sent you only a few years forward in time."

"I'm lucky you forced me so far into the future?"

"I'll admit, the disease you have now won't kill you with the same indiscriminate pain as the Poly Plagues, but it was the best I could do." Dr. Jennings shrugged his shoulders. "If they withhold the Patch, there's enough evidence in this building to convince anyone you're the leader of the PLM. I simply need to give them the name of this building, and the Patch is mine. I will have the privilege to see justice served and you to take the blame."

"How can you access the Patch?" Mike asked. "You don't live in Eau Claire—you live in the other Eau *Clare* without the *i*."

"You figured out my secret city too?" Dr. Jennings shook his head. "Of course, it would take a criminal mind to understand that type of deception."

"It still doesn't get you the Patch."

"I've had time to work out all the details. I have dual citizenship. I think you even visited my living quarters, although I have never lived there. This house is in my Eau *Clare*, and, as Gary Cooper, it provides me many luxuries— including solitude as the sole resident in my own city. Yet once I change my Bio Pulse, I can as easily become an Eau Claire resident with a boring name and access to the Patch. Then I'll move on to another city where I've made similar living arrangements, the king in my own kingdom. I could never live like they do." He flicked his hand up to indicate the rest of the city. "Crammed together, forced to live like prisoners. My separate cities are my sanctuaries, what distinguishes me from the rest, making this life tolerable."

"Let me see if I have this right," Mike said. "You have stolen another person's identity. Hell, you've taken an entire city's identity. The same crime I was sentenced for and you still want to see justice served. Tell me you see the irony."

289

"Oh, I see the incongruity, Mr. Newhouse. But times change, as you said, and wise men change with them, not against them as you did."

"Why are you telling me this anyway?" Mike asked.

"It amuses me. I have no one I can discuss my incredible feats with for obvious reasons, and I know so few people who go back as far as you and I."

Mike had other questions, but he saw no advantage to prolonging the conversation. He had work to do and remained quiet. The doctor stared at Mike with a stillness and intensity that was physical in its impact. Mike held his gaze, but he understood this was something the warden enjoyed as well and closed his eyes to meditate. The warden tried to engage Mike with taunts and information.

"I listened to you struggle to fit in as I'd predicted." Dr. Jennings waited for a response. "I heard your pitiful performances. I was there when you lusted after a woman who electrocuted you."

Mike remained still, and his Bio numbers did as well, forcing Dr. Jennings to pursue other interests.

Mike sat for hours, drifting in and out of conscious sleep. He sensed the warden stand and walk past. When the warden's back was turned, Mike dove at him, hoping to catch him off guard in a last effort to confront his jailer. An electric shock threw Mike back with a zap as the warden walked through the door.

Mike lay on the floor until the sun rose the next morning. The effects of the electric charge were temporary, but events of the previous day, along with the disease, had caught up with him. He hoped to start the morning with new energy and ideas. He had neither. Mike checked each room he could on the third floor and found nothing but curiosities.

Using a beautiful heavy floor lamp with a Tiffany shade, he pounded a hole through an interior wall allowing him access to the other side of the third floor. He checked the rooms and again, found no exit. The warden had clearly occupied this side with a made bed, operational bathroom, and even a kitchen with food. Mike spent hours searching the third floor, careful not to come within range of any proximity sensors. He threw objects at the windows hoping to break them, but the electrical field acted as an invisible wall. The harder he threw an item, the more violently it was repelled, which gave Mike an idea.

He had to wait until the next morning to implement his new plan as another day had slipped away. He made himself a satisfying dinner from the food available, uncertain if leaving food was short-sighted of the warden or part of his plan to ensure Mike died of his disease, not hunger. He slept in the warden's bed until the sun woke him.

He saw no way around the proximity sensors, making the only logical choice to go through them. The most easily accessible sensor was located above the stairway. Mike spent several minutes testing its outer limits then marked a line at the edge of the sensor's range with a piece of broken sheetrock.

He stood in front of the line and prepared his body for a different kind of time travel, a journey through space so slow it would confuse time. He moved imperceptibly forward, shifting his weight to one foot, allowing the other to glide forward. Guru had taught Mike the technique as part of his own style of walking meditation. The idea was to focus on the whole body and feel the weight transfer from one area to another as muscles fired, not to simply move a limb, but to support its graceful arc.

Mike had tried the technique several times in prison but never achieved the state of grace Guru described as getting lost in time.

"It's similar to walking on a road you've only ever driven on at sixty miles an hour," Guru said in a park years ago to a much younger Mike, "seeing the detail that had always been a blur."

Since his visit to Eau Claire, Mike had learned patience, in part from jumping 131 years forward, reacquainting him with time on a new level. He hoped his intimate relationship with time would be enough. As he reached the first step, he felt time's full embrace like a mother hugging her son after war.

He finally understood what Guru meant, feeling he could stop time, analyze a strand of it, replace it in any order, and still make sense of time. The slower his body moved, the faster time rushed around him. It reminded Mike of a curiosity he learned in sixth grade about midpoints. He could divide the distance between any two points by finding its midpoint and continue dividing the distance into infinitely smaller pieces. He divided time into smaller and smaller pieces, moving his muscles through each location with the sensation of sprinting through the world, while from the outside appearing not to move at all.

He was tired and refreshed at the same time, as if he were stretching his legs on a long run. As he neared the finish line, a point on the floor he estimated to be the sensor's end, he sped up time and his movement, but he had underestimated the sensor's reach. A surge of electrical energy threw him forward.

His whole body fell limp from the electrical jolt and offered no resistance in his descent down the stairs, a poor reward for an outstanding achievement. Mike slid down several steps before coming to rest on the landing. He lay on the floor, but smiled, knowing he had made it to the other side. After assessing his body for a few minutes, he stood and felt better than expected, his whole body having been too relaxed to create friction against the stairs.

Mike first checked that no other barriers barred his way out as he proceeded to the first floor and spent a few moments searching through the piles of material there. The warden had talked about evidence, and Mike remembered he had found his original shirt and pants in the hands of others. He wondered if his shoes or other personal items were hidden somewhere in the building.

Mike found a pile of garbage in a metal bin, stacks of old papers, boxes of books, old lab equipment, several framed paintings, and an extensive coin collection. He didn't find what he needed and was too tired to look longer, which made his decision on what to do next more difficult.

He brushed dirt off himself and fixed his hair before he stepped out of the lab onto the quiet walkway. Looking back at the three-story building that had been his temporary prison, he saw nothing to distinguish it from its surroundings. Mike walked back to the square near the train, where he finally felt a safe enough distance from the warden's building to stop. He wondered the status of the Patch and asked an older woman walking by.

"Where did you come from?" she asked.

"Sorry, my BP isn't working lately."

"Oh, I know what you mean," said the woman. "My favorite health store was closed."

"Have you heard any news on the Patch?"

"It's delayed. They mentioned complications. The other cities are worried. I can't blame them, but it sounded as if they've worked out a compromise."

Mike thanked her and found the nearest Clean Screen. He walked back and forth in different stages of undress and felt as if he'd lost three pounds of dried sweat. His next priority was food, and although it became more difficult to find someone willing to help as uncertainty in the city increased, Mike knew he had the talent.

"Excuse me, can you tell me the time?" Mike asked a man in the nearest health store and was flooded with nostalgia at the quaint but never-used expression in Eau Claire, thinking of the people he had met, marks he had snared, and great conversations he had started with that one simple question.

"It's 1:56," said the man sitting at the counter. "You give up on the city already and turn off your BP?"

It was much later than Mike had thought. He guessed his trip through the proximity sensor had lasted thirty minutes, not four hours.

"I guess I need a Bio Boost, but I can't find one," Mike said, reading his mark clearly. "They tell me they're out of parts. You spend twenty-five years in a city and these spectators come in and run down the resources. They haven't got a sustainable bone in their bodies."

"Tell me about it," said the man and Mike's bowl of stew was all but ordered.

After a meal he felt better and thought more clearly. He decided to turn on Philip's BP in short bursts while walking. He learned the disease had progressed enough to keep Eau Claire preoccupied with the epidemic, making him and Philip somewhat lesser priorities. After he looked up Gary Cooper and discovered that Mr. Cooper and his Eau *Clare* no longer existed, Mike was uncertain what to do about the warden.

He didn't know the warden's identity in the real Eau Claire, although he must have been close when he visited the warden's unit. Dr. Jennings' lab and building were useless since Mike's possessions were most likely the only evidence anyone would find. He had used his BP for only twenty seconds, but it was enough time to destroy any faint plans of going to the city for help.

He thought about visiting the library and paging through a book until either everyone died or the city administered the Patch, but he suddenly realized exactly where he wanted to be and raced off to the Park District. He didn't ask permission as he strode through a home used as a make-shift medical complex. He found Gina sitting in bed, looking better than he had ever seen her, with the glow of someone who had recently fallen in love.

She jumped up and nearly tackled Mike and only stopped him from hitting the floor with her tight grip.

"I was so worried. I had people looking for you, but they said you disappeared." Gina examined Mike. "They've decided to release the Patch."

"Good, but wait 'til you hear what's happened. I decided to turn on my own BP and instantly—"

"On two conditions," Gina interrupted. "First, no one can leave or enter Eau Claire for the next fifty years. The second is that Outsiders are no longer welcome in Eau Claire and will be refused entry to any city within a hundred-mile radius to discourage people from going cross-country." Gina turned away from Mike. "They haven't decided whether to let you stay or if they'd give you the Patch in either case."

Mike took Gina by the shoulders to turn her around, but he didn't have the strength and walked to her other side. "It doesn't matter." He lifted her chin to look into her eyes. "I found him. I found the leader of the PLM."

Gina brought her forehead to his. "Nobody cares anymore. They have their solution. It's like watching you get electrocuted again." Gina's tears landed on Mike's chin.

"Mike, you're a hard man to find," Dave said, walking into the room, oblivious to the intimate moment. "There's a Council meeting tonight at 8:00 to decide if you're allowed to stay in Eau Claire. I don't know if Gina's told you, but the consequences have become more complicated."

"Dave, I found the leader of the PLM. I know where he lives and I can identify him."

"That's great, great," Dave said. "Hey, once we have this nasty epidemic taken care of, I'd love to hear your story."

"But I can identify him. When he comes for his Patch, I can point him out."

"We've already begun administering the Patch in twenty-four different locations. I'd be more concerned about your meeting tonight. The distribution of your Patch will be determined at the meeting as well. Hey, see you tonight."

THIRTY-EIGHT

Mike wanted to tell Gina about Gary Cooper, Eau *Clare*, the building, and even Dr. Jennings, although he wasn't sure how to describe their relationship. Before he knew what to say, before she could tell him about her fears, two Observers escorted Mike out. Gina was their first test subject, still under observation, and Mike, as the Observers reminded him, was an infectious nightmare with an important meeting in less than five hours.

After making one more failed attempt to see Gina, Mike meandered to his studio. The idea of a performance came to him when he discovered the meeting was to take place at the Fairgrounds, near the Furnace. He decided to create a whole new presentation. In a flurry of creative activity, Mike didn't have time to second guess ideas or debate the outcome, only to create.

With fifteen minutes to spare, Mike made his way to the Fairgrounds with the sun low in the sky. Tired, feverish, hungry, but determined, he focused on outcomes. He knew what had been missing in his other performances—a goal he could understand, motivation in the form of self-preservation. He would have been nervous if given time. Instead he slid on his entrepreneurial mask and treated his presentation as a trick, a game, a hustle.

Twenty-five Supervisors who made up the Council sat in a half circle on a stone ridge, illuminated by lights as a crowd of tens of thousands gathered around, forcing Mike to fight his way to the center. He heard a few insults with his BP turned on, but was surprised by the civility of the crowd. Most of the people came out for entertainment, relieved to be alive and recovering, anxious for a performance. Mike didn't know what to expect from a Council meeting as he stepped onto a large, flat stone in front of a semi-circle of seated Supervisors. Once on the stone, the crowd quieted until Mike thought he heard the low rumble of the Furnace.

"Mr. Newhouse, you come before us today, June 13, 84 so we, the city representatives, may determine your citizenship in Eau Claire," said the only standing Supervisor at the apex of the semi-circle in a booming voice that carried easily by the natural acoustics of the area.

Nothing distinguished the speaker from anyone else, except for his rigid posture. "As an Outsider, you were accepted into this city on a one-year trial basis and in your first ninety-six days you have been involved in three separate disease outbreaks." Chatter among the crowd grew as Mike realized today was his birthday. He almost laughed. The standing Supervisor asked for quiet and the noise dissipated. Mike hummed *Happy Birthday* to himself while the Supervisor continued.

"The treatment for the last outbreak was negotiated with other Regions only hours ago, forcing Eau Claire to agree to fifty years of isolation with no trains allowed in or out of the city. Generations would experience the ramification of such a restriction, except for the fact that Eau Claire will have no new generations. For decades not a single birth will take place because we have been forced to extend our life spans to survive. These changes redefine citizenship and intensify the city's commitment to each individual. The first decision this Council must make under this new reality is what to do with the Outsider at the center of all three health disasters."

Mike attempted to speak but was cut off by the booming voice.

"The first option before this Council is to allow Mr. Newhouse citizenship in Eau Claire, knowing it's a fifty-year commitment and knowing his history for contamination." Mike didn't like the way the speaker was presenting his options, but he remained quiet. "The other option is to banish Mr. Newhouse to the Outside, where he has lived for the past forty-four years prior to his eventful and short stay here. Furthermore, if we banish the Outsider we must decide whether to do so with no treatment of the current disease as recommended by this Council Lead, or with treatment in defiance of my recommendation. Before we begin deliberations, the subject is allowed to address the Council."

The Supervisor sat down.

Mike wasn't sure what to say. He thought of trying to explain Gary Cooper and Eau *Clare*, but he knew it would be dismissed as crazy talk. He stood tall.

"The problems this city has endured over the past three months have been caused by the PLM." Mike heard the swell of chatter race through the crowd and waited until the murmurs died down.

"I am not, nor have I ever been, involved with the PLM. In fact I helped find seven members. But I don't think this meeting is about proof or claims or who's involved. It's about blame. To that I have no answers, no solutions. I am simply a man out of time." Mike turned his gaze from the crowd to the Supervisors around the semi-circle.

Without asking for permission, Mike activated his holographic presentation. Twelve giant holographic people, three times normal size, sprung up from his Bio Pulse, each representing a number on a sixty-foot clock that hung in the darkening sky with an image of the city of Eau Claire glowing in the middle.

The character at one o'clock spoke first, a white-haired old man with a slight resemblance to Chester, the ghost who didn't trust cow pies. "Time has always had a face. For thousands of years, starting with the sundial and progressing to the wristwatch, time-keeping devices used a circular face." The image of Eau Claire faded to the face of a clock with an hour, minute, and second hand. The ticking of the clock grew, heard over the light orchestral music Mike had programmed in the background.

"It gave time personality, a face from which to smile or frown or accuse. Time eventually went digital before becoming the audio signal we know so well, that voice in our heads. Gone is the face, the personality, the beating heart." The ticking drowned out the music before it faded. The crowd remained silent.

A woman with Sara's expressive face and wearing a simple flowing gown stood tall at two o'clock. "Whether Time is excited or bored is hard to say. We didn't employ it for that reason. We have enslaved Time."

Images of Eau Claire citizens distracted by their BP data filled the center of the circle. "We've captured Time to keep track of our every move, chronicle our day, and give our lives meaning. We have never been an equal partner with Time; we have always wanted to control it."

An eight-year-old girl with his daughter's eyes, Ren's defiance, and the gapped-tooth grin of his great-great-great granddaughter stood from her seated position at three o'clock. "Time is a teacher—older, wiser, and with plenty of lessons to reveal if we would only listen. Yet all we hear are the latest rumors in seconds, minutes, and hours. We throw tantrums and fight Time's guidance, confident we're right or simply too engrossed in our own entertainment to care." Images of misbehaving children erupted from the fading clock face. "We run pell-mell through life and only stop to listen when it's time to come home, pleading for fifteen more minutes."

A twenty-year-old man with Paul's large head, turned at four o'clock. "We let time seduce us, whispering sweet nothings in our ear and making promises she never keeps. She is beauty. She is power. She's a whore." Women in skimpy clothes and high heels never seen in future Eau Claire walked across the clock face. "We don't want her love. We want her power and think we can buy it or take it by treating her poorly, only to discover she's stolen our wallet filled with years and dreams."

A man in his thirties, resembling Stanley, stood at five o'clock. "She is our daughter. One minute wanting to hold our hand, the next, amazed at what the city contains. We feel special because she's a part of our lives." Images of children throughout Eau Claire flashed in the center. "But she's no more our possession than we own the day. We think we're in control, when all we want is for her to love us because our lives have no meaning without her."

A pleasant looking woman resembling Gina sat on a chair obscuring six o'clock. "Time is a friend we think we understand, but we barely know. She's multi-dimensional, showing us only one side, while we miss the depth and breadth of her true nature. What do we really know of time? That she is reliable? Accurate?"

Numbers on a digital clock spun to the thousandth of a second in the center of the circle. "We don't know if she is happy or what happened to her before we met. We enjoy the relationship, but we wonder what we've missed."

The man at seven o'clock, who looked similar to Guru, explained that time was like a city and required constant care. "Seconds, minutes, and hours must be recycled, cleansed by death and reused in birth. Curiosity and wonder wash away hatred and prejudice."

A band conductor stood at eight o'clock, explaining the intimate relationship between music and time. "It's a bond that's brought us closer together by giving us a language with which to communicate with time."

Nine o'clock was a man, old and close to death, who spoke of his reconciliation with time. "I look forward to being Time's partner once again, not as the two strangers we've been, both afraid of rejection."

An old woman at ten o'clock described how time was like an Outsider. "Time surrounds us, living in the void around the city, welcomed as long as he pleases us, with the idea that we can simply discard him when he fails, never seeing the bigger picture."

At eleven o'clock stood a woman holding a baby. "Time is a baby that needs our care and protection, she said, "until one day when we'll need Time to take care of us."

Mike stood at twelve o'clock, growing even larger in size, at the top of the circle, now seventy feet in the air. "Time is a con artist, building our trust through the years, telling us what we want to hear, the whole time studying us for our weaknesses. To him, it's a game." An image of a man dealing Three Card Monte filled the sky.

"We appear to have choices—jobs, volunteer activities, musical groups, artistic outlets, what to eat for dinner. But

Time has stacked the deck, allowing us to believe we've decided, when it was what he wanted us to choose all along. He's corrupted us with our past and befriended the present to own our future. He skims off the top, taking a few idle minutes no one will notice until he has collected enough *I love you's* never said, risks never taken, and full moons never noticed."

Mike's timing was perfect as the moon rose into view. It was one day short of full, but Mike hoped no one noticed.

The holographic images froze as Mike spoke from the stone. "The Council has a choice to make. I know of time. I've jumped through it, measured punishments by it, tried to catch up to it, saw people cheat it. I'm a man out of time and I offer a solution. Spin the wheel."

The characters moved around the edge and the clock hands spun, producing a ticking noise with each rotation, increasing in volume and speed until the edge of the clock was a blur of motion, and the ticking vibrated in the chests of all present. The blurred characters disappeared, replaced with outcomes such as *Outside with Patch, Outside without Patch, Stay in Eau Claire, Fresh Start, Have a Party, Spin Again*. The clock hands came to rest, both pointing straight up as cathedral bells clanged twelve times.

"Instead of watching the hands spin to Time's beat, why not free ourselves of Time and spin the hands using our own power. Unaffected by the past and unconcerned with the future, leaving us free in the present, free to go forward or back, fast or slow, free of certainty, consequences, and predictability."

Mike asked for a volunteer while he produced a miniature holographic clock that matched the one in the sky. "Spin the wheel. Take control of Time." He stood back and waited, not sure what would happen next. A few of the Supervisors looked concerned, but none interrupted as the crowd stared at the small clock floating in front of Mike.

A wave of murmurs crested over the crowd and after ten seconds, which felt like ten minutes to Mike, an older woman stepped out of the crowd from Mike's far left. As she came closer, Mike recognized her as Betty Manderfield. At 111, she was a ghost Mike had talked to earlier. Mike didn't see the circular Patch that most people wore on their neck near their carotid artery and it didn't surprise him. She was sweating and looked tired. He put his arm around her and helped her onto the stone.

"Thank you, Betty," he whispered.

"I've wanted to push time around a bit," she said softly. "And you looked lonely up here."

Mike hugged her before he moved the miniature clock face where she could reach it and showed her what to do. Betty touched the wheel, grabbed both clock hands, and with all of her strength sent the hands flying around the clock face which mirrored the large clock in the sky. The hands made a clickity-clackity noise that intensified until they stopped on *Go Back in Time and Pretend it Never Happened.*

Betty squeaked out a cheer. "I think I'm a winner," she said to the Supervisors. Mike kissed her on the cheek and told her she could leave, but she said she wasn't going anywhere and sat on the stone with her legs dangling over the edge.

Mike addressed the crowd. "Anybody else can come up and spin the wheel." He looked at the Supervisors. "We can keep spinning until you get the answer you want. I even have different outcomes if you don't like these." The twelve outcomes turned into twelve more, then back to a watch face with a second hand gently ticking in the background. "Time is watching. What will you decide?" Mike sat next to Betty and held her hand. They talked quietly, ignoring the Supervisors.

"To tell you the truth," Betty said, "I was hoping I'd land on *Have a Party*. I could go for a party."

"I should've talked to you before I programmed it, but I'll make sure we have that party."

THIRTY-NINE

Ellen, Mason's granddaughter, now ninety-seven, never left Eau Claire. It was one of the safest places during the Poly Plagues, and the items her grandfather left her made her life bearable and her family safe in a world of misery. Her house, the one her grandfather helped find decades ago, was located inside the ring of bio filters.

Ellen had looked through the survival kits months after her grandfather's death, thinking his mind must have been more compromised than she'd thought. When his predictions started coming true, however, and the tools he left became invaluable, she moved her box up from the basement and sent the others off to her brother, sister and two cousins. But by then the migration had escalated, and delivery was uncertain.

Ellen used the knowledge and the tools to save her family until each item in the box was expended or obsolete. The only item that remained was a letter, with a name and date on the outside. Ellen read the letter when she first opened the box and nearly threw it away, but she kept it for sentimental reasons.

Late in the fall of 2105, she invited her granddaughter Hope to the house. Hope was a common name for babies born in the decade after the Poly Plagues ended. Hope had recently had a child of her own and brought the baby to meet her great-grandmother. It was Ellen's first great-grandchild, and she inspected every square inch of the child before engulfing her in a protective hug. She made the kind of noise people do with babies and said how she looked like her son when he was born.

They had tea in the small room upstairs where they laid the baby in dappled sunlight while they talked. Hope was surprised by her grandmother's formality, knowing her as a laid-back, scientific, seen-it-all kind of woman. Ellen took out the old box, dusty and battered, and told stories Ellen knew her granddaughter had heard many times.

Hope tried to pay attention, hearing the seriousness in her grandmother's voice as Ellen told the stories in more detail, showing Hope the old predictions that had lost their power in retrospect, along with the ancient BPs and used vaccine vials. She needed her granddaughter to understand.

"Every prediction on this list has come true." Ellen waved the notes Hope had seen several times. "These Bio Pulses look ancient to you, but fifty years ago they were invaluable, with functionality that didn't exist in any other devices. And these vaccines," Ellen opened the cases to show the empty vials, "were used up before you were born, but they kept us alive when friends and neighbors died every day."

"Grandma, I've heard this all before. Why are you telling me now?"

"You were born after the Poly Plagues and I know many of the things in this box seem old and outdated to you, but it still holds a few surprises."

She pulled something out of the box that no else had seen in the fifty-three years since she first opened it—a letter, old and brown, made of paper seldom seen now. On the front of the letter was a name and date written more than fifty years ago. Hope looked at it and recognized her daughter's name and birth date. "I wanted to give Gina this letter myself, but I don't think I will be alive when she is ready to receive it."

"Grandma, you'll probably outlive us all," Hope said.

"This is not about me, it's about the future. Please make sure Gina gets this when she's ready. I know you think this box is a dusty old relic, but it saved this family and I want to fulfill my grandfather's wishes. I hope you will feel the same about mine."

FORTY

Mike worked on his performance, and the next day he and Gina led another expedition to the Outside, looking for resources to support the increased Eau Claire population. With trains no longer supplying Eau Claire with new plant varieties or unique provisions, the Outside became the natural alternative for additional supplies. The city designed a grid and schedule to make sure the operation was sustainable. Mike and Gina's roles were cultural, leading the art community on excursions to the Outside and fostering a greater awareness of nature. Mike wanted to charge ten credits a trip, but Gina wouldn't let him.

Mike still received congratulations from random people for the Time piece he performed five months earlier for the Council and repeated a week later as part of a large party for Betty Manderfield, who died shortly after. It was the first BP-free party in decades and such a success the city decided to make it an annual event in Betty's honor.

Eau Claire's new target population increased to 112,000, making it a Tier-Two city. More than six thousand people refused the Patch, which led to the biggest Furnace celebration ever and brought Eau Claire to only eight thousand above its population goal.

Kevin's recovery took the longest of anyone's in Eau Claire, most likely complicated by the exotic flu strain he had contracted earlier. An application of a second Patch was required to bring him to full strength. He needed monthly scans and an annual visit by Dr. Donavan, who finally came to Eau Claire and was the only person allowed to enter or leave the city. He insisted on following Kevin's case along with conducting a longitudinal study of Eau Claire residents.

Eau Claire's quarantine delayed Mike's hope of visiting Sonia, his great-great-great granddaughter by fifty years, but he enjoyed their weekly electronic visits. Sonia's face had taken on a mystical quality as if his daughter were now looking over him. Ren and Mike took several trips to the Outside, where Mike continued her mentoring in meditation and Ren helped him with his first-ever physics class.

Following Mike's performance to the Council, one Supervisor left, asking loudly, "I wonder what time it is?" One by one the rest of the supervisors stood and blended into the crowd until the Council Lead finally did the same. They never voted and no one mentioned the incident again, except Dave. "Hey, nice performance, Mike. Keep up the good work."

The city searched Dr. Jennings' building the day after they issued the Patch to Mike. On the first floor, they found items that Mike had discovered. Upstairs they located hand-written notes on old sheets of paper containing detailed information about Eau Claire, a list of people celebrated at each Furnace ceremony, and considerable data about Mike Newhouse. The socks and shoes Mike wore when he time traveled were discovered in a second-floor bedroom along with several pieces of pottery he'd made.

Mike ran into Dr. Jennings once, a few months later. His name wasn't Dr. Jennings, but Lawrence Hobbs. Mike wasn't wearing his BP and surprised Dr. Jennings/Lawrence Hobbs.

"Don't worry, you'll get used to prison life. Fifty years will go by in no time." Mike said as he clapped Dr. Jennings on the back and made him jump. Gone was the warden's confidence and control. He even looked smaller, less significant. "But you've got to watch yourself in the Clean Screen." Mike smiled and couldn't stop smiling the rest of the day. He thought there could be no better reward than locking the warden up in the prison he'd helped to create.

· · · · ·

Gina was in their unit, reading a letter her mother had given to her when Gina turned twenty-five. She had read it many times in the last twenty-one years, but she sat down to read it one last time before putting it away as a keepsake.

July 19th, 2048

My dearest Gina,

I am your great-great-great grandfather. I'm sorry we will never get the chance to meet, although I feel I know you better than most people. I'm not sure I should be writing this letter, but I'm certain I already have.

I don't know everything your future holds nor do I want to share with you all the things I do know, but I think it's important I inform you of two items. First, on March 9, 2151, a man will come to Eau Claire. He'll call himself an Outsider, and this will be mostly true. I believe you can trust this man, and you may fall in love with him. The difficulty is that my knowledge is limited. You must determine for yourself his trustworthiness. As for falling in love, I will leave that in your hands.

311

You are probably wondering if I'm a madman. I don't want to tell you how I know what I know only to give you proof I'm not a madman. I wrote your name and birth date on the outside of this envelope fifty-seven years before you were born. You graduated from Eau Claire High School in 2122 with a degree in Water Management and a GPA of 3.78. I could go on, but I don't want to tell you things that haven't happened to you yet, so I'll stop there.

The second thing I need you to know is another man will come to Eau Claire, or perhaps he never left. He is involved with a group called the Prolong Life Movement. This man will have similar knowledge that I do, but with no regard for the wonderful city of Eau Claire. Please do what you can to minimize his impact. I ask this because I feel responsible for whatever problems he causes and risks he creates.

I want you to be safe and happy, and I debated for months about whether I should write this letter. But what I know of you, our shared love of finding things that are hidden, makes me believe you would want to know these things. By writing this letter, I also have the opportunity to say hello and wish you a wonderful life. You're an extraordinary person and have a great life ahead of you. Enjoy each day and have a solar chocolate soufflé at Ground Earth for me. It sounds wonderful, and I've never been able to make it myself.

With all my love,

John Mason, your great-great-great grandfather

312

. . . . .

Gina folded the delicate and brittle document, putting it away for good. She smiled at the many implications, then did what she always did after reading the letter, visited Ground Earth for solar chocolate soufflé.

Mike met her there, and for the first time in her life, Gina shared her soufflé. She explained to Mike, as best she could, about their strange connection, her obsession with the PLM, and a letter she received from her great-great-great grandfather, John Mason.

Mike listened to Gina's story, nodding between bites of soufflé. He was intrigued, then confused. Finally, when Gina mentioned John Mason, it all clicked. Mike nearly choked on his soufflé. He pondered the possibilities, then cast them aside in favor of new beginnings with the radiance of a man who had embraced his relationship with time.

ACKNOWLEDGEMENTS

I'd like to first and foremost thank my wife, Ellen. She is my alpha reader, preposition fixer, no-nonsense editor, always challenging me to make sense. She creates a safe place to write and gives me confidence, simply with her presence. Like all of our journeys, I've written this book hand-in-hand with her. To my sister, Therese, my spiritual guide in all matters of literary funkiness, whose enthusiasm and blunt critique moved the story forward. To Carol Hollar-Zwick, who jumpstarted this book into publication with her kind offer to apply her formatting expertise. To my first readers who slogged through much longer, less defined versions years ago: Bill Jones, Ken Zwick, Jan McHugh, Tom McHugh, and Carol Hollar-Zwick. To Colin McHugh, for his insight into algorithms, keywords, and the social media dance of publishing a book. To The Mill: A Place for Writers, where this novel started as a struggling short story. To Jill Swenson for her insight and Jean Long Manteufel for her timely push. To all the Millennials and those to come, I hope this book offers encouragement for a better future. Sometimes the only way to a better place is to have traveled through a much messier one.

ABOUT THE AUTHOR

Christopher Kunz is a writer and small-city philosopher who moved from Minneapolis to find his community in Neenah, Wisconsin, where he lives with his wonderful wife, neglected lawns, and impossible gardens. *Doing Time* is his first novel.

Made in the USA
Monee, IL
02 May 2020